CHRISTOPHER BUSH
THE CASE OF THE PURLOINED PICTURE

CHRISTOPHER BUSH was born Charlie Christmas Bush in Norfolk in 1885. His father was a farm labourer and his mother a milliner. In the early years of his childhood he lived with his aunt and uncle in London before returning to Norfolk aged seven, later winning a scholarship to Thetford Grammar School.

As an adult, Bush worked as a schoolmaster for 27 years, pausing only to fight in World War One, until retiring aged 46 in 1931 to be a full-time novelist. His first novel featuring the eccentric Ludovic Travers was published in 1926, and was followed by 62 additional Travers mysteries. These are all to be republished by Dean Street Press.

Christopher Bush fought again in World War Two, and was elected a member of the prestigious Detection Club. He died in 1973.

THE LUDOVIC TRAVERS MYSTERIES
Available from Dean Street Press

The Plumley Inheritance
The Perfect Murder Case
Dead Man Twice
Murder at Fenwold
Dancing Death
Dead Man's Music
Cut Throat
The Case of the Unfortunate Village
The Case of the April Fools
The Case of the Three Strange Faces
The Case of the 100% Alibis
The Case of the Dead Shepherd
The Case of the Chinese Gong
The Case of the Monday Murders
The Case of the Bonfire Body
The Case of the Missing Minutes
The Case of the Hanging Rope
The Case of the Tudor Queen
The Case of the Leaning Man
The Case of the Green Felt Hat
The Case of the Flying Donkey
The Case of the Climbing Rat
The Case of the Murdered Major
The Case of the Kidnapped Colonel
The Case of the Fighting Soldier
The Case of the Magic Mirror
The Case of the Running Mouse
The Case of the Platinum Blonde
The Case of the Corporal's Leave
The Case of the Missing Men
The Case of the Second Chance
The Case of the Curious Client
The Case of the Haven Hotel
The Case of the Housekeeper's Hair
The Case of the Seven Bells
The Case of the Purloined Picture
The Case of the Happy Warrior
The Case of the Corner Cottage
The Case of the Fourth Detective
The Case of the Happy Medium

CHRISTOPHER BUSH

THE CASE OF THE PURLOINED PICTURE

With an introduction
by Curtis Evans

DEAN STREET PRESS

Published by Dean Street Press 2019

Copyright © 1949 Christopher Bush

Introduction copyright © 2019 Curtis Evans

All Rights Reserved

The right of Christopher Bush to be identified as the Author of the Work has been asserted by his estate in accordance with the Copyright, Designs and Patents Act 1988.

First published in 1949 by MacDonald & Co.

Cover by DSP

ISBN 978 1 913054 07 6

www.deanstreetpress.co.uk

INTRODUCTION

Labouring under Suspicion
Christopher Bush's Crime Fiction in the Postwar Years, 1946-1952

SEVEN YEARS after the end of the Second World War, Christopher Bush published, under his "Michael Home" pseudonym, *The Brackenford Story* (1952), a mainstream novel in which a onetime country house boots boy, having risen for some time now to the lofty position of butler, laments the passing of traditional English rural life in the new postwar order, as signified by the years in which the left-wing Labour party held sway in the United Kingdom (1945-51). The jacket description of the American edition of *The Brackenford Story* reads, in part:

> *The Brackenford Story* is the story of a changing England. William saw the political enemies of the Hall gradually successful, whittling away the privilege it stood for. He saw squire begin to sell his land, the taxes increase, the great Hall sold, the beautiful trees along the drive cut down. And then with a Second World War, nationalization, rationing, pre-fabricated houses and queuing. William recalled with gratitude the kindness of his masters and their sense of responsibility for others. He saw that the bad old days of Toryism were not so bad after all. And he never lost his sense of outrage at the loss of something he felt was worthy of preservation.

A few years earlier, in July 1949, Anthony Boucher, the postwar dean of American crime fiction reviewers and a highly socially conscious liberal (small "l"), wrote with genial bemusement of the conservatism of British crime writers like Christopher Bush, in his review of Bush's latest crime opus, *The Case of the Housekeeper's Hair* (1948), making topical mention of a certain anti-Utopian novel penned by a distinguished dying tubercular English writer, which had just been published in June. "However much George Orwell, in *Nineteen Eighty-Four*, may foresee the forcible suppression of 'crimethink' under 'Ingsoc,' English socialism in 1949 takes pleasure in exporting mystery novels which disapprove of the Government and everything about it," Boucher observed with wry irony. "Like most of his colleagues, Christopher Bush is tartly critical of the regime; and an understanding of his unreconstructed Tory attitude is necessary if you're to hope to understand the motivations of this novel."

In both the detective novels and mainstream fiction which Christopher Bush published between 1946 and 1952, Bush, like many other distinguished mystery writers of the Golden Age generation (including Agatha Christie, Dorothy L. Sayers, Georgette Heyer, John Dickson Carr, Edmund Crispin, E.R. Punshon, Henry Wade and John Street), indeed was critical of the Labor government and increasingly nostalgic about a past that grew ever more golden in blissful, if perhaps partially chimerical, remembrance. Yet keeping Bush's distinct anti-left bias in mind, fans of classic crime fiction will find between the covers of the author's crime novels from these years--*The Case of the Second Chance* (1946), *The Case of the Curious Client* (1947), *The Case of the Haven Hotel* (1948), *The Case of the Housekeeper's Hair* (1948), *The Case of the Seven Bells* (1949), *The Case of the Purloined Picture* (1949), *The Case of the Happy Warrior* (1950), *The Case of the Corner Cottage* (1951), *The Case of the Fourth Detective* (1951) and *The Case of the Happy Medium* (1952)--fascinating observation of postwar social malaise in the age of British imperial decay and domestic austerity, as well as details about the rise of rationing, restriction and regulation, the burgeoning black market and, withal, that ubiquitous flashily-dressed criminal figure from Forties and Fifties Britain: the spiv (dealer in illicit goods).

Puzzle-minded mystery readers also will find some corking good no-nonsense "fair play" mysteries. "Few writers can equal Christopher Bush in handling a complicated plot while giving the reader a fair chance to solve the riddle himself," avowed the American blurb to *The Case of the Corner Cottage*, while Anthony Boucher applauded Bush's belated return to the American fiction lists after the Second World War, declaring: "It's good to have Mr. Bush back after too long an absence . . . he presents the simon-pure jigsaw-puzzle detective story with unobtrusive competence." Concurrently in the United Kingdom, author Rupert Croft-Cooke, who himself wrote fine detective fiction as "Leo Bruce," pointedly praised Bush's "urbane and intelligent way of dealing with mystery which makes his work much more attractive than the stampeding sensationalism of some of his rivals."

In the pages which follow this introduction by all means attempt, dear readers, to match your keen wits against those of that ever-percipient gentleman sleuth, Ludovic Travers. Frequently in tandem with his old friend Superintendent George Wharton and with occasional input from his smart and sophisticated wife Bernice Haire, the former classical dancer, Ludo continues to hunt, in his capacity as a sort of special consultant to Scotland Yard (or "unofficial expert," as he puts it), more not-quite-canny-enough crooks. Additionally Ludo, a confirmed fan of American crime films like *The Blue Dahlia* (1946) and *Call Northside 777* (1948), comes to find himself in ownership of the Broad Street Detective Agency, perhaps the finest firm of private inquiry agents in London. In these old and new capacities in the postwar world Ludo confronts his greatest cornucopia of daring and dastardly crimes yet.

Curtis Evans

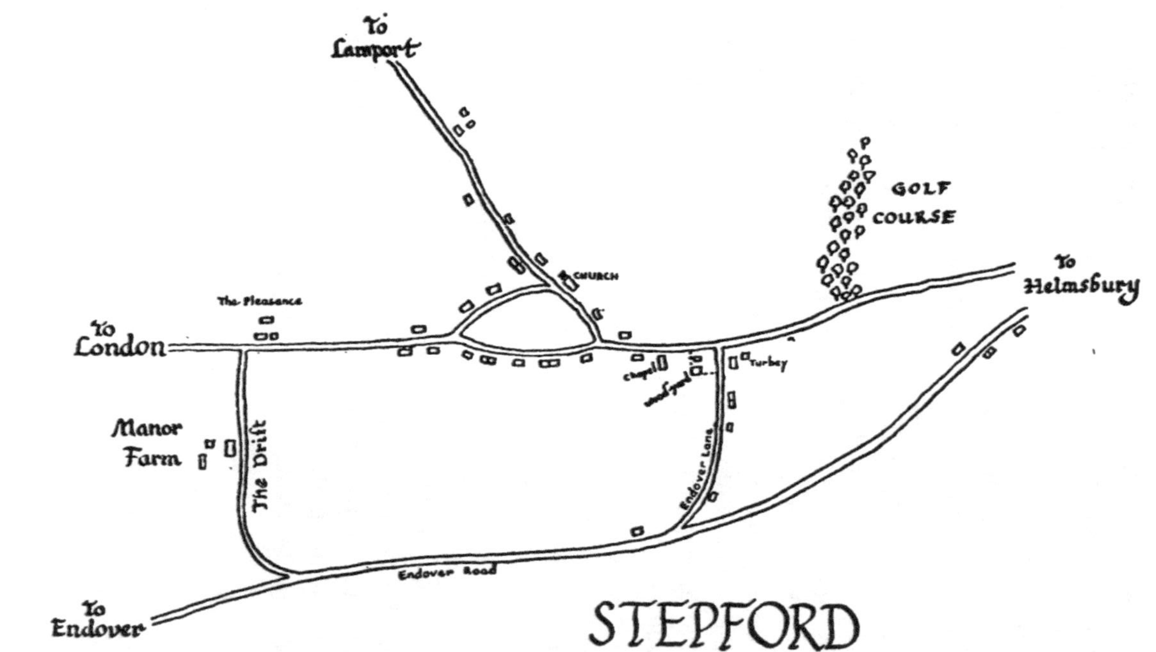
To Lamport
GOLF COURSE
To Helmsbury
The Pleasance
To London
CHURCH
chapel
Post Office
Turkey
Manor Farm
The Drift
Endover Lane
Endover Road
To Endover
STEPFORD

Chapter I
TALKING OF CARPETS

I REMEMBER that afternoon particularly well—a Tuesday, and, to be exact, the 27th of January, 1948. The following Thursday my wife was going to Switzerland to spend a month with her sister, and on the Friday I was due at the little East Anglian village of Stepford to spend a fortnight with a cousin of mine whom I had not seen for some considerable time. So when the telephone bell went and it was George Wharton's voice that I heard I was just the least bit perturbed. Let me explain.

More years ago than I care to remember I happened to be called in by Scotland Yard as an unofficial expert in a certain line that seemed to have a bearings on a somewhat abstruse murder case of which a—then unknown to me—Superintendent Wharton was in charge. We happened to hit it off together, and, to cut a long explanation short, I was later called in again. The thing became a habit, and probably because someone had forgotten to strike my name off the duty roster. In any case George Wharton and I worked together at intervals from then on. Where a murder case seemed to require the attentions of so important an official as Wharton, instead of the usual Chief-Inspector and Sergeant, there was I, teamed up and on the pay-roll.

The years made George a good friend of mine, and he was a great favourite with my wife, and yet I had learned to associate a sudden call from him as foreshadowing an imminent job of work. Keen as I am on working with George, I was not at that particular moment anxious to be hustled away to heaven knew where or heaven knew what. There was my wife's departure to be supervised, and I was looking forward to my own holiday with Bernard Ampling. He was older than I—a retired schoolmaster and a bachelor—but uncommonly good company. His was a snug little place and he had promised some honest-to-God food, and I knew we should have some golf. And after a strenuous early winter I was entitled to that holiday.

But there was no need for apprehension. George wasn't wanting me, as so often in the past, to meet him somewhere at a second's notice. What he was proposing was to drop in that evening if we weren't too busy. I said we'd both love to see him and he must certainly come in time for a service meal.

"I thought you might be in too much of a muddle," he said. "You know what I mean. Bernice going away and one thing and another."

That made me think. George was apologising, and that meant that he had something to conceal.

"Not at all," I said politely—and waited.

"As a matter of fact I may be away myself for a day or two," he went on. "Still, I'll tell you about that later."

He added a mumbling something that might have been anything and then rang off. Bernice had been giving an enquiring look or two, and I told her she was right. It was George Wharton and he would be coming along for the evening meal.

"But why so lugubrious?" she asked me. "It's always great fun when George Wharton comes."

"I suppose it is," I said. "I ought to be quite pleased, too, for other reasons."

Her eyebrows lifted enquiringly again.

"He says he's going away and probably on some job or other," I said. "My idea is that he guesses I'll be thinking he might have taken me with him. He'll probably do a whole lot of specious explaining, and all to no purpose, because the last thing I want just now is a job of work."

"Darling, you really shouldn't be so uncharitable!" she told me, so I left it at that. For Bernice, while she listens to my occasional outbursts against George's little ways, persists in regarding him only in the light of those company manners which he so charmingly displays on his visits to our flat in St. Martin's Chambers. George, to her, comes under the heading of "old darling". Speaking charitably and with the candour of a friend, I find him far more complex. Mind you, I like George. I respect him for many things and admire him for many more, but I also know him at times to be as tricky, as blandly smug, as carefully secretive and as vociferously righteous as a combination, say, of Tartuffe, Chadband, Count Fosco and Ah Sin. That such tricks of his trade were originally mere camouflage for the undoing of the criminally wary is no complaint of mine. My quarrel is that he has allowed such tricks and capers to become so much a part of his makeup that he is no longer aware that they are tricks at all.

But he was certainly at his company best that Tuesday evening, and from the moment when he handed Bernice a really fine bunch of early daffodils. I almost asked him if it had been tough going getting over the cemetery wall. Bernice upbraided him delightfully for spending so much money, which just shows the different way we look at things. But to get to George's job of work.

For once I was wrong, and there were to be neither apologies nor propitiation. George was off the following morning for professional calls and conferences in West Suffolk, Cambridgeshire, West Norfolk and South Lincolnshire. Spread over some months there had been a series of isolated thefts from country churches. The various police authorities had got nowhere, and now the Yard was acting as a kind of co-ordination, and George would try to get results from a piecing together of what little information there was.

"What sort of thefts, George?" I wanted to know. "Poor boxes and that sort of thing?"

He gave me a glare. Then he remembered in time that a fool, when he happens also to be host, should be suffered reasonably gladly. The glare became a smirk.

"Not petty thieving," he said. "Carpets principally. One or two fine old pieces of furniture, but principally carpets and rugs. ... What's the matter?"

Bernice and I had looked at each other with something of a wild surmise. My fingers rose to my horn-rims—a nervous trick of mine when at a sudden mental loss or on the edge of discovery.

"You tell him, Ludovic," Bernice said, but I knew she was bursting to tell the story herself.

"It's really your story, darling," I hypocritically protested. "You were the one things happened to."

Bernice led off and I added a touch or two, and the story was this.

The previous September we were going to Norwich where I had a job of work for which petrol was provided. A long week-end was all that was needed, and then, as we had hoarded petrol of our own, we decided to extend the trip by starting off four days early and loitering on the way. Suffolk is my native county, and there were scenes I wished to revisit and places unknown which I certainly was wanting to see. Bernice was keen on church architecture, and, since East Anglian churches are about the finest in the country, my original idea seemed a happy one. Forthwith we mapped out an itinerary that would take us through the less frequented parts of Essex and Suffolk, and so through Cambridgeshire to the Fens, and ultimately to Norwich from the west.

It was at a little village which I will call Blifield that our adventure occurred. We had lunched at a town on the route and that afternoon were cruising along quiet roads and lanes. It was a lovely autumn day, and under the hot sun the homely countryside looked drowsy with sleep and thirst. Meadows were parched from the drought, and so early had harvest come that fields already had their stubbles ploughed. Cattle lay in the scant shade of hedges, and horses stamped the ground and swished their tails against the incessant flies. I was feeling a bit drowsy myself, and when we came suddenly to quite a pretty village and caught sight of a church with a remarkably handsome steeple I decided to let Bernice explore while I took a nap.

The church lay along a narrow lane a good two hundred yards from the nearest house. Superb elms fringed the churchyard and a small wood lay between church and village. The lane itself forked about a hundred yards from the church and gave two approaches. I was not sure if I could reverse the car if I took either branch, so I drew up one and backed into the other, and there were steps and a gate opening on a path that led to the church porch. I couldn't see it because the hedge was too high, but what I did have full in view was the nearer stretch of the branch lane that was facing me.

Bernice had been gone quite a short time when I heard a car change gear somewhere along that lane and apparently near the church. Then suddenly the car shot into sight. It was medium sized and black, and just before it hurtled round to the main lane I caught a glimpse of the driver—a youngish man with a sallow face and thin moustache, and his felt hat pulled well down over his eyes. It was the merest flash of a view that I had, and I was only just aware, for instance, that another man sat alongside him, for that car swerved violently round the bend at the fork and was gone in a cloud of dust. The risk the driver had taken made me shudder, for had another car been coming, however slowly, along the main lane the two must have crashed head on.

Almost at once Bernice appeared.

"You're back soon?" I said. "Nothing worth seeing, was there?"

"A man scared me," she said. "I think he's still in the church."

I should have laughed if she hadn't looked so genuinely frightened. Just as she neared the porch, it appeared, a man had suddenly bolted out, and just when her feet left the grass for the gravel of the path. It was as if the sound of her feet had woke him up when he should have been on duty.

"Not this door, lady, further along there."

She thanked him and went in search of the door. It turned out to be a small door that gave direct access to the vestry, but it also was locked! No twisting of the handle and no pushing with a shoulder could alter the fact, and as it was so clearly the door that the man had indicated she turned back to tell him about it. But he was no longer in the porch, and, still more curious to note, that main door was now ajar! Then puzzlement became alarm. Perhaps the man thought she was alone. *Maybe he was waiting for her inside the porch door.*

It's a poor husband who can't be bellicose on behalf of his wife. I locked the car and pocketed the ignition key and we went back to the porch. Bernice hadn't heard a car drive off, and prob- ably because she had been on the opposite side of the church and had been making a fairish noise herself. The man who had spoken to her looked like a tradesman in his Sunday best, she said. He was also middle-aged, plump and rather tall.

The porch door was still ajar and I stepped inside, and there was the same utter stillness and cool and queer ecclesiastical odour that had met us before in a score of country churches. Then while Bernice waited, I explored that church and I could guarantee that never a soul was in it. Then when I told her about that car she had the sudden feeling that the men were thieves. Nothing had been tampered with as far as I could judge, and yet what other explanation was there? The man in the porch might reasonably have been on watch while a confederate was inside on some dirty work. Bernice had been momentarily lured out of the way and he had warned his confederate and the two had bolted out of the church to their car and then headlong off. From just outside the porch, by the way, the roof of my car could be plainly seen, so the watcher had guessed at once that Bernice was probably not alone.

Bernice insisted that we should call at the vicarage, but when we found it no one was at home. At the post office I got the telephone number, and that evening I rang the vicar from our hotel and told him what had happened. He seemed both grateful and perturbed and said he'd ring me himself later. It was after dinner when he did so, and then he was very relieved. The only thing to attract thieves, he said, was a fine oriental carpet presented to the church many years before by the then lord of the manor, but by the mercy of providence the doctor's wife had taken it home—as previously arranged—a day or so before to give it its annual treatment against moths.

When we got back to London we found a letter awaiting us. It said the police had been making enquiries and two men answering roughly to our furnished descriptions had visited the village in the July and therefore possibly to explore the contents of the church. It added—and we were in hearty agreement— that unless a church was full in the eye of houses or cottages, its treasures were at the mercy of thieves, for with that kind of gentry fear of sacrilege was a mighty poor deterrent. Even if a church was locked, a visitor could collect the key and then it would be easy to make a false key—bulky though it might be—for a subsequent surreptitious visit. In the letter I wrote back I mentioned some of the fine carpets and rugs and specimens of early furniture which we had seen in churches and which had made our mouths water. Had I been criminally inclined, more than one of those specimens might now be adorning my flat.

"I think you were right, Bernice," George said. "In any case it's interesting. It may be even more so when I hear what people have got to say on my trip."

"Carpets and rugs seem the likeliest stuff," I said.

"Easy to put in the boot of a car," he said. "That's more than you can do with a Tudor or Chippendale chair."

"And how profitable!" That was Bernice, and her tone seemed to have an unseemly regret. "I need a new carpet in this room, but it'd be criminal, even if I could get one, to pay the prices they ask. Look at the advertisements in the papers!"

She instanced some friends of hers and the fabulous price they had made of an old carpet they no longer needed.

"I know," George said. "And when you get to the genuine oriental article you're in bigger money still. And there's a first-class market."

"Who are the thieves? Black marketeers and so on?"

"Most likely," George told us. "The sort of people who can get false number-plates and registration books and licences and so on—just in case."

"A private collector couldn't be at work as well?"

George chuckled to Bernice.

"A guilty conscience," he told her. "Maybe when you're both out of this flat I'll have it searched."

"I'm not overburdened with brains, George," I told him with false modesty, "but if I'd lifted a carpet or two I'd have enough sense to keep it well out of sight. But you don't believe then that a crank of a private collector might be doing some of the thieving?"

George shrugged his shoulders and he refused to commit himself. By that time the following week, he said, he might know a great deal more.

"By the way," I said, "when I'm at Stepford you might be reasonably close at some time or other. Why not slip along, if it's only for a meal. Bernard Ampling's a most delightful chap. You'd like him no end."

"Where is this Stepford place exactly?"

"Two miles this side of Helmsbury."

"A nice little town, Helmsbury," George said. "I think I like it as well as any country town I've been in. What's it got? About ten thousand people?"

"I doubt it," I said. "But I know it's got two churches and a couple of cinemas—and, of course, a first-class golf course. And it's an easy run to the sea. That's what helps to make it a good sort of place to retire to."

I wrote the address for him in case he might be able to pay a visit:

> *Bernard Ampling,*
> *The Pleasance,*
> *Stepford,*
> HELMSBURY.

"He's a retired schoolmaster," added Bernice; "and at Halstead, Ludo's old school."

"He's not the stage kind of schoolmaster," I said. "He's been a great sportsman in his time."

"He's very, very charming," Bernice said, and then added an unconscious something that was almost blasphemy. "He and Ludo are such opposite types and that's why they get on so well together."

Now a man can't very well argue his own merits, and I forgot that none-too-happy remark till I was in bed that night and waiting for sleep. Then it struck me that Bernice had been shrewdly to the point when she had described Bernard and myself as opposites. Or hadn't she? Wasn't there a paradox that she had altogether missed? Permit me once more to explain.

Bernard's brain is the kind that I admire, for it is so little like my own. Your mathematician and your advanced physicist have an intellectual depth and resource far beyond my shallow own. Mine is a brain that must be darting hither and thither and would wilt under the concentration that the higher mathematics have always seemed to me to demand. I like knowing a goodish deal about a whole lot of things instead of being a specialist in any one. I like my leisure to be varied, too: to be high-brow and low-brow, and free of the bounds of a single hobby. I like, for instance, the surreptitious studying of my fellow men. I like crossword puzzles of the more abstruse kind, but I've no use for chess, for that isn't my kind of problem. Mysteries gnaw at me like an aching tooth, and yet my flibbertigibbet sort of brain has to find a quick answer or none at all.

Now the paradox is that, while Bernard and I are so much unlike, he has been just as catholic in the matter of sport. I have heard him say that there is far more fun in playing a lot of games fairly well than in playing one near to perfection. But in sport our only meeting place is golf—at which we are about on a par. My six-foot-three always made me too lath-like for games of the robuster sort, and my eyes—useless without glasses—made me squeamish of cricket and the risk of a rising ball. But we do have one thing in common—a passion for what are known as antiques. He, like myself, inherited some good pieces and has all his life collected more. And there again our taste in common is for furniture; for whereas my second love was always china, his is pictures.

That somewhat scatterbrained portrait of a couple of people brings me naturally to a third—George Wharton. Sometimes I've been tempted to call George's brains mere astuteness; not, I should say, because of any intellectual arrogance on my part, but only in some peevish, irritated moment. Mind you, there are times when I must be a rasping, fretful irritation to George himself, particularly when some imp of inconsequence makes me regard with a maddening flippancy something that ought to be serious.

But George's brain is really the worrying, tenacious kind, that gets teeth into a problem and burrows away relentlessly till something happens. You see what I mean even if the metaphors are hopelessly confused. George also has an excellent memory, and his vast experience is a private encyclopaedia to which he is able to refer. And what Bernice said about Bernard Ampling and myself applies as well to Wharton and myself—that in spite of little tiffs and divergencies we work well together because we have so little in common—except an equal urge to tackle the problem in hand.

But I wasn't thinking about anything like that when I neared Helmsbury. Basic petrol had gone and it was a train that took me there, and on that desperately slow journey with rain lashing the windows and little to be seen outside, I began thinking of those thieves whose activities Bernice had interrupted. I thought how annoyed that driver chap must have been when he went into the church and found no carpet there, and I imagined he was hunting the vestry for it when Bernice's appearance kyboshed the whole business. By modern prices, so the vicar had told us, that carpet was cheap at four hundred pounds. A couple of people, working like those two we had seen at Blifield, could with little trouble and less risk pick up a thousand or two in the course of a concentrated week.

Then I wondered if, after all, a private collector had any hand in that series of thefts. I thought, if furtively, of a set of eight perfect Chippendale chairs that Bernice and I had seen in the gallery pew of a certain church, and a dated Henry the Eighth chair we had seen in a certain vestry, and it seemed to me that, provided the articles were stolen from a district sufficiently remote, a collector needn't keep them in a private place for private gloating, but could ironically and pridefully display them to his less knowledgeable friends and even maybe to a jealous dealer. And so engrossed was I with those thoughts—and myself, of course, as the knavish collector—that I became aware only just in time that Helmsbury was the name of the station which a porter was vociferously calling.

I got my two bags down and scrambled out to the platform. Helmsbury is a junction, and quite a few people were scurrying through the driving rain to the shelter of the main station. As I, too, moved off, peering through the rain for a glimpse of Bernard, I nearly knocked a man off his feet.

"I'm so sorry!"

He mumbled a something and hurried on, and then I knew that somehow his face had been vaguely familiar. Somewhere I had seen him before, and as I trudged through the rain I suddenly remembered where. That thinnish, sallow face and the dark moustache, and the felt hat pulled well down over the eyes. And then I smiled to myself as I knew it couldn't be. The face of the driver of that car in the Blifield lane had been seen for no more than two seconds at the most, and the face of the man who had just turned annoyedly at my apology had been little more than as quick a blur.

"Hallo, there! What a perfectly horrible day!"

There was Bernard, looking scarcely a day older than when I had seen him three years before. Just what happened I don't recall, but I know he insisted on taking one of the bags and I imagined we had a word or two of stilted conversation.

"That man there," I suddenly said. "The one in the brown hat, just going through the barrier. Do you know him?"

But whoever it was had already gone through and I had to explain that I thought him someone I knew. I realised, too, that I had been so engrossed with those ideas of mine in the train that I'd been off-hand with Bernard, or even rude. But he seemed to have noticed nothing, and a minute or two later we were chatting away in the taxi that was taking us the two miles to Stepford.

CHAPTER II

A HOLIDAY BEGINS

THERE WERE many reasons why I had not seen Bernard Ampling for so long a time. When his mother was alive—my Aunt Margaret as she was—I paid almost regular visits to Stepford, and then the relationships between Bernard and myself were rather unusual. He was much older than myself, as I have said, and so I had not only an aunt but—in my younger days, at least—a kind of uncle as well, and a generous, helpful one at that. But as the years go by, ages cease to count and we had grown together, as it were. I perhaps was a bit more decrepit than my years, and he was uncommonly fit and active for his, and that seemed to make us more or less the same age.

Soon after the fall of France he had been asked to undertake some specialist work for the Government, and in 1943 he had been sent to Canada and had stayed there till the end of the war. Thereafter I always seemed to have too many claims on my rare holidays, or else my work just cut across times that were suitable for himself, and we had seen each other once in town and no more.

"Let me see; when were you here last?" he asked me as our taxi waited at the traffic lights just short of the High Street.

"I think it was on a flying visit when I was on leave in 1942," I said. "Just before your mother died."

"Of course," he said. "That wretched war is always getting in the way of my memory."

"Many changes, are there?"

"Very few," he said. "Ellen stayed on, of course, and acts as housekeeper."

"I shall miss your mother," I told him. "I was very fond of her—not that everyone wasn't. You're very like her you know."

"And she was very like your mother," he said. "You and I ought to be alike according to that, but we aren't."

But we weren't all that unlike, as I said, except perhaps in the matter of height where I had the advantage or liability of six inches. He was slim, too, like myself, though far more wiry, but his face had that tan of weather that mine had never had the chance to acquire. The really attractive thing about him was the look of perpetual amusement or ironic contemplation that lay in the eyes and the wrinkles at their corners, and the humorous quirk, as I'd call it, at the corners of his mouth. He looked, in fact, as if there was always something to enjoy; or maybe it was an endless and amused appreciation of the fact that he'd escaped marriage.

"The antique shop still there?" I asked, squinting through the rain as we moved along the High Street.

"The same shop, but much larger," he said. "That frightful old swindler, Tidman, has gone and a new man has it. New, I say, but he's been here—let me see; it must be four or five years. Frosbeck his name is."

"I just remember Tidman," I said. "I suppose the slump hit him."

"There was an awful slump, of course, but I think he had the wind up about the bombing. Helmsbury took a nasty knock or two. Look out there, for instance."

There was a large open area that was probably a cleared site, but I didn't remember Helmsbury sufficiently well to know what had once been there.

"Frosbeck bought the business fairly cheaply," Bernard went on. "He must have done awfully well, too, during the latter part of the war, what with the two big American aerodromes almost on our doorstep. By the way, there's a second antique shop now. Another comparative newcomer named Corbit opened up at this end of High Street. A rather smaller shop than Frosbeck's."

"What's he like?"

"I don't altogether trust him," Bernard said: "There's no good reason why I shouldn't. Perhaps it's his manner. A bit too ingratiating, a touch too plausible. You know, Uriah Heepish."

"What's his stuff like?"

"Rather too much reproduction. His shop's absolutely stiff with fake brass and showy pictures. You know the kind of thing. And he's just a bit too plausible for my liking. That kind of thing always seems to me to let an antique dealer down. He's far too obsequious, if you know what I mean."

I agreed that obsequiousness wasn't the hall mark of a reliable dealer, at least as far as my experience went. I'd always found that a dealer of any standing had the quietness of manner and the kind of natural dignity that comes from a confidence both in himself and his stock, and, perhaps more than all, from continual contacts with customers who had the now esteemed dangerous assets of birth and breeding.

"Frosbeck's very different, I gather."

"From Corbit—yes. He's a really well-read man. Quite a good fellow in every way. He plays a good game of bridge into the bargain."

We were well out of the town and I grimaced as I saw the water standing on the sodden fields.

"Doesn't look too promising for golf," I said.

"I doubt if we'll get a game for a day or two, however quickly it dries up," he told me. "The last game I had was on Monday, and it was no fun at all. Simply one long squelch. And we've had a lot of rain since then."

I suddenly sat up in my seat. There was the mound of sawdust that marked the sawmill-timberyard, and we were passing Endover Lane that ran alongside it.

"Back in Stepford," I said, "and it feels pretty good, golf or no golf. Any changes in the village?"

"None of any consequence," he said.

"Truebent still at the woodyard?"

"Oh yes. Truebent's still there. Just a bit older, like all of us."

"Didn't he use to play a thundering good game of bridge?"

Bernard grinned.

"He certainly did—and does, as I sometimes find out to my cost. He's the devil of a chap to be up against when you're trying to bluff."

"And what about the vicar? He's still here?"

"Yes, Langdon's still here. He and I share a gardener. We neither of us need a full-time man."

We were now going through the village proper, and the sight of the tiny chapel had recalled a someone else.

"What about that cabinet-maker you used to employ sometimes? Is he still here?"

"Turbey?"

"That's the chap. He used to live just down Endover Lane. A regular fruity sort of character he used to be."

"He still lives in the same cottage, but he works now for Corbit."

"Is he still as religious as ever? I remember his ticking me off for a spot of swearing."

"Oh yes," he said, and seemed rather amused. "Turbey's still a vociferous Methodist. His wife comes in three mornings a week to help Ellen. She's not so vociferous. But here we are."

The car was slowing. We had passed the church and the main cluster of cottages, and now we were through the village and the car was drawing into the little driveway of The Pleasance.

The house, a smallish one of the mid-Georgian period, looked precisely as when I had seen it last, for that had been in a mild winter. There was the same lawn with the crescent rose-beds and the circular sweep of drive, and the same trellis-work as a screen between garage and house, and the same lopped elms just visible beyond and above the kitchen garden. Ellen Cockley was waiting at the door. She had been cook in Aunt Margaret's time and would now be well over sixty, but she didn't seem to have altered much except perhaps that her hair was greyer and she was wearing a black dress with a white collar instead of the uniform in which I always seemed to remember her. She remembered me, too, and it was nice to be greeted as if I belonged. Bernard had called her the housekeeper, but it was clear from the start that she was definitely the mistress. But her homely Suffolk was still there. As soon as I had spoken to her, my collector's curiosity had got the better of my manners, and I was staring round at the new chest in the hall and wondering if the barometer was the one that I ought to know.

"You can look at all them things later on, Mr. Ludovic," she told me briskly. "You get up to your room and get them damp things off. Mr. Bemard'll show you where. Tea'll be ready soon as you're down."

It might be as well if you knew the lie of the land, and luckily it was the easiest house in the world to memorise. You came through a porch to a largish hall and cloak-room. On the left was the drawing-room-lounge and on the right the dining-room. Behind the dining-room and communicating by both door and serving hatch was the kitchen, and behind the lounge—it had always been called the drawing-room in Aunt Margaret's time—was the former breakfast-room, now Ellen's sitting-room. The upstairs geography was just as easy. Stairs led to it from the hall. My bedroom was that above the lounge and Bernard's was above the dining-room. In a space corresponding to the downstairs hall were the bathroom and lavatory. Above the kitchen was Ellen's bedroom, and alongside it a spare room. Not a large house, as you see, but the rooms were of quite good size and lofty and well-proportioned. The ceilings of the main rooms were beautifully moulded, and the lounge had a particularly fine fireplace.

My bedroom was Bernard's old room and so it was new to me, and in it were some pieces that I hadn't seen before, including a walnut tall-boy that had quality in every inch of it. The insatiable curiosity I have about most things becomes shameless where other people's antiques are concerned, and I thoroughly investigated that room before I even began to unpack. I thought it a beautiful room, and the bed was comfortable, and there was an excellent view. A minute or two later Ellen was calling up the stairs that the scones were getting cold.

"I thought we might as well shut out the weather," Bernard said when I came into the lounge. It certainly looked snug with the curtains drawn and a good fire burning, and I had the quick, unworthy thought that maybe Bernard had realised that artificial light and cheerfulness would enhance the beauty of even that lovely room.

"Come on, my dear fellow," he told me. "We'll have a look at things later. Ellen was getting very concerned about these scones."

But I couldn't help talking about them during tea. So many things seemed to be new.

"I don't say it grudgingly," I told him, "but these must have cost you a packet. I've given up serious collecting. Modern prices terrify me."

"I do very little of it either," he said. "Quite a lot of things I had at Halstead and they came here with me. Then I really had to replace the heavy Victorian stuff when Mother died and I did buy fairly freely. Luckily it was during the slump and I could realise now at a very big profit. Even things that I bought soon after my return from Canada have appreciated quite a lot—that knee-hole desk, for instance, and that chiming bracket clock."

"Well, give me the good old days," I said, "when you never knew what you were going to pick up. Like that Chelsea cup and saucer I got for half a crown. Nowadays everybody knows far too much. Rarely a hope of picking up a bargain."

"I wouldn't say that," he told me with his ironic grin. "The easiest people in the world to get bargains from are the dealers. They have to know so much about everything that they can't possibly know everything about anything. That's where the expert comes in. You know infinitely more about china than most dealers, unless it happens to be a particular dealer's special hobby. Take those two miniatures, for instance. I bought them from Frosbeck only about a month ago."

They were hanging above the mantelpiece. Ellen came to remove the tea-tray, and when she had gone I took them down.

"What are they?" he asked me quizzically.

"This sort of stuff is your speciality, not mine," I said. "You tell me."

He went to the writing-desk and brought me his glass. I gave my spectacles a clean and then had a look. It was superb work—no doubt about that. The eyes and hair of the woman were uncannily meticulous, and yet the general effect was perfection itself. The man's was obviously a first-rate portrait, and his complexion had a velvety sort of texture like the bloom on a plum.

"Right, are they?"

"The backs are open," he told me. "Look at the skin. Look at the ivory."

I had a look. The gold-beater's skin at the back had the colour of old leather, and the thin disc of ivory on which the miniatures were painted had a slightly greenish tinge.

"They're pretty good," I said, "the miniatures, I mean. And genuine, as you say, though you know far more about that than I do. Whose are they?"

"Plimer's."

My eyebrows lifted.

"And they cost you?"

"Twenty guineas the two. And at the present moment they're insured for two hundred."

"Good lord!" I said. "And Frosbeck didn't know."

"I was lucky," he said. "Just happened to go in the shop when he was looking at a small collection he'd bought at a private house. There were about ten or eleven if I remember rightly. I had a look and asked him what he'd take for those two. Twenty guineas, he said, and I gave him the cheque."

"Wonder what he'd think if he knew?"

The old ironic smile was there again.

"Shall I tell you?"

"He does know?"

"It's like this," Bernard said. "Frosbeck's a good sort of chap and you don't like getting too good a bargain from someone who's more than a dealer. Whom you play bridge with occasionally, for instance. I didn't tell him what they were worth. I left that to him. I just told him, and only a day or two later, that I didn't think he'd charged me enough and I was feeling just a bit unhappy about it."

"What'd he say?"

"He said he'd made a good profit and if I'd come into the shop a very few minutes later than I did he'd have made the thorough examination of them which he hadn't had time for. All he asked was that if I ever wanted to sell I'd give him the first offer. He flatly refused to take an additional cheque which I offered him."

"And when you come to look at it, that's the way to do—and to keep—business," I said. "You've been a good customer of his?"

"I've bought several things," he said, "but rarely at what you could call bargain prices. Frosbeck and I never mix up business with friendship, and that's the way I prefer it."

We went along to the dining-room to have a look round, and I was staggered by the changes. I remembered it as a dull, stodgy room—the kind that though spotlessly clean yet looks dusty and even grubby. Now the heavy mahogany stuff had all gone, and so had the red carpet that used to cover every inch of the floor.

The wall-paper had gone, too, and the walls had a warm sort of biscuit-coloured distemper that showed up the frames of family portraits. The Chippendale grandfather clock was the only thing that I recognised, for the furniture was now Heppelwhite. A particularly fine Vauxhall mirror hung over the fireplace.

"I bought that from Frosbeck," Bernard said. "Thirty guineas I paid him for it."

It was a stiffish price, but it was worth it, I said. Then I really noticed the floor.

"The old flooring wasn't too good," he said, "so I had it up. Turbey got hold of some old oak and laid this floor in his spare time. It's come up to a lovely polish."

"I like the rugs," I said.

There was one each side of the Heppelwhite table and another in front of the sideboard.

"They're not bad," he said.

"Old, are they? I'm an absolute ignoramus about rugs."

"I don't know an awful lot about them myself," he said. "This one's a Bokhara, and that one Kirghiz. The other I haven't bothered about identifying yet."

"You've acquired them recently?"

"Yes—and no." With the grin there was a kind of sideways, deprecatory shake of the head. The look became more personal and more quizzical. "You're still fond of mysteries?"

"I suppose so," I said, and didn't see what he was driving at. "They're still part of my bread and butter. Why do you ask?"

"Well, here's one for you. This is the one room of the house I don't let the vicar enter."

I thought for a minute and then gave it up.

"What's the answer?"

"I'd rather not tell you just now," he said. "But talking of rugs, I've got Holman's *Oriental Rugs and Carpets* if you'd like to dip into it some time."

I said I'd be only too keen, but as it happened I had no chance to open the book that night, for just after dinner the vicar dropped in to fix a change of arrangements about the shared gardener. He said he wasn't staying for more than a minute, but it turned out to be two hours.

"Let me see," he had said to me. "Didn't Bernard tell me that you're associated with Scotland Yard?"

I admitted I was the minutest of cogs in a pretty big machine.

"Must be fascinating work, tracking down criminals," he said. "Still, everyone to his trade."

"It wouldn't be up my alley!" Bernard told him. "I'm afraid I should find myself pretty often on the side of the criminals."

Langdon laughed. He was evidently only too used to Bernard's contrariwise methods in argument.

"Oh, I'm serious enough," Bernard told him. "Aren't we all criminals nowadays? Even you, vicar."

He instanced a certain matter of extra petrol in those recent good old days when there had been such a thing as basic, and Langdon's rubicund old face took on a deeper colour. And of course that led to talk of the black market, and that led to talk about the Government, and that required a drink. We were still gabbling away when the bracket clock struck the hour.

"Is that nine?" the old vicar asked naively.

"It's ten," I said.

"Heavens!" he said, and got at once to his feet. "Ethelberta will be notifying the police that I'm missing. I must simply scramble."

The rain had ceased, but it was blowing a gale. Bernard and I saw him off at the front gate and watched the light of his torch flickering in the blackness of that tempestuous night.

"Who's this Ethelberta he was anxious about?" I asked as we turned back to the house.

She was since my time—a sister who was keeping house for him now that his wife was dead. Then back in the house, while he was telling me more about her, it suddenly struck me that he had been remarkably generous, or else forgetful, in arranging with Langdon to take over the gardener's insurance.

"Langdon wasn't imposing on me," Bernard said, and as if he wasn't too anxious to talk about it. "It's none too good a living and he's been hard hit by recent legislation. I can afford the insurance—far better than he can."

We neither of us felt like going at once to bed, so we had another drink. I had a look at *The Times* again and Bernard picked up the Helmsbury *Courier*. I, as curious as ever, had looked to see what he was reading, and I said I liked those local and provincial papers.

"Very essential in the country," he said, "especially out here in the long grass. You get the cinema programmes, let alone all the local news."

A minute or so later he was giving a chuckle, and he looked up, to catch my eye.

"Just another row at today's town council meeting," he told me. "Always scrapping, those fellows are. Truebent seems to be in it this time. He and a frightful old ruffian called Drew." He chuckled again. "I must pull Truebent's leg about this when I see him."

I was having a look at the headlines:

SCENE AT COUNCIL MEETING
COUNCILLOR DREW HINTS AT FINANCIAL SCANDAL

He went on with his reading and I with mine. Then he put the paper aside and asked if I'd have yet another nightcap. I said I'd had enough and I was feeling a bit sleepy.

"And what did the scandal turn out to be?" I asked him.

"No one knows yet," he told me amusedly. "Apparently Drew got Truebent's goat about something and they had a few words. Drew said that before Truebent started finding motes in other people's eyes he'd better take the beam out of his own. Truebent challenged him to be more explicit, and old Drew promised that at the next council meeting he certainly would be. He said there'd be a scandal that'd rock the whole town."

I said local councils were stiff with back-scratching and jobbery and I hoped Truebent hadn't let himself in for something.

"He's quite capable of looking after himself," Bernard told me and still amusedly, and with that we went up to bed.

* * * * *

I slept like a log. There was a tap at my door, and before I was sufficiently aroused to call a "Come in!" the door opened and there was a woman with a tray. I sat up, blinked, then hooked on my glasses.

"Good morning," I said.

"Good morning, sir. Here's your tea, and a letter."

"You're Mrs. Turbey?" I asked her as I took the tray. "I know your husband very well. How is he, by the way?"

"Keeping very well, sir. He'll be sixty next week, if he's spared. Shall I draw the blinds?"

"Do please," I said, and I said to myself, *"if he's spared."* Rather an old-fashioned Methodist flavour about that. But little of the vociferous Methodism of Turbey—as Bernard had called it—about his wife, or ought I to have said *spouse*? Turbey, as I remembered him, was quite fat, and irritatingly cheerful. She was spare and desiccated, with a highly coloured face, and lips that were thin and rather blue. Turbey, as I remembered him, was always singing the songs of Zion, but her harp had apparently been long since hung on the willows.

The door closed on her and it suddenly struck me that she must have come remarkably early to work. But it was after half-past eight, and I remembered that Bernard had said there was no need for hurry in the mornings. And, wonder of wonders, the sun was shining. I got out of bed and had a peep through the open window and it certainly seemed as if we were in at long last for a really fine day. Then I had a look at my letter. I had guessed it was an air-mail letter from Bernice, but it had a Cambridge postmark, and almost at once I spotted the writing as George Wharton's.

Dear Travers,

Nothing much doing at present and it looks as if this business may take longer than I thought. It's the old story. If action had been taken earlier we might have got more evidence and done something about it. As for the carpets and rugs, the descriptions given me have been so far about as much use as a sick headache. Not a single identification mark beyond what might apply to hundreds of similar rugs. Still, I gather it's hard to describe such things beyond their general colour and a rough idea of the pattern.

Also in the handbooks of most churches, the kind that you find on a table inside the door, price twopence or threepence, there seems to be no mention of carpets and rugs, they being taken for granted. I have got one though with an account of a missing picture and another—I haven't got a spare of that—with picture and description of a Chinese Chippendale chair that seems to be very valuable.

I've been giving a lot of thought from time to time about these stolen things, and I can't get away from the idea that since the thief seems always to have been very knowledgeable he'd have some idea of the best market. If he could sell, for instance, to an unscrupulous collector he'd get far more than from an ordinary fence. Or he might sell to an unscrupulous antique dealer who had a safe market in mind.

If I know you as well as I think I do, I know that a good part of your time will be spent in the antique shops of the town and district. I know that's a pretty hopeless chance, but you might keep your ears and eyes open. You remember that route of mine? Think it over and ask yourself if where I am and where you are don't mean something, though my own preference is for Ipswich. There are always rascals in the antique trade.

There are more unlikely things than that I might slip along some time next week for an hour or so. Will warn you in good time. You can keep the little handbook.

Yours as ever,

GEORGE W.

PS. A rather peculiar thing about that stolen picture. About a fortnight ago a man called on the vicar at Hickford and asked for a detailed description. He wouldn't say who he was, but the vicar gave him a handbook like the one herewith.

I had a look at that handbook which was for the Church of St. Peter, Hickford Parva, Cambridgeshire. The picture was quite a small one, twenty inches by fourteen, and was said to be by Zurbaran, the seventeenth-century Spaniard. It had been presented to the church by the widow of a Colonel Russton who had brought it home after the Peninsular War. It was described as both interesting and valuable because it was so much smaller than anything known of the artist's, if one excludes, say, part of a triptych.

A fulsome description followed, penned by the donor. I saw it as just one more Crucifixion theme with Spanish treatment and colour, and I realised that the handbook had probably never been brought up to date all the years it had been printed. Then it struck me that I ought to show Bernard the photograph and description and hear what he made of it, and then I changed my mind. At my job one learns to be secretive by nature. Even my wife—or Wharton's wife—never knows more than the general public about a case on which we may happen to be engaged. Official business was official business, I thought to myself, and in this case it was Wharton's business and not particularly mine.

But as I was dressing I did wonder what it was that Wharton had so cryptically mentioned in his letter about his itinerary and my present position, and how he preferred Ipswich. When I saw what he was driving at I wondered why I had not seen it before. Wharton's itinerary made a kind of rough arc at distances varying from thirty miles to over a hundred around Helmsbury, or, if it came to that, around Ipswich. Suppose the thief or thieves lived at Ipswich, then all their thefts had been made at the ends of spokes, as it were, that radiated from the Ipswich hub. Had the thieves had a London headquarters, then the thefts would have been along an arc facing inwards towards London.

A gong went downstairs, and I went down, too. Ellen asked how I had slept, and then Bernard appeared and I told them both that I had slept like the dead.

"Harris has cleaned and oiled both your golfing shoes," she said. "And mind you're not back late to lunch. Half-past twelve's the time on Saturdays."

It was too wet underfoot for golf, he told her. What we might do would be to take the ten-fifteen bus to Helmsbury and come back by the twelve-ten. I said that would suit me fine.

CHAPTER III
THE BROWN FELT HAT

THE GLASS had risen far too steeply for Bernard's liking, and though the morning sun was the finest we had had for days and the wind had died down, there was a feeling in the air that the wind might at any time begin rising again. I quoted the old Suffolk saying of my boyhood—more wind, more wet—and Bernard added that more wet meant even less chance of golf. Also he had seen the early morning sky and his prophecy was that though we might get even two fine days there was more wet to come. It was a prophecy that turned out amazingly correct. That very afternoon the wind rose again and by night was once more a howling gale. And yet if the weather had kept fine things wouldn't have turned out as they conveniently did. Take the matter of bridge.

"It strikes me that we oughtn't to let the weather get us down," Bernard said at breakfast. "We can't play golf in a gale even if the course dries up, which it won't. What about some bridge? To-morrow afternoon might be nice if Ellen could fix up tea."

I said I was all for it. I got practically no bridge nowadays and it'd be great fun provided the other three weren't experts.

"Falkner might make one," he said. "He's the headmaster of the grammar school, and since your time."

He rang Falkner, but Falkner regretted he was already promised forth. So Truebent was rung, and he said he'd be delighted to come.

"Good," Bernard said. "I've got Ludovic Travers staying here. You remember him, I expect."

I don't know what Truebent said, but Bernard did a bit of leg-pulling.

"What's this about you and old Drew? Don't say he's caught you dipping into the till?"

After that it seemed to be Truebent who was doing the talking. When Bernard hung up, he wasn't looking quite so ironically cheerful.

"Truebent sounded to me as if he had a guilty conscience," he told me, and then glanced at the hall grandfather. "Hallo! We'd better be hurrying or we'll miss that bus."

We just made it. It was a short enough ride and yet a depressing one. I don't mean because the bus was packed, or because I couldn't help seeing the flooded bunkers of the golf course, but what always depressed me was the bungalow suburb that began just where the golf course ended. We got off at the Memorial, which is at the Stepford end of the High Street, because I was to be shown some of the bomb damage. The better-class residential part of the town lay, by the way, to the north and east, along the Ipswich and Newmarket Roads.

There seemed quite a few cars, principally those of farmers, I was told, for Saturday was a smaller market day and the big day for shopping and there'd be matinees at both cinemas. There were certainly plenty of people about and it was because we had to work our way carefully along the narrow and crowded pavement that I missed Corbit's antique shop. Bernard said there'd be plenty of time to come back to it after mid-morning coffee.

A minute or so later we were at Frosbeck's. The shop facade had not been altered in the least, but the display in the window was very different from the heterogeneous assortments that had always comprised it in his predecessor's time. Now it consisted of one or two nice pieces of furniture and a central sofa table on which was an apple-green tea service. To a dark backing were fixed a mirror and a couple of pictures.

We went in the shop and there was the familiar smell of potpourri and furniture polish. Before I'd time for more than a quick look about me, a plumpish man with a straggly moustache was coming towards us, and from his green baize apron I guessed he was some sort of foreman. His smile showed that he knew Bernard well enough.

"Morning, sir. You'd like to see the guv'nor, or can I do anything for you?"

"Just a word with the guv'nor, Tom," Bernard told him.

"He'll be along in a minute, sir." His voice lowered as he nodded across at the office. "Mr. Drew's in there, but he'll be out in a minute."

"No hurry," Bernard said. "We'll just have a quick look round."

Tom flicked a finger to his cap and moved off to the door beyond us.

"That's Tom Polter, the general factotum," Bernard told me quietly. "A very knowledgeable chap. Used to be with an Ipswich firm."

The office seemed little more than a space partitioned off in the far corner. Through the glass of its one wall of board—the other was largely door—I could see the broad back of a tallish man and there was a front view of a short, thin man, and the fingers of the thin man were holding his chin and fidgeting nervously, and he was making wry faces as if either disagreeing with what the taller man was saying or else listening to disagreeable news. Then suddenly the thin man was shrugging his shoulders as if to give the whole thing up. The taller man turned towards the door and there was the sound of the knob. Then the thin man emerged from the office and the other followed him.

The thin man was wearing a hat and so he couldn't be Frosbeck. He looked about sixty, and what held my attention was the peevish, cantankerous look and the thin, malicious lips. Then as we moved the two caught sight of us. The thin man gave Bernard a curt nod and no more, and his cold eyes took me in. Frosbeck gave a nod, too, and a smile, and went on in the thin man's wake, and the two stood for a minute on the pavement just outside the door.

"That's the famous Alfred Drew," Bernard told me, "the one who had the scrap with Truebent at the council meeting. He doesn't like me much. He always looks like a rather scrawny bantam-cock. Plenty of money, though. He's said to have a finger in practically everything in the town."

The shop door was being closed and Frosbeck was coming towards us.

"Sorry you've had to wait."

I suppose the war should have made us used to beards again, and yet it had been a surprise to see a bearded man, and in a queer way it was like going back to one's boyhood. And Frosbeck was very like an uncle of mine: a fine figure of a man whom I could just remember. But he didn't look old. His hair was a badger grey and almost white at the temples, and yet I was sure he wasn't much over fifty. The face was full and the lips thick, though by no means sensual, and the dark eyes had a curious melancholy that gave the face its charm. His voice was a res-onant baritone—just the voice for that breadth of chest—but there was nothing about it of the bluff or hearty. It was like his manner: quiet, even reserved, and yet somehow always friendly.

"We're not here on business," Bernard told him. "This is my cousin, by the way—Ludovic Travers. This is my good friend William Frosbeck."

We shook hands and Frosbeck was asking if I was a collector.

"No you don't," Bernard told him amusedly. "I'm not going to allow him to be inveigled into swelling your bloated profits."

"There'll be time, I expect," Frosbeck told him with some-thing of the same amusement. "You're going to be a resident, Mr. Travers?"

"I'm only a guest at the moment," I told him, "but I do hope to get down more frequently than I have done. I've known this shop for a good many years, by the way."

"He's a pretty good bridge player," broke in Bernard. "He says he's had no practice lately, but if I know anything about him he's a dark horse."

"You'll have to get a game or two for him," Frosbeck said, and that led naturally to the invitation for the Sunday after-noon. Frosbeck said he'd be delighted, and he'd bring Truebent in his car.

"I never knew such a town for rogues and rascals," Bernard said. They both chuckled and the joke had to be explained to me. With petrol severely rationed, Frosbeck, or perhaps Truebent, was a kind of free taxi for the small bridge circle, especially when a session happened to be at The Pleasance. In the back of his car Frosbeck then carried a picture or a piece of furniture, and in the extreme unlikelihood of his being stopped by the local police there was the evidence that he had been calling on a possible customer. As for his passengers, well, aren't we enjoined to give people lifts?

"It's your own neck you're sticking out," Bernard told him.

"I know," Frosbeck said, "but I hate being dependent on buses, and crowded ones at that. Besides, they never seem to coincide with the end of a rubber." He gave me a smile. "All this doesn't horrify you, Mr. Travers?"

"Not a bit of it," I told him. "As a matter of fact I'm all for it. Everything in the last two years seems to have conspired to make criminals of us, and I was one of the first to succumb."

"We mustn't start talking about the Government or we'll be here for lunch," Bernard said. "We'll expect you sometime before three o'clock, then, and it'll be up to you and Truebent how you get there. Now I think Travers would like a quick look round. Anything new, is there?"

"I don't think there is. What are you particularly interested in, Mr. Travers?"

"Getting wonderful bargains," I said.

He gave a chesty chuckle.

"Strangely enough, I think most of us are. Any particular line in bargains?"

"Well, china's my hobby, or was."

"Why not show him that jug?" Bernard said. "Let's get him to give an opinion."

That scared me at once and I began making deprecatory remarks about my competence to judge anything, but the jug was being put in my hands. It was a far from unusual type: like a Worcester jug and of the cabbage-leaf pattern, with a mask under the spout. The leaves were moulded in low relief and the under-glaze decoration was blue.

"Well," said Bernard when I'd looked at it and felt it. "What's the verdict?"

"For what the opinion's worth," I said, "I don't think it's Worcester. If I had more time at it I might be more certain, but I still think it's one of those copies that used to be made by Turner of Caughley."

Bernard was staring and then grimacing. Frosbeck smiled as he took the jug back.

"Exactly my own opinion, but I wanted to be sure. I'm very grateful, Mr. Travers. I think I can confidently label it now as Caughley."

"A whole lot of people wouldn't," I said. "They'd call it Worcester and leave the customer to find out—perhaps."

Frosbeck said nothing, but there was a smile with the slow shake of the head. What neither he nor Bernard knew was how lucky I'd been over that jug, for I had inherited one, and then after our marriage Bernice had hated the sight of it. It clashed with everything, she said, so I had got an opinion from an expert and had then parted with it to a dealer. But as George Wharton used to impress on me in my early days, there's a time to prattle and a time to be dumb, and I wasn't spoiling my new reputation. By a stroke of luck I'd made a personal hit with Frosbeck, and I knew from experience that when one gets on friendly terms with a dealer there's often the chance of a genuine bargain.

We had a look round the shop and its two back annexes and there were heaps of things I'd have loved to buy if the prices hadn't been prohibitive. And yet, as Frosbeck said, he sold no end of stuff to London dealers who then had their own profit to make. Bernice, by the way, had asked me to look out for a decorative mirror, but the only one of the kind that Frosbeck had was marked at forty guineas, which was fifteen more than I was prepared to pay.

"Don't let's be despondent, Mr. Travers," he said. "I hope to attend a sale near Ipswich on Monday and there's a mirror there which strikes me as just the kind of thing you want. If I buy it I'll bring it back in my car and you can see it on Tuesday."

I said I'd be very grateful, and then Bernard was looking at his watch.

"Come in whenever you like," Frosbeck told me. "If I'm not in the shop I may be above in the flat."

"Tom Polter'll know where you are," Bernard said. "And while we're here we might as well go out the Back Street way."

I didn't know that particular piece of Helmsbury geography, but from the back room where we were a short passage led to Back Street. This was a narrowish road serving as a back entry to the shops on that particular side of the High Street, and on its far side were storerooms and warehouses. Frosbeck's garage was there, and the premises above it were his workshop and his store place for surplus stock.

"This is my favourite view of your shop, you know, Frosbeck," Bernard said quizzically. "I always have a look here before I go in the front way."

"Why's that?" I asked.

"Well," he said, "here's where all the new stock's unloaded. If ever I see a lorry standing outside here I spring very nimbly round to the front and get at the head of the bargain queue."

"I must remember that," I said, and Frosbeck told me that I probably knew Bernard's liking for a joke. I could have told Frosbeck quite a lot about that. Once I'd met a man who had been a contemporary of Bernard's at Cambridge and he told me what a vital spark my so-called uncle had been. How he had escaped being sent down for various practical jokes and escapades my informant didn't know. Now, of course, Bernard was in the staid sixties, and yet it would never have surprised me if he were suddenly to indulge in some practical joke or other even of the most flagrant kind. But Bernard was speaking, and his tone was serious.

"Alfred Drew doesn't look less miserable these days? Is he anything of a customer? I'm only asking because I've often wondered what the devil he does with all his money."

"He doesn't buy a lot nowadays," Frosbeck said. "He knows a lot, mind you, and he's a very shrewd buyer."

"One thing's a certainty," Bernard told him. "However little he spends with you, he spends much less with Stanley Corbit."

Frosbeck gave a wry smile.

"Yes," he said slowly, "I rather expect he does."

That was about all, and that last part about Drew and Corbit had been Greek to me. When we moved off, Bernard cut back a few yards and there was a passage that brought us to the High Street. Just across the road was a rather nice tea-shop. The morning rush was over and upstairs we found a table for morning coffee.

"I like Frosbeck," I said. "Everything about him seems so un-affected and genuine."

"His reputation is exceptionally good," Bernard told me. "For one thing, he doesn't stand in with other dealers. Corbit, as you can imagine, is very definitely in the ring."

"How do Frosbeck and Corbit get along? Any bad blood between them?"

"Not a bit of it. I know they go into each other's shops, and probably do each other good turns. I've myself heard Frosbeck recommend a customer to try Corbit's for something he didn't happen to have himself. That's the only way to carry on business in the same town."

I quite agreed. Then I was asking about Frosbeck's native county, as I hadn't been able to place his accent, and probably because he hadn't had any. Bernard said he couldn't say.

"Probably a Londoner," I said.

"He told me he'd always been in business in the provinces," Bernard said. "He's a widower—I know that—because one day he happened to let it slip."

"What's his bridge like?"

"Very solid. He calls well and doesn't miss a lot."

"Isn't there bridge at the local club these days?"

"Bridge of a sort," he said, "but somehow the membership seems to have reduced itself to a series of Blimps. The atmosphere's too stuffy for me. I'd rather play with people who're still alive: people like Frosbeck and Falkner and Truebent. I don't give a damn *who* people are. It's *what* they are that interests me."

There, for the first time on that visit, was the uncle of a few years ago. An apology seemed definitely needed.

"I wasn't speaking from any snobbish point of view. I know perfectly well you haven't a pennorth of snobbery in you. Neither have I, for that matter—or I hope so."

He leaned across and gave me an avuncular pat.

"My dear chap, I know you haven't."

Our coffee and biscuits came, and I remarked that the man Drew hadn't seemed too pleased at the sight of him.

"For an excellent reason," he said. "I had a hand in queering one of his pitches. I told you he had a finger in nearly every pie, and this particular business cropped up just after I got back from Canada. I was a member of the golf club committee and we got wind that a syndicate with Drew as the hidden moving spirit was trying to buy the land across the road opposite the fourth and fifth holes. The idea was to buy it, and then unload it as building lots. I was made chairman of a sub-committee and we had to work underground to try to stop that appalling eyesore along the Stepford Road. That, by the way, was when I heard most of what there was to know about old Drew. I always think of him as old, though I don't suppose he's as old as I am. Perhaps it's because he's such a shrimp. But about that land. The upshot was that the club bought it behind the back of the syndicate and old Drew's never forgiven me. He really ought to be grateful. The new Town Planning Act would have left the whole property on his hands."

"What was that bit about not buying anything at Corbit's shop?"

That was a longish story, Bernard said. Corbit and Drew were thick as thieves when they first came to Helmsbury. Alfred Drew's wife was a native of Helmsbury—she had died soon after the return—and so there was a reason for his retirement to the town, but Corbit had no apparent reason beyond the fact that he and Drew had been business partners in London. Bernard was in Canada when things happened, but there came a definite cleavage between the old partners. Drew touched nothing that didn't turn to gold, while with Corbit things went just the other way. Local talk was that Corbit opened that antique shop because he'd lost most of his money and had therefore to go into business again to make a living. Certainly he gave up a very nice house on the Ipswich Road for a much smaller one just short of the bungalow suburb on the Stepford Road.

"You mean that Corbit was jealous of Drew?" I said.

"More than that," he said. "The real split came over Nelson Corbit, Stanley's son, and Drew's daughter. I forget what her name is. Nelson had a business in London and used to come down here at week-ends I'm told, and he was very friendly with Drew's daughter. Then there was the very devil of a scandal: Nelson Corbit's firm got nobbled for black-marketeering—something to do with illegally manufacturing cosmetics—and he had to pay a terrific fine, with twelve months thrown in for luck. When he came out—that was a year or two after I got back here—Drew's daughter went to town and married him. There was a devil of a row between Drew and Stanley Corbit and the culmination came one day when Corbit knocked the old boy down in the High Street. I don't know how Drew angered him, but it was a dirty trick. Corbit's a hulking sort of chap compared with Drew."

"Didn't Drew bring an action for assault?"

"Oh no. He's not that sort if you know what I mean. Old Drew would prefer to settle things in his own way."

"And has he?"

"Not that anyone knows. But if I know him, he's biding his time."

"What about the married couple?"

"The marriage went phut in no time. She got a divorce and I believe is still living in town, though she comes down occasionally. Nelson Corbit seems to be down here for good. I don't know what he does for a living, but I rather think he helps his father."

It had gone half-past eleven and we had to be making a move. Bernard said there was some fish that had been ordered by telephone and after he'd collected it he ought to get on the telephone to Ellen. Now the bridge had been definitely fixed, she might want something else brought in besides the usual tea-cake.

"You won't want to follow me around," he said. "Why not have a quick look at Corbit's? Our bus starts from the Market Square. Better be a bit early if we want seats."

There was certainly a tremendous difference of class between Corbit's shop and Frosbeck's. In Corbit's window was a jumble of the second- and third-rate: Staffordshire figures and the cruder kind of pottery and lustre, and a mass of questionable brassware, and some poor-quality samplers, and a fake Napoleonic portrait on glass.

I stepped into the shop and a man was on me practically at once, and his hands were clasped in front of him and his shoulders had an obsequious stoop.

"Good morning, sir. Anything you're particularly interested in?"

It was a quiet and unctuous voice.

"I'm a collector of Whieldon," I said. "I suppose you don't happen to have any?"

He was black-haired but bald except for a fringe round his neck and above his ears. The lips were full and the nose hooked, and there was a paunchy look about him. A much younger man than Drew and strong enough to have snapped the old boy in two.

"Whieldon?" he said. "Not at the moment. I have one rather nice piece of Walton. A tree-backed figure of Friendship."

"I know it," I said. "The two boys clasping hands beneath a tree and a dog at their feet."

"You would like to see it?"

His face had lighted, but I shook my head.

"Sorry, but I'm interested in nothing but Whieldon. You haven't any good-quality walnut?"

"There's this piece," he said, and led the way to the back of the shop. In the comparative gloom where it couldn't be too closely inspected stood a walnut chest of drawers, and in spite of the bad light I could see that it had been heavily restored. Besides, a dealer nowadays can't keep good walnut in his shop.

"It's a nice piece," he said, and his eyes were watching my reactions. "I can let you have it cheap."

"It's not the kind of thing I want," I said.

"Only twenty-five guineas. You could sell it again at a profit."

"I'm sorry," I said, "but I'm really not interested."

I turned back and he followed at my heels.

"If you would be so good as to give me your address I should only be too glad to notify you when I have any Whieldon."

"That's very good of you," I said. "All I'm interested in is good-quality stuff in collector's condition."

I gave him a card and he made a great show of putting it in his wallet, and that was that. I thanked him again and he thanked me again and out I went to the High Street. A fish out of water was what I thought him, with the right methods for the wrong sort of customer, and the wrong sort of stock for a first-class trade.

A glance at my watch showed me that the bus left in ten minutes' time, and I stepped off the pavement and lengthened my stride. My bus was drawn up in Market Square and it looked pretty full, and there was no sign of Bernard. Then I found a downstairs seat at the back and within a couple of minutes the downstairs aisle was packed with standing passengers. I saw Bernard coming and he saw me and gave a wave. I indicated that there might be a seat upstairs.

It was just as he signalled that he understood that I caught sight of the man in the brown felt hat. He was coming straight towards the bus and I could see him perfectly and full-faced. There wasn't a doubt that it was the man into whom I'd barged on the railway station platform, but whether or not it was the driver of that car in the Blifield lane I wasn't so sure. If anything, I thought he was. Either that or practically that man's double.

"That man there—just coming towards us," I said to the man who shared the seat with me. "Do you happen to know who he is?"

He had a look and then shook his head.

"Sorry, I don't. I'm a stranger here myself."

By then the man was beyond the bus and out of sight, and it would have been hopeless for me to have tried to make my way out. Besides the conductress was getting in behind and at once the driver started up his engine. In a matter of seconds we were off.

After lunch that day I wrote a letter to Wharton and told him about the two encounters with the man in the brown felt hat. I said I could guarantee nothing, but it certainly looked as if the man either lived in Helmsbury or had his headquarters there. Wharton himself must be the judge as to whether or not the information was of any use, but in any case he couldn't say that I hadn't been trying to help. I addressed the letter to Cambridge and posted it that afternoon when Bernard and I went for a country walk.

CHAPTER IV
TWO DISCOVERIES

ONE WHOLE DAY in Stepford already gone. That was what I thought when I woke on the Sunday morning, and so far things had been a long way from bad. Ellen brought up the early tea and said it was a fine day, but very windy, and that latter I could hear for myself. But the night's gale seemed definitely abating, and all I was hoping was that on its heels wouldn't come more rain.

Bernard said rather apologetically at breakfast that he usually went to church. The congregations were so small that he felt it a bit of a duty to rally round Langdon, so to speak. I said I'd like to go, too.

"Fine," he said, "if you'd really like it. Lunch won't be till after one o'clock, so we might take a short walk afterwards."

"Round the Circle?"

"So you remembered it," he said, and smiled. I said that of course I remembered it. That had always been a natural work from The Pleasance, even if it was more like a square than a circle. Just opposite The Pleasance was the lane known as The

Drift that led past Manor Farm. Then one turned sharp left again into Endover Lane, and so home past the sawmill and through the village. Our walk from church would of course be the reverse way.

We went to church, where Langdon preached a somewhat woolly sermon to a congregation of certainly less than thirty all told. After it we had a word with Ethelberta Langdon, who again was after my time. She was tall and thin, and with quite a pleasant manner. She and Bernard seemed excellent friends, and there seemed, too, to be some kind of secret between them.

"You had a slight alarm on Friday evening?" he asked her, and in a tone that was either quizzical or amused.

"Friday?" she said with a quick frown. Then she laughed. "But of course. No, I wasn't alarmed. I knew you'd have everything in hand."

That was all, and he didn't elucidate to me when we moved on. The little chapel was where the cottages were beginning to thin out, and the morning service there was over, too. Ahead of us we caught sight of a broad back which I thought I recognised.

"That's Turbey," Bernard confirmed. "He's a regular on Sunday mornings. His missus stays at home and cooks the dinner."

Bernard's a good walker and my long shanks cover the ground at a fast rate, and that morning we had to step out smartly if we were to be home on time. The wind was a bit of a nuisance, but it certainly was bracing. Turbey's walk was rather of the stately kind and we overhauled him just as the three of us turned into Endover Lane.

"Morning, sir," he said to Bernard, and flicked a quick finger to his bowler hat.

"Morning, Henry. You remember Mr. Travers?"

I certainly remembered him well enough even if he did look even fatter and quite a bit older. His mouth gaped at the sight of me.

"Whuh, bless my heart and soul!" he told us in his broad Suffolk. "I should think I jolly well do remember him. And how are you, sir?"

His very hand was as pudgy and warm as I'd remembered it.

"I'm pretty well, thank you, Turbey. And you're looking as bonny and cheerful as ever?"

"And why not, sir?" His look, and I couldn't help thinking it a crafty one, included Bernard as well as myself. "Why shouldn't we be cheerful, sir? Religion weren't never designed, so we're told, to make people miserable."

"Good for you," I said, for the want of something more apt, and then—we were almost at his cottage—Bernard cut in:

"What particular faking's going on in that workshop of yours at the moment?"

"Faking, sir?" Injured innocence wasn't the word for his look. Then he grinned, and I thought for a moment he was going to dig me in the ribs. "Mr. Ampling's just the same, sir. He never don't alter. Allus will have his little joke."

"You've run across nothing lately?"

"Not the sort of stuff *you'd* be interested in, sir." He paused, head sideways. "There's a print, though, what I'm framing for old Mrs. Denton. It look rather good to me. If you like it she might sell it to you."

"Where is it?"

"In the shop, sir. Won't take you a second to look."

A private lane, wide enough to admit a car or cart, led alongside the cottage to where a workshop stood some distance back at the side of the garden. Turbey hauled a key out of his best trousers pocket, undid the padlock of the door and motioned us in. It was a big, spacious shop, with all the lovely smells of resinous wood and paint. The floor was thick in sawdust and strewn with shavings and the bench chock-a-block with tools, and I saw quite a good lathe. There was plenty of timber, too, standing in the corners, and there was also a wreck of a bureau which Turbey was evidently about to restore.

"Here's this here print, sir," Turbey was saying, but I wasn't interested in that print; not only because I know nothing about prints, but because I had caught sight of something, and a something that gave me enormous pleasure. It was almost fifty years since I had seen one like it, and that was in the cottage of an old servant of our family whom my mother used to call to see when

I was a boy. It was a large portrait of Charles Haddon Spurgeon, in a bird's-eye maple frame and hanging on the wall between the double windows above the bench. The photograph was on maroon cardboard, and around and beneath it was the lettering in silver. I discovered I could remember almost every word of that text.

> "I have fought a good fight, I have finished my course, I have kept the faith: henceforth there is laid up for me a crown of righteousness, which the Lord, the righteous Judge, shall give me at that day."

"No use to me at all," Bernard was saying about that print. "It's in pretty bad order, too. Thank you all the same for letting me see it."

I drew Turbey's attention to the framed photograph and told him where I'd last seen one like it. He seemed very gratified.

"And I lay it never did you no harm, sir."

"Harm?" I said, a bit puzzled.

"My old mother's, that was, sir. Allust keep it there, right under my eye, so to speak, when I'm workin'. Good as a tonic that is, sir."

"Give me something out of a bottle," Bernard said, and brought the conversation back to earth. "We must be getting along, Turbey. Always grateful, you know, if you've anything to show me."

We left Turbey locking the shop and humming a hymn tune.

"You know," I said as Bernard and I quickened our pace down the lane, "if Turbey weren't so transparent I'd think he was a bit of a rogue. I don't trust that obtrusion of religion."

Bernard laughed.

"My dear chap, you've got it all wrong. Turbey isn't transparent. He's as crafty a rogue as ever I've known."

"But what about his co-religionists? Do they think him an old humbug?"

"The trouble is that everyone rather likes him," he said. "Even when he swindles and overcharges, he's got such a plausible way with him that people come up asking for more. He's swindled me more than once, but I still go on employing him occasionally. I don't mind so long as he confines his rogueries to over-charging. After all, I do find him useful in various ways."

"He had a nice lot of wood in that shop of his," I said.

"And he lives right against the woodyard," Bernard told me amusedly. "He and the foreman there are probably as thick as thieves. Did you notice the stout padlock Turbey had on the shop door?"

"Didn't you say he worked for Corbit?"

"I did."

"Then isn't he double-crossing Corbit in a way to offer you things? Oughtn't he to give his employer the first offer of anything he gets wind of?"

"Turbey believes in free trade," he said. "The better the commission, the freer it is."

"A nice lathe he had there. Looked as if it cost a packet."

"Turbey's well enough off," he told me. "He recently bought the property he lives in. That cost him fifteen hundred pounds."

"It's not a lot of money as things go nowadays," I said.

"That's not the point," he said. "It's a devil of a lot of money for a working man like Turbey, even if his missus does work, too."

In the afternoon we had our bridge, and most enjoyable it was. Before it came the amusing ritual of justifying the use of Frosbeck's car, for Frosbeck had brought with him a small needlework picture in which Bernard was supposed to be interested, even if it didn't get any further than the hall table. Truebent had come with him, and he said he remembered me well. I remembered him well enough, too, even if he had aged a bit more than Bernard had suggested. There was now a lot of grey in the black of his hair and an even heavier look to his blue, clean-shaven jowl. But the eyes were just as alert, and his mouth had the same old humorous twist.

He had always prided himself, I remember, on being thought of as the rough diamond type with a heart of gold, though that, with him, was a kind of inverted snobbery, for he'd had a good enough education and could find the manners of a gentleman when he had need of them. The cut of his plus-fours and the rakishness of pullover and necktie were the kind one sees on a stockbrokers' golf train on a Sunday morning. Truebent, by Helmsbury standards, was big business, and he didn't mind how many people were aware of it.

But that afternoon he was both subdued and on his best manners, and Bernard said afterwards that he'd never known him so decorous. Maybe that scandal that old Drew was threatening to unearth was more serious than most people thought; at any rate, Bernard didn't rally him about it, and it was quite sedately that we settled down to our game. Then during tea Frosbeck did make an oblique reference to Drew.

"I saw Margaret Drew out with her father this morning," he said. "Apparently she's down here again."

"Is she the one who married Corbit's son?" I said.

"She's the one," Frosbeck said. "I believe she's reverted to her maiden name."

Truebent cut clean across that line of conversation. How was I spending the time in Stepford?

"Sort of hither and thither," I said. "I'd rather like to have a look round the old woodyard some time when you're there. I love watching big stuff being sawed."

"I'm there practically every morning," he told me. "Drop in whenever you like."

Bernard said he had a committee meeting at the golf club on the Wednesday morning, so I said I'd drop in then. That about ended the talk and we got down to our game again. It was just short of seven o'clock when we stopped and I had the pleasure of paying everybody, not that it was ruinous. At threepence a hundred it came to just under ten shillings.

"You had some filthy cards," Truebent told me. "We must give him his revenge, Frosbeck."

"What about Wednesday?" Frosbeck said. "I shan't be free till the evening, but what about half-past seven at my place?"

Truebent thought he could make it. Bernard accepted for us both.

"But how do we get home?" he said. "The last bus leaves at ten to ten."

There was general amusement at that.

"Have it your own way," Bernard said resignedly. "But I'd honestly feel much happier if you'd let us have a taxi."

"It's establishing a bad precedent," Truebent said. "Besides, Frosbeck never uses all his petrol. You're not weakening, are you, Ampling?"

"Personally, no," Bernard told him. "All the same, I'd hate to see Travers up at the local bench."

"I'll bail him out and Frosbeck can pay his fine," Truebent said.

The usual thanks, and off they went. We went with them to the door, but the rain was coming down in torrents and we stayed in the porch.

"Damn the rain!" Truebent said feelingly. "I'm doing some pumping at the quarry and this'll about fill it again."

"It's poor Travers I'm thinking of," Bernard said. "We'd both been looking forward to quite a lot of golf."

"Why not spend the day at Ipswich?" suggested Frosbeck. "I'm going to that sale tomorrow and can give you a lift and pick you up afterwards."

"That's most extraordinarily kind of you," Bernard said, "but I don't know that even Ipswich will be much fun if it's raining like this. Don't think us ungrateful, but may we leave it till the morning? If the weather report's at all promising we'll be glad to accept."

That was how it was left. And the morning, as it happened, turned out to be fine; at least it wasn't raining, and the weather report, so Mrs. Turbey told me when she brought the early tea, had mentioned only occasional showers.

"No letters?" I asked disappointedly, for I'd rather expected one from Bernice.

"Nothing for you, sir," she told me, and as if it had been presumption on my part. "Only a parcel for Mr. Ampling."

I finished my tea and then thought I ought to make dead certain about Ipswich before I dressed, so I went across to Bernard's room.

"What about it, Bernard?"

There was no answer. I looked inside and he wasn't there, and I guessed he was in the lavatory. Then I caught sight of something on the table just inside the door. It was lying on some brown paper and corrugated packing, and was evidently the parcel which, according to Mrs. Turbey, had come by the morning's post. My shameless curiosity got the better of me yet once more and I took a step or two inside the room. Bernard had evidently been investing in yet another picture, I thought, and I wondered, nevertheless, why that picture was unframed. It was painted on wood and was roughly about a foot and a half by a foot. And just as those realisations went casually through my mind, I was realising something else. It was a something so startling and so incredible that my face suddenly flushed and my fingers were at my glasses. Then I had another look. There seemed never a doubt about it. That unframed picture was the Zurbaran Crucifixion that had been stolen from Hickford Parva church.

I closed the door quietly and slipped back to my room, and just as I entered it I heard Bernard humming cheerfully to himself as he came back from the lavatory.

"What about Ipswich?" I called to him. "Everything set?"

"Most certainly so," he called back to me. "A quick breakfast and we'll catch the nine-ten bus."

I washed and shaved and dressed, and my fingers were all thumbs. I knew that what I had seen couldn't just be true, but that was only an accepted and formal delusion, for at the back of my mind I knew it was true. Then all at once I knew what I'd do. Once I knew that, I didn't hesitate. I went straight to his room, humming fairly loud to give him warning. Once inside that room I'd pretend to catch sight of the picture and then, of course, he'd simply have to say something about it.

"What about clothes?" I called, as I drew near.

"Just anything," he said.

The door was ajar and I gave a perfunctory tap and walked in. He was manipulating a bow tie at his dressing-table mirror. But that side table was now bare. Picture, wrapping and string had all gone.

"Far too handsome," he said, as he ran an amused eye over me. "Thank God you'll be wearing a rain-coat."

"Ready?" he said, when he'd put on his coat and taken a last peep at himself in the glass. "Let's go and gobble this breakfast or we'll be missing the bus."

Before half-past nine we were at Frosbeck's shop. Tom Polter said the guv'nor was upstairs and we were to go straight up. Now we were in the shop there was no need to use the side door, for stairs led up from an inner room. Frosbeck heard us coming and opened his living-room door to admit us.

"I'm glad you're coming," he said, "and I think we're in for a fine day. Have some coffee."

We said we'd scarcely finished breakfast. I caught his eye, and he was smiling, for already I'd been staring round that room.

"I'll be ready in five minutes," he said. "Make yourselves at home. Cigarettes are on the mantelpiece."

He went through to his bedroom. I remarked to Bernard that the flat looked a snug little place.

"Very snug," he said. "Just one bedroom and this room and a kitchen. That'll be his housekeeper," he said when I cocked my ear at a sound that came through the other door. "She's here all day, but sleeps out."

I helped myself to a cigarette and took a look round the room. Like most dealers' private rooms, it had a piece or two with which the dealer was loth to part, or maybe they were family pieces. A really nice Sheraton bookcase had a regular library of reference books, some fairly new and some that looked hopelessly old. Brent's *English Miniatures* caught my eye and I was just about to have a look at it when I heard Frosbeck coming.

"Ready?" he said. "We'll have to go out at the back. I've got the car there."

It was a large car, for, as he said, it often had to do duty as a van, but the back seats were extraordinarily comfortable. When we were out of the town he passed something back to me.

"The sale catalogue. Like to have a look at it?"

We had a look and it didn't seem very important as sales go. The various items typed heavily as antiques were vaguely described, and among them was the mirror.

Lot 87. ANTIQUE carved wood mirror in design of fruit and foliage.

That was all it said, so I asked Frosbeck if he had actually seen it. It was a somewhat naive remark, but he didn't appear to think so, or else he was tactfully ignoring the suggestion that a dealer might trust wholly to a catalogue.

"Oh yes," he said. "I was at a special view on Friday. It's a very nice mirror indeed."

Then Bernard was asking him about some pictures that were mentioned, and it wasn't long after that that we were in the suburbs of Ipswich. Frosbeck dropped us at the far end of the Woodbridge Road where we could get a bus to the centre of the town, and we were to be there again at four o'clock that afternoon.

What happened to us in Ipswich doesn't matter, except that we had what ought to have been for me an enjoyable day. And the reason why it wasn't was because of that damnable picture that I had seen that morning on Bernard's bedroom table. All day long that picture kept getting between me and the things which I saw and which I should have enjoyed, and with every new return of bewilderment and surmise there would be new additions of furtive suspicion of which I was only half-heartedly ashamed.

By the end of the afternoon this was the jumbled accumulation of ideas. First was a kind of justification. Who was I, in fact, to blame Bernard for possible black-market purchases when I myself would jump at the chance of buying, say, butter and fowls and eggs? You see the fallacy in that? It was already making Bernard guilty, although at the same time I kept insisting and with the same half-hearted assurance that he couldn't be. And yet there was Bernard himself to weigh down the scales. Bernard, the once irresponsible who might still regard the irregular acquisition of collector's items as an amusing and ironical adventure.

Above all, there was the matter of those two oriental rugs which Langdon was not supposed to see, and the ironic challenge that had been in Bernard's eye when he had told me so. There had been that remark he had made to Langdon on the Friday night, and with a very definite irony—that he himself was often inclined to be on the side of the criminal. And yet, as far as I remembered, there had been no oriental rugs in Stepford church, and if there had been any—and stolen—since my time, then why hadn't Langdon mentioned the matter when Bernard had given him so excellent an opening by mentioning my connection with Scotland Yard.

Then as a rebound was the knowledge that Bernard Ampling was the last person to be so irresponsible as to risk the reputation of a lifetime to acquire, even at a tenth of their value, things which he could well afford to buy, and in the open market at that. Even the viciousness of post-war financial legislation hadn't altered the fact that he was still—by post-war standards—a wealthy man. And back of all the suspicion I could always see the Bernard Ampling whose probity and sterling character I'd never in all my life had the faintest reason to question.

But by the time we were waiting at the rendezvous for Frosbeck's car I was able to thrust things to the far back of my mind. Even if Bernard had suddenly gone mad, I could tell myself, I'd never say a word to George Wharton. George had once boasted to me that where duty was concerned he'd apprehend his own father. Maybe, maybe not, and I'd never in any case have made such an assertion to George, and now I was saying to myself that duty and I would part company before I dropped even the remotest hint of what I might know.

Frosbeck's car put an end to speculation, and especially as he had the mirror with him. Bernard and I examined it as we moved on.

"It's a beauty," I said. "I like it enormously. But what about price?"

"Much more reasonable than I thought," he said. "Allowing a tiny profit for me, it'll cost you twenty-five guineas."

"Then it's mine," I said promptly, and Bernard added as promptly that he'd give me a fiver profit on it straight away.

"You're sure you're charging enough?" I asked Frosbeck.

"If it's for yourself—yes," he said. "At that price I think you should give me the first offer if you want to sell."

That was more than reasonable, and when we got back to the shop I insisted that he should write all that down on the receipt and guarantee, and have his own carbon copy. When he thanked me for the cheque he said he'd put the mirror in the car when he took us home on the Wednesday night. New screw-pins were needed in the mirror back and he'd fix some copper wire for hanging it. Cord was far too unreliable.

"If you like," he said, "Polter can fix that now and I can run you and the mirror home."

"No you don't," Bernard said. "Fair's fair, and I'm damned if we're going to use any more of your petrol."

So that was that and off we went to the tea-shop. It was now quite fine overhead, and although it was five o'clock it was still quite light. That was why I saw so clearly the man in the brown felt hat, even though he was on the other side of the street.

"There's the man I asked you about the other day," I said to Bernard. "Who is he, do you know?"

"That's Nelson Corbit, Stanley's son," he told me. "The chap I was telling you about. The one who married old Drew's daughter. Did you think you knew him?"

All I could say was that I'd taken him for someone else.

On the Tuesday morning we browsed, and in the afternoon we went to the Ritz cinema in Helmsbury and saw quite a good picture and then had tea. After dinner I was called to the telephone. It was Wharton.

"Too much of an imposition if I turn up for lunch on Thursday?" he wanted to know.

I said I was sure we'd both be delighted.

"Then expect me somewhere about midday," he said. "But about that letter of yours? Anything new?"

I told him about the Monday afternoon's discovery of the identity of the man in the brown hat.

"Connected with an antique shop, is he? Sounds promising."

"I'm far from certain he's the Blifield man," I said.

"Still it's worth looking into," he said, and merely added that he'd be seeing me on Thursday.

I told Bernard who it had been and he seemed very pleased. I told him a goodish deal about George—the best side, of course—though there was never a word about the job on which George was at the moment engaged. About that I intended to play scrupulously fair. If George liked to mention or even discuss his work, that was his concern. But I must admit that I was wishing that he would and because that seemed the likeliest chance of bringing Bernard himself into the open.

That word open was the operative word and one that somehow summarised my thoughts on that Tuesday night. After another day in Bernard's company I was more of the opinion that I had been very much of a fool to have thought him capable of the things my Ipswich thoughts had imputed to him. And yet I was just as certain that he was engaged in some business or other that was devious, to say the least of it, and there still remained the undeniable fact that he was in possession of either the stolen Zurbaran or an exact copy. If everything was open and aboveboard, why hadn't he shown that picture to me? I'd seen every other picture in the house, and why should there be a distinction made about the Zurbaran?

And so to the Wednesday morning. Bernard went off fairly early to his committee meeting—something to do with new plans for draining the golf course—and when I'd seen him on the bus I shamelessly made my way to his room. I didn't dare stay more than a minute, but in that minute I could see never a trace of the picture. Then I thought I knew where it was, for a drawer in one of the chests was locked.

It was a dull and blustery morning and I quite enjoyed the walk to the woodyard. Maybe I should have been a carpenter myself, for anything to do with wood always fascinates me, and as soon as I was inside the gate I was sniffing the resinous tang of pine and the more acid, sappy smell of oak. On my left was that monstrous heap of sawdust that now straggled through the roadside hedge, and to the right was pile after pile of felled trees, oak principally, but some pine and elm. When the sawdust ended on the left along Endover Lane there were stacks of sawn timber in the open and under cover. Away to the right by the big sheds was the whine and whirr of a saw.

Truebent must have seen me coming, for he was at the office door as I drew near. He was wearing another and older suit of plus-fours, and the hand that I shook didn't look as if it had done any manual work for years.

"Come along in," he said. "What'll you drink?"

I said it was pretty early, but if he had it I'd have beer. He seemed to have a regular bar there, and we both had beer, and then we sat talking for quite a time. I'd said how quiet the place was compared with when I'd seen it last, and he was saying he wasn't much more than a caretaker. Everything was controlled, and all his time and that of his clerk was spent in filling in forms. Then he was telling me how the whole business worked nowadays, and it seemed to me that he was doing little more than working on commission for the Government.

I wouldn't have a second beer, and so we went along to the sawing-shed. I'd remembered a dozen men working there, but now there were four.

"Things have got to a nice pass," he told me, "when a man gets the miserables looking round at what's supposed to be his own property."

Then he was asking if I was in a hurry. I said I wasn't.

"Let's get out of here," he said, "and go and have a look at the pumping. Then we might have a drink at the Roebuck."

His was a big American car, but he didn't drive it fast. It must have taken us quite ten minutes to get to what he called the quarry, which was a mile through the town on the Ipswich

Road. I should have called it a gravel and stone pit, not that the name matters. The road mounted and curled round one side of it, but the main face stretched well to our right, and we drew in off the main road by an unmetalled road that was badly cut up.

F. SHEFFIELD
GRAVEL AND STONE MERCHANT
Tel. Helmsbury 14

That was the rather faded wording of the board by which Truebent drew the car up. His own concern was the pumping plant, the engine of which we could see working about a hundred yards to our right. Normally, as he said, water drained or seeped away, but six weeks of heavy rains had made a miniature lake along the working face and stopped all work. Once the lake had been pumped dry a hardcore road would be laid and a new drainage system installed.

We went along the railway-sleeper track that made a temporary road, and Truebent had a word with his foreman. I had a look round, but daren't leave the sleepers or I'd have been up to the ankles in orange mud. We were there about ten minutes, perhaps, and then moved off again. Truebent was in a much better humour. If the rain held off for only a couple of days the back of the job would be broken.

As we were going through the town we caught sight of Bernard, and Truebent pulled the car up. Then the three of us went on to the Roebuck for a drink. After it Bernard refused flatly to let Truebent take us back to Stepford and wouldn't listen to his plea that he had to go back to the woodyard in any case. From the wink and the nod that Truebent gave me it was plain that Bernard had guessed right. At any rate we left Truebent having yet another drink with a business friend, and went home by bus.

In the afternoon we browsed, and that evening dinner was early and we were well in time for the bus that was to take us to Frosbeck's for bridge. And that moment seems the one for explanation and apology, since everything that has gone before it has been only a kind of prelude, and maybe a dull one at that. But at least it was a prelude to murder, and in it you met the actors in the drama or tragedy to come. And though I was not to be aware of it, it was to come within a matter almost of minutes.

CHAPTER V
ENTRANCE—AND EXIT

WE WENT IN by the side door and up the stairs to a lighted landing. The door on its right led to the kitchen and that immediately ahead opened into Frosbeck's lounge or living-room. He must have heard us coming, for he was at the open door just as we got to it.

"I'm afraid we're just a bit early," Bernard said. "The bus was on time for once."

"All the better," Frosbeck said as he drew back to let us in.

"You're looking very hot and bothered?" Bernard told him.

"I expect I am," Frosbeck said. "We're going to be five, for one thing—not that that matters—but up to a minute or two ago I thought we mightn't even be four."

"Everything all right now?"

Everything was. Truebent had rung in the late afternoon to say he might be late and mightn't it be better to get another player. Frosbeck said he was to come when he was able and they'd be expecting him. Then he thought that Truebent might have meant anything by the word *late*, so he rang his house to ask him at what time exactly he could come along. But there was no reply. What seemed best then was to get a fifth, so Falkner was rung. But he was out, though expected at any moment, and so Frosbeck had to wait till Falkner rang him as requested. But Falkner, thank heaven, had been able to come.

"My dear fellow, what a business for you!" Bernard told him commiseratingly. "You really shouldn't have given yourself all that trouble. We'd have been just as happy spending an evening here with you."

It was the kind of natural, unforced thing that Bernard would say, and Frosbeck seemed to appreciate it.

"Something I was almost forgetting," Bernard was going on. "There's something for you to collect from The Pleasance when you take us home tonight."

Frosbeck's eyebrows lifted. Bernard nodded what seemed an affirmative to the unspoken question.

"You'll find a book of words attached," he said, and then we heard more steps on the stairs, and there was Falkner.

He was a much younger man than I'd anticipated; about thirty-five, perhaps, with an excellent record in the war and appointed to his present post immediately after demobilisation. I liked the look of him, and it turned out that he had a brand of humour that was quite his own. Later in the evening, when he made some amusing retort to Bernard, I couldn't help thinking what various brands of humour there were; Bernard's little ironies, for instance, and subtle innuendoes as compared with Truebent's saloon-bar kind of humour that left out nothing and hinted at even more.

With few preliminaries we got down to our game, and by preliminaries I mean drinks. In fact there were no drinks. It was an unwritten law that at those private games there should be nothing but late-in-the-evening refreshments—coffee, say, and sandwiches. Drink—except perhaps for Truebent—was hard to come by, and damnably expensive, and everybody's means weren't the same. I thought it an excellent arrangement. But to get to the bridge. Never did I know cards play such capers. I got to four hearts, for instance, on six to the ace, queen, ten, plus two outside aces, and when my partner gave me two outside kings I was a bit annoyed that I hadn't redoubled Bernard's double. In a minute or so I was glad. He had six trumps himself, including king, jack, nine, and was bare of my best outside suit, and I went down three tricks. And that was how the cards went, and that rubber took no less than an hour and a quarter, and one needed an accountant to tot up the score. Just as Falkner and I made it two hundred to us, steps were on the stairs again and there was Truebent. He, too, was looking hot and bothered and was full of apologies. He hadn't, for instance, had time to change his clothes.

"You look uncommonly smart to me," Bernard told him, and Frosbeck was telling him to cut the cards.

"Why aren't we all cutting?" Falkner said.

"I'll sit out this one," Frosbeck said. "I'll have to be making the coffee in a few minutes in any case."

But we wouldn't have it, and we all cut in. I drew the seven of clubs and thought I was in, but it turned out to be the lowest card. Not that I worried. I'd had my eye on those two books of Frosbeck's and there were one or two rarities that I wanted to consult. Brent's *English Miniatures* was one, and I settled down in the corner of the chesterfield, with now and again a look towards the players to see how the game was going.

I made my way carefully through the book, for one couldn't but linger over the marvellous coloured reproductions. Then at last I came to Andrew Plimer, and for the first time in that book I came also to phrases in the text that were underlined in pencil. *An uncanny meticulousness of detail in the drawing of hair* and *a velvety bloom that was apt to pall* were two of them, and there was a marginal line along the passage that dealt with Plimer's fondness for white in the dresses of his women sitters. Frosbeck then had been reading up Plimer, and the amusing thing was that he had done so after Bernard had got his bargain. The stable door had been shut when the horse had gone, for had he read up Plimer before, Bernard would surely never have got away with those two miniatures at so absurd a price.

Or was it absurd? After all, Frosbeck had said he had made a good profit, and maybe he had made just as good a profit on the balance of that small collection which he had bought. And, as I remembered it, he had been in something of a cleft stick. He had bought the collection so cheaply that he simply couldn't lose money on it, and therefore he had made no serious preliminary examination. Then, just as the collection arrived home, in walked Bernard and had picked the two Plimers and asked the price. Frosbeck didn't wish to show ignorance by any hesitation, so he quoted what to some people would have been quite a lot of money, and which would be a good profit for himself. Nor was he upset when Bernard quoted the deal as a bargain, for one essential in the antique trade is to put an occasional first-class bargain in the way of a valuable customer.

There was a burst of laughter at the card-table and I put the book back and went to see the cause. Bernard it appeared, had made a bluff call and had been left in, and it had cost him and his partner a packet. I drew up a chair and watched the next hand, and that was the one that ended the rubber. Then we debated whether or not it was worth while beginning another before coffee. Frosbeck said he'd be only about ten minutes, and Truebent was keen to go on. So we went on.

As a rubber it was a farce. Bernard and Truebent went down on a hand, and then Falkner and I got two quick games with tremendous hands, the last a lay-down little slam. In what seemed well under ten minutes Frosbeck was bringing in a tray. There was an uncut cake as well as sandwiches.

"You didn't make this coffee?" Falkner asked incredulously.

"Frosbeck's coffee is the best in Helmsbury," Bernard said. "I don't know how he makes it, but it's always extraordinarily good."

Frosbeck said it was his housekeeper's recipe and the secret was in putting in plenty of fresh coffee and when it was made adding a piece of butter the size of a marble. That settled the grounds and brought out the full flavour. And it wasn't a long business. He'd guarantee to start from scratch and have hot coffee on a table inside five minutes—provided, of course, the kettle was near the boil. I mention that talk because it was that that made me look at the clock. Truebent had come in at about ten to nine. His first rubber had taken twenty minutes, and the second one under ten minutes, and it was then just after half-past nine. I'm not saying, mind you, that I noticed those times with anything ulterior in mind. I'm just saying that those were the times, and one reason why I noticed them was because I was wondering how many more rubbers there'd be, and then realising that that would depend on how long those rubbers took.

After that delightful scratch meal of coffee, sandwiches and homemade cake, Falkner cut out and we played a twenty-minute rubber. Then Bernard was out and it was almost eleven o'clock when that final rubber ended. Truebent was the first to go; in fact he practically dashed away. For one thing, he had left his car in Back Street and it would be in the way of Frosbeck's car. When the rest of us came down his car had gone. Falkner left us and Frosbeck got his own car out. That mirror of mine was on the front seat.

The night was dry, black as ink even if the stars were shining, and in the air there seemed almost a touch of frost. When we got out of the car Frosbeck was moving off again. Bernard reminded him that there was something for him to take back, and as soon as we were in the hall he was sprinting upstairs. By the time I'd laid my mirror carefully on the hall table he was coming down again and he was carrying a largish parcel. To me it looked like a picture in a frame, and it was about the size of the Zurbaran Crucifixion.

I'd already said good night to Frosbeck, so I went through to the lounge and switched on the light. Frosbeck's car moved off, though not till a minute or two later, and then at last Bernard came in. He was suggesting a night-cap and then bed, and over that small whisky we talked about the evening's bridge.

As I waited for sleep that night I couldn't get that mysterious picture out of my mind, and the thoughts of it and the speculation kept me long awake. What Frosbeck had to do with that Zurbaran I couldn't imagine, unless it were he who had unlawfully acquired it and had tried to sell it to Bernard. Bernard probably had taken a specialist's opinion and now was merely sending the picture back. But snug though that line of reasoning was, it didn't somehow convince. For one thing, I couldn't imagine a man like Frosbeck being concerned in anything at all questionable. And that solution of the affair didn't answer one other question—why Bernard had kept that picture in his bedroom and had never mentioned its existence to myself.

Mrs. Turbey's mornings at The Pleasance were Mondays, Wednesdays and Fridays, so it was Ellen who came up with early tea on the following morning. George Wharton was due for lunch and Ellen was a bit flustered, and Bernard and I were having orders to get up at once so that breakfast could be got out of the way.

That morning, too, I had woke with an idea. It was not so much a brain-wave as a logical happening of which I ought to have been aware before.

"Mrs. Turbey's all alone now at the cottage?" I asked Ellen.

"Oh yes," she said. "The daughter was married last year. They tell me she's got a green ration book."

That, I gathered, was a kind of synonym for expecting a baby.

"A nice wedding, was it?"

"Real nice," Ellen said. "They had it at the chapel at Helmsbury."

Bernard had happened to mention that wedding when we were talking about the Turbeys, and out of that mentioning had come the idea. After breakfast, then, I wrote a long letter to Bernice while Bernard was pottering about in the garden. It was a fine morning, by the way, but a stiffish wind was blowing and the weather forecast had promised gales.

Bernard wasn't anxious to go down town, so I caught the eleven-o'clock bus alone. It was to the office of the *Courier* that I went, and there I got permission to look through the files of back numbers. Not only did I find what I wanted, but I was able to buy a copy of the number concerned, and after that I posted my letter to Bernice. As I paid a special air-mail rate, I was hoping for a reply within a week.

The post office was almost adjoining the town hall, at the back of which were police headquarters. A car was drawn up outside and a plain-clothes driver was sitting on the running-board smoking a cigarette and reading a newspaper.

"This doesn't happen to be Superintendent Wharton's car by any chance?" I asked him.

It *was* Wharton's car, and Wharton himself was inside the building. The driver was a Sergeant Matthews, who said he knew me. While we were talking, Wharton came out, and the local Inspector—Umberson—with him. George looked amazingly smart. He was wearing a heavy brown overcoat instead of the old blue one with the faded velvet collar, and his vast weeping-willow moustache had been brushed into an almost recognisable shape. He shook hands solemnly and as if he'd just suffered a bereavement. I asked him how long he was staying and he said he'd be away and gone in the morning. Umberson had just advised him that the Roebuck was the best hotel.

We soon altered all that. I rang Bernard from the police station and he said he'd be delighted to put George up. Umberson said he'd see that Sergeant Matthews was looked after, so George said he'd drive the car to Stepford himself. It looked to me as if Umberson was just a bit relieved to have so important a personage as Wharton at rather a further distance than the Roebuck, and he was giving the whole proceeding a blessing as if he himself had been responsible. He said he knew Mr. Ampling, and he had played golf with him once or twice, and he said it as if he'd vetted both Bernard and The Pleasance and was graciously pleased to give a clean bill of health.

When George drives a car the whole of England is a built-up area, and when I once twitted him with his funeral driving he gave me an apt retort—that however he drove he was still alive. But I didn't dare speak to him till we were through the town and on the straight stretch past the bungalows.

"Umberson help you at all, George?"

"More a courtesy visit than anything," George said off-handedly. "No church thefts in this immediate neighbourhood."

Then he gave a snort.

"He was all flustered. You'd have thought he had a murder on his hands instead of some man or other being missing." He snorted again. "They don't even know if he's missing. He just didn't turn up last night, so his daughter said." He gave a third snort. "Some local big bug. A councillor or something. That's why Umberson's making all the fuss."

I don't know what made me ask it, but I did.

"Was the missing man's name Drew?"

"Might have been," George said. "Probably was."

His hands were grimly clutching the wheel and his eyes as grimly on the road ahead, for we were past the woodyard and in the village proper. He jammed on the brakes and crawled to pass a stationary grocer's van. Then came the last short stretch of straight to The Pleasance, and he ventured to speak again.

"You know him?"

"Drew?" I said. "Well, I've seen him. And I've heard quite a lot about him. His daughter married that man I told you about—the one I think is the man I saw at Blifield church."

Then I had to tell him the house was just ahead, and in a moment or two we were turning into the drive. Bernard was at the door as we drew up, and through that open door there was coming from the kitchen the very pleasant smell of roast chicken.

An hour later that chicken was very much of a ruin. We had ended the meal with a glass of excellent port and had gone to the greater comfort of the lounge for coffee. Wharton had been excellent company, and now he was even more genially mellow. I was cynically thinking that he had every reason, what with free quarters in a hospitable house and an expense account to pocket afterwards.

"You've got a wonderful place here," he said appreciatively.

"It was my father's," Bernard told him deprecatingly. "I may have added a thing or two here and there, perhaps, but—well, there we are."

Wharton said it was enough to make a poor policeman's mouth water. He'd one or two pieces himself, he said, and maybe if he could have afforded it he'd have bought more, for he'd always been interested.

"I am still," he went on. "As a matter of fact I'm interested at the moment in rather a peculiar way. I don't know if Travers has dropped you a hint."

I said I hadn't, but there we were. George said that Bernard was an honourable man, so to speak, and then blew the whole gaff about the job that had brought him to East Anglia.

Bernard seemed most interested. I, as you know, was interested, too, but chiefly in Bernard's reactions.

"Why doesn't one hear about all this?" he asked Wharton. "I own that I did read a paragraph about a stolen picture, but I don't suppose one person in a thousand has the least idea of what's been going on."

"Shortage pf space in the papers, for one thing," Wharton told him. "Lack of co-ordination for another. You get an isolated theft reported—if it isn't crowded out—and then perhaps another one, but the various authorities concerned aren't in direct touch. It isn't seen as a whole. That's what I'm supposed to be trying to correct."

"What *was* the picture that was stolen?" asked Bernard. "As far as I remember it was merely mentioned in the snippet as being a valuable picture, believed to be by Zurbaran. Fairly recently, too, I think."

Wharton lugged a mass of papers from an inner pocket and handed him what I recognised as a copy of the brochure I had upstairs. Bernard nodded to himself as he read it. When he handed it back he was giving a rather puzzled smile.

"Very interesting. And, do you know, I think I may be able to help you. Somewhere or other, quite recently, I've seen a picture like that."

Wharton fairly shot up in his seat.

"Don't be too optimistic," Bernard told him, and the smile was now wry. "It's one of those things you have vague ideas about and no more." He shook his head. "Give me time, though, and I'm pretty certain I'll remember it."

Had it been myself, there'd have been snorts and even blasphemy, but even George couldn't very well try any gingering up of his host's memory. He just waited for a moment or two with a suggestion of expectancy, then changed the subject to the missing Drew. That made things involved. I had to tell Bernard why I'd been interested in Nelson Corbit. Bernard said he wasn't wholly surprised. Stanley Corbit's antique shop wasn't flourishing enough to keep both himself and his son.

We must have sat talking for more than an hour what with Wharton being given the ramification of the Drew-Corbit history as Helmsbury knew it, and though Wharton didn't take any notes I knew from the pursing of his lips and his occasional grunts that he was fixing everything firmly in his mind.

"Do you know," he said, "I'd rather like to run my rule over this Nelson Corbit. Where do you think I'd be likely to find him?"

"You might try the father's private address," Bernard said. "I'll look up the number for you."

George said I'd better do the ringing and he gave me an idea of what I was to say. It was all very conspiratorial, with the three of us in the hall.

"Hallo," I said. "Who's speaking?"

"It's Mrs. Corbit."

"Oh, Mrs. Corbit, I'm a friend of Nelson's." I should have told you that to disguise my voice I was holding a handkerchief in my teeth. "Can you tell me where I can get hold of him?"

There was quite a silence. I was wondering if the line was dead, and then she was asking who was speaking.

"Goldberg," I said. "Reuben Goldberg. You must have heard him talk about me."

"I don't know," she said, and then hesitated. "Nelson isn't here. He's had to go away."

"You don't know where?"

"No," she said. "He often goes away."

"Maybe he's gone up to town to see me," I said.

"I don't think he has," she said. "He didn't take his things. Even his father doesn't know where he's gone."

"Thank you, Mrs. Corbit. Perhaps I'll be seeing him when he gets back."

"What was the name again?"

But I hung up. All the better if she hadn't exactly remembered the name.

"Away is he?" Wharton asked, and all I could do was tell him precisely what I'd heard. And that was all for the moment. Tea was due in a very few minutes and Wharton and I went upstairs for a freshen up. I remembered something I had meant to ask him—if he had learned anything about that mysterious man who had called on the Hickford vicar and asked for a detailed description of the stolen Zurbaran. But there was nothing new, George said, except perhaps that the man had given the vicar to understand that he was a picture dealer who had heard of the theft and had happened to be passing through the village.

* * * * *

I woke in the morning with a badly furred tongue. Wharton had gone down town soon after tea the previous evening and had not returned till dinnertime, but after that meal we had sat yarning and smoking till best part of midnight. No wonder my tongue was furred and my throat a bit relaxed, for the lounge had been blue with tobacco smoke, and most of it from George's pipe.

I hooked on my glasses and looked at my watch. It was twenty minutes to eight, and I knew that the noise that had woke me hadn't been the gale—that had been blowing all night—but the entry of Mrs. Turbey, who always arrived by the half-past seven bus from Helmsbury. Then suddenly I heard the women's voices in the hall, and almost at once there was the quick patter of feet outside my room. Another moment or two and there was Bernard's voice on the landing. Ellen was talking excitedly. I slipped on a dressing-gown and took a look out. Bernard came to meet me.

"An extraordinary thing's happened. Old Drew's body's been found. Turbey found him lying over the hedge by the woodyard when he was going to work."

I was fingering my glasses.

"What was it? An ordinary death? Or something else?"

"Turbey went to the woodyard and rang for the police," Ellen broke in.

Bernard said we'd better tell Wharton.

CHAPTER VI

WHARTON TAKES OVER

IT WAS NO MORE than ten minutes later when Wharton pulled up his car just short of Endover Lane. Mrs. Turbey could have had no opportunity to spread the news, for nobody could be seen but a uniformed constable, though three cars were drawn up in the main road just beyond. Wharton flashed a warrant card at the constable, and I followed at his heels.

A group of men were standing at about fifty yards down the lane and as if they were having a conference, and the only one I recognised was Umberson. Turbey stood just a little way back, leaning against his bicycle. Umberson came to meet us.

"A nasty business," he said, "and rather funny after what we were talking about last night."

"Murder—or what?"

"He'd a nasty crack on the skull," Umberson told him. "He might have got that from all sorts of things, but what about him being here?"

"Mind if we have a look?"

Umberson seemed only too glad, and even if he'd been the other way he'd have been too late, for Wharton had kept on walking and now we were getting our first glimpse of Drew's body. It lay on the extreme edge of the sawdust: mound, where that mound straggled into the hedge. A poor hedge it was, too. Whether or not the sawdust had killed it I didn't know, but I could see it was little more than a series, of thorn stubs that made a rough boundary between woodyard and lane.

Drew lay on his back, face to the sky, and he was wearing a dark overcoat: the one, I thought, in which I had seen him in Frosbeck's shop. His hat was lying against a thorn stub, where it had apparently been caught. A piece of wood was under the skull to protect it from the sawdust and Umberson said the doctor had put it there after he had examined the wound.

"He was obviously put there," Umberson said, and waved a hand at the body.

"When?"

"That's a bit of a puzzler," Umberson told him. "The doctor says he's been dead about thirty-six hours."

"Then he was put there last night?"

Umberson hesitated. Wharton gave him a look of barely controlled impatience. "Make up your mind one way or the other," was what I was expecting him to say. Then he let out a breath instead and asked to speak to the doctor. Umberson beckoned him forward and made the introduction.

The doctor—Hadcote was his name—was a man of about forty, who certainly knew his job, and I don't say that because he was prompt in his answers but because those answers were given quietly and assuredly. He confirmed what Umberson had said, that death was due primarily to a blow on the base of the skull. Drew's skull was particularly thin. What time had elapsed between the blow and the actual death couldn't be more than approximated till after the post-mortem.

"But you think it was about thirty-six hours ago?"

"Approximately, yes."

"And when do you think the body was put here?"

"Soon after death," he said and gave a quick look at Umberson.

The beginnings of a wry smile were at Wharton's lips. Somebody had slipped up, and he knew it.

"And why do you say that?"

"When I moved the body the sawdust was perfectly dry underneath."

He said it quite calmly, as though what followed must be obvious.

"Yes," said Wharton, as if to himself, and his lips pursed and he was looking up at the sky. "Thirty-six hours ago was Wednesday night. What was the weather like here?"

"Fine all day," Umberson said. "Blowing half a gale, but everything was drying up nicely."

"And when was the next rain?"

"Not till you came down to the station last night," Umberson said. "You said it was raining then, and when we went out it was coming down proper."

"It began at about half-past five," Hadcote said. "I had to go out to a patient."

"And that was the first rain for over two days," Wharton said, and pursed his lips again. Then he was stepping over the scarcely discernible ditch and straddling the body. He hoisted it by the shoulders and looked underneath. He steadied the body with his knee and pulled out a handful of sawdust. He let the body down and the sawdust trickled through his fingers.

"Well, that's logical enough," he said. "He was put here on Wednesday night."

Then on went his antiquated spectacles, and he was peering at Umberson over their tops.

"Only one little difficulty. Why wasn't the body discovered before?"

His look was a sort of answer-me-that-one. But Umberson had an answer.

"I think it was to do with the wind."

"The wind?"

"Yes, the wind and the weather."

Wharton didn't see it. Then he began to have glimmerings. And he caught sight of Turbey.

"That the man who found the body?"

Umberson said it was, and he showed where Turbey lived. Every morning he cycled to work, starting off at half-past seven.

"He works in the town?"

"That's right. At Corbit's, the antique dealer."

A bell rang somewhere in Wharton's brain. He beckoned to Turbey. Turbey gave me a look as if I ought to do something about it, then he went forward, still holding his bicycle.

"You needn't bring that damn bike," Wharton told him. "No one's going to steal it." And then more genially: "At least I hope not."

"Turbey and I are old friends," I said. "It was Mrs. Turbey who brought us the news this morning."

Turbey was in his working clothes and vastly different from the returning worshipper of the Sunday morning. He hadn't shaved, and his collar was dirty and his tie little more than a string. Across his shoulder, over the ancient waterproof, was a knapsack, from which peeped out the neck of a bottle of what looked like cocoa. Usually, too, he was humming a hymn tune or even singing aloud, but now his harp, too, was very much on the willows. The whole man was somehow deflated.

"You're a countryman," Wharton told him genially. "Suffolk born and bred—eh?"

"Yes, sir."

"A bit of a weather prophet, I'll bet."

Turbey gave me another look.

"Weather's important, isn't it, Turbey?" I said. "When you've got to cycle to and from work the weather makes a bit of difference."

"You're right, sir," he said, and then ventured to have another look at Wharton.

"Wednesday night. Where was the wind?" fired Wharton.

"There weren't none, sir. It didn't git up till after midnight. By morning it was a regular gale."

"Where from?"

"Nearly due south, sir. Over yon way, that's where it was comin' from."

"There we are!" Wharton told me. "Soon as I clapped eyes on him I knew he was a weather expert. I bet he could tell us everything about the wind from Thursday morning onwards."

His eyes had shifted invitingly to Turbey.

"I reckon I could, sir," Turbey told him. The old Turbey was slowly coming back and he spoke with a bit of an air. "When I was comin' home last night—that'd be just after five, sir—the wind'd shifted right round to the north-west, where it is now. And it blew a regular gale all night."

"Good," said Wharton, who must have known most of that himself. "But to go back to the Thursday morning. Did you happen to look this way then?"

A nod back at the body told Turbey what he meant. Turbey said he might and he mightn't, if Wharton knew what he meant.

"But obviously you saw nothing," Wharton said. "Let's suppose the wind had partly blown the sawdust over the body. Suppose only the stomach, say, had been showing, or a leg. Would you have noticed?"

Turbey reckoned he wouldn't.

"And I'll tell you for why," he said. "If I'd seen it at all, I'd have thought it was a bit of timber or something. Like all them other bits there."

Oddments of wood and billets he meant, protruding through the heap or even lying in the clear.

"And what was the difference this morning?"

"Well, sir, I could see nearly all of him. 'Whuh,' I said to myself, 'what's that there? Look almost like someone a-layin' there.' And then I seed it was."

Wharton said he was a first-class witness. Umberson said he might go if the Superintendent had finished with him. Turbey hoisted up his bicycle, and as he mounted it he was giving me yet another look. What he was wanting to convey I didn't know. It was somehow as if he was expecting me to look after his interests—whatever they might be.

"Well, if the north-west wind uncovered the body there ought to have been signs of it," Wharton was telling Umberson.

"There were," Umberson said. "The sawdust was all blown against it from that way. We took a photograph or two before the doctor moved the body. Turbey had moved it, too, when he got over to see who it was."

"But you're sufficiently sure to be working on the basis of the body being put here on Wednesday night?"

"Absolutely."

"I'm inclined to agree," Wharton said. "But just one other little point. Why shouldn't the body have been *buried* here? Whoever buried it in this sawdust didn't expect it to be found perhaps for days. Or it might be weeks."

Umberson ventured on a smile.

"The wind'd never have uncovered it, sir, not if it had been actually buried. Sawdust is tricky stuff. It dries quickly on top, but the wind wouldn't burrow into it, so to speak. All it'd do would be to blow the very top layer to and fro. It'd blow a kind of drift against the body, then a shift of wind'd blow it off again."

"I think you're right," Wharton said. "But we've still not mentioned the main point. Why was the body *here*? You saw the soles of his boots?"

Not only had Umberson duly noted the soles, but he was producing an envelope in which was a mixture of mud and sawdust. He had cut it from the sole of a boot.

"Hang on to that," Wharton told him. "It's the most important piece of evidence you've got. Perhaps you'd better have a good look at it under a glass. Did you find any footprints?"

Umberson said there hadn't been time. But the ground wouldn't be disturbed. He'd have an extra man on duty to see to that.

"And you might find whatever it was that struck him," Wharton said. "What your opinion is I don't know, but I'm pretty sure he was killed here. He came here for some reason or other and he walked through soft ground and on sawdust. Then he was struck down. And we still don't know why he should come here."

"Ah!" said Umberson looking towards the lane end. "Here's Mr. Truebent, who owns the woodyard. I asked him to come along."

"He doesn't know why?" Wharton asked quickly.

"He hasn't a notion," Umberson said. "I just said I wanted to see him—that's all."

Truebent didn't seem the least perturbed as he came down the lane. Surprised—yes; particularly perhaps at the sight of me. I merely shrugged my shoulders.

"Morning, Fred. What's going on?" he was asking Umberson.

"Morning, Donald."

He waved a hand in the direction of the body. Truebent looked that way, then his mouth gaped.

"Looks like old Drew!"

"It is Drew," Wharton said quietly. "Have a look at him, Mr. Truebent."

It was at Wharton that Truebent looked. Then he moistened his lips and straddled across. He didn't seem to notice that one foot was ankle deep in mud. His head shook, then he squelched his way out again.

"It's Drew all right," he said. "But what the devil is he doing here?"

"You haven't any idea?" Umberson asked him.

His hands rose and fell.

"Not the faintest idea." His eyes opened wider. "Was he . . . I mean . . ."

"He was killed," Umberson said. "Murdered, I suppose you'd call it. The back of his skull was stove in."

Truebent's eyes screwed up as if in pain.

"Oh, my God!"

There was a moment or two of silence, and it was a silence that Truebent must have felt. And eyes were watching him.

"Why should he have come *here*?" he said. "What the devil was he doing here?"

"You didn't ask him to come here for any reason?" Umberson asked quietly.

"I? Why should I ask him to come here? I hated the sight of the old swine. Why should I want him here?"

"Don't know," Umberson told him, and the quietness of his voice was somehow ominous. "Unless it was perhaps to talk over that business of last Friday."

"Last Friday?" The eyes had narrowed enquiringly, and then suddenly the fingers of a hand were clenching. He took a step towards Umberson.

"Here, just what are you suggesting? That I killed him to keep his mouth shut?"

"Now, now, Don," Umberson told him, and just as quietly. "I didn't say any such thing. All the same, it's what a lot of people might think, you know. But you didn't kill him, though?"

"Kill him? What sort of a bloody fool do you think I am. Besides, Drew had nothing on me, and I can prove it. What if he did open his mouth wide. I should worry. Hot air. That's all that business of Friday was."

"Well, I'm glad to hear it," Umberson said. "You going to the office?"

"Where else—now I'm here."

"Then I'll be seeing you later," Umberson told him. "I shan't keep you very long. Just to clear things up for the records."

Truebent went scowlingly back to his car. The ambulance backed in and the doctor departed with Drew's body. Umberson strolled with Wharton and me to the end of the lane, for George had said we ought to be getting back to a belated breakfast.

"I reckon you'll be taking this over," Umberson told him. "I can't get away from the idea that everything's mixed up with that business we were going over last night."

"Maybe," Wharton said, "and maybe not. Meanwhile it's your headache—not that Mr. Travers and I aren't prepared to help."

"And what's the first line you think I should take?"

"None at all," Wharton told him. "Carry on with that routine job of looking for footprints and the weapon. Have a friendly chat with Truebent by all means, but don't antagonise him—and that's all. No worry; no panic. When the doctor tells you exactly when Drew was killed then you can take your coat off and roll up your sleeves. Then you can start testing alibis."

Umberson nodded.

"There *is* one little precaution you might take," Wharton went on, "not that I need tell you your job. Keep an eye on Nelson Corbit, if he's back home again. Just in case."

Umberson nodded.

"Now we'll be moving on," Wharton told him. "I'll probably be at Mr. Ampling's place for some time yet if you should happen to want me." He held out a hand. "Good luck. And don't forget: no hurry, no panic. No one's going to bolt. If they do, the case is ended."

Wharton moved his car on to the lane and then reversed.

"Umberson'll make a mess of this," he told me as soon as we were heading for home again. "I don't like all that Donald and Fred business. Worst of these small towns. Everybody has to be hail-fellow-well-met with everyone else."

George was visualising himself already as in charge of that case, and that slight on Umberson meant nothing. Had anyone else questioned the integrity of the police George would have blasted hell out of him.

"What was that Friday last business Umberson was talking about?" he was wanting to know.

I gave him a rough idea.

"So Drew was making disclosures," Wharton said, and he was giving what you may already know as his Colosseum smile—

that of a lion who picks for himself a particularly plump Christian. "And making them today. Handy for Truebent, whatever you like to say."

And then he was shaking his head. George hated to think of that case ending so quickly.

"Too easy, though. This isn't an open-and-shut business."

"And Truebent would have been worse than a fool to put Drew's body on his own sawdust," I said, and then we were at the drive again and Wharton was craning up and down the road before he turned in.

We were all apologies. Bernard said there was nothing for which to apologise and so did Ellen when she brought the breakfast in. As for Wharton's staying on till next morning, Bernard said it would be a pleasure if he stayed for a week. As we ate, we gave an account of what had been happening. Bernard agreed that things didn't look too comfortable for Truebent.

"I'd wager a considerable deal," he said, "that Donald Truebent couldn't possibly commit a murder. I've known him for years. Known him well."

Wharton hypocritically agreed.

"It needn't have been murder, of course," he said. "A blow struck in anger." He shrugged his shoulders for the rest.

"I like Donald Truebent," Bernard said. "I'd hate to think he'd be concerned in a thing like that. I don't say he's an angel, mind you. What businessmen are? But sharp practice or political or parochial jobbery are vastly different things from concealing a killing—manslaughter I believe you'd call it."

Wharton and I went up to shave. I finished my toilet first and went along to his room, for there were things which I had felt a sudden wish to talk over. And yet I hardly knew how to begin, for the whole thing boiled down to a defence of Truebent and with it there was mixed a far too keen realisation of the difference in the reactions of Wharton and myself to the events of the morning. For me they had been far too unexpected and sudden, and they had concerned people with whom I was already familiar. To him, on the other hand, those actors—if I may call them so—were merely names, and what he had had was a fine enjoyable hour in the centre of the spot-light and giving to Umberson an exhibition of detection as one of the fine arts.

"How do you like Ampling?" was the roundabout way in which I actually began.

"He's one of the best," George told me emphatically. "He's what I call a gentleman. None of you lah-di-dahs."

That was somehow an obscure glance at myself, and why I didn't quite know, unless it was that I was not a particularly sporting type.

"You think he's got good taste?"

George stopped in the act of brushing his hair.

"You've only to step inside the house," he told me, and glared.

"Then if you'd trust his taste in everything else," I said, "why don't you trust it in the matter of his friends? Do you think he doesn't choose his friends with the care that he chooses his pictures?"

"Just what are you driving at?"

"At Truebent," I said. "Bernard Ampling says, and I agree, that Truebent couldn't have killed old Drew. If there'd been a quarrel and he'd lost his temper and cracked him over the skull, he'd never have hidden the body. He'd have rung the police and taken what was coming to him. That's the kind he is."

"I haven't disagreed, have I?" he told me with deceptive mildness. "Didn't I agree when you said he'd have been a fool to have hidden the body in his own sawdust?"

I'm suspicious of George when he retreats, and retreating he was. The answer I'd expected was one that I'd heard a score of times before: that you couldn't say any man was not a murder type, and the less of a murder type a man was the more erratic his actions were likely to be once he had actually committed a murder. So I retreated, too; at least I switched the argument aside.

"Other people had an interest in the death of Drew," I said.

His grunt had a note of contempt.

"That sticks out a mile, doesn't it? That Stanley Corbit knocked him down, didn't he? And what about the son? Didn't

Drew stand in the way of the marriage to his daughter?" He grunted again. "At least, that's what I gathered."

"Something funny about those two, George," I suddenly said. "If you look at it from a different angle, oughtn't it to have been the other way about? Shouldn't Drew have killed both Stanley Corbit and Nelson Corbit?"

"How do you mean?"

"Stanley Corbit knocked him down publicly and Drew didn't bring a case against him. And why should Nelson Corbit have a grudge against Drew? After all, he did marry Drew's daughter. And pretty badly he treated her by all accounts. It was Drew who always disliked Nelson Corbit. After that business with his daughter he should have hated him enough to kill him. That's overdrawn, perhaps, but you see what I mean."

"Cross your bridges when you come to them," he told me. "All the same, you're forgetting one little thing."

He wanted me to ask what it was, and I did.

"You think Nelson Corbit was the man you saw at Blifield. You claim that Drew had a pretty big grudge against him. Suppose Drew had discovered just what little games Nelson Corbit was up to. Suppose Nelson knew it. Then what?"

"That's getting pretty far ahead," I said.

"No further than you've got yourself," he told me. "But if you and I take over this case that'll be one of the reasons—because it's got a bearing on those robberies."

Then he was telling me that we ought to be getting downstairs, and his manner was suddenly so genial that I was more suspicious than ever. That connection between old Drew and the Corbits seemed to me to be very far-fetched and little more than a specious wangling. George, in fact, was anxious to take over the case, and, if so, there wasn't a shadow of doubt that take it over he would. A Superintendent of Scotland Yard is a mightily important person and has a mighty big say.

Bernard was asking what we'd like to do, and George said he was in our hands, at least till the afternoon. When George admitted that he'd had one or two attempts at golf Bernard suggested we three should put in an hour or two on the drier part of the course and then lunch at the Roebuck. In a few minutes it was all fixed up.

What happened on the golf course doesn't matter, though I must say that George insisted on using little but a number three iron, and with it he hit the ball a tremendous crack, even if where that ball subsequently went was nobody's business. Then we had a drink in the bar, and so to the hotel for quite a respectable lunch. Sergeant Matthews drove us back to Stepford. George was seeing Umberson and doing some telephoning, and wasn't to be expected back for tea.

As we passed the Embassy Cinema—and that was at about a quarter to two—we saw a queue that stretched right round the front and up a side street. Sergeant Matthews told us what it was. *Gone With The Wind* had at last reached Helmsbury and was on for the whole week at the Embassy. There were two performances daily: one at two and the other at seven, and Matthews himself had gone to the later one the previous night.

Two things only need recording for the rest of that day. As Bernard and I were finishing tea, I remarked casually that it was a curious thing that he should have seen somewhere a picture like that stolen Zurbaran.

"Yes," he said. "It does seem a rather curious coincidence."

"You don't happen to have remembered where you actually saw it?"

"Strictly between ourselves," he said, and his eyes were disturbingly steady on mine, "I was guilty of a certain amount of subterfuge. In fact I knew all along where I had seen it."

My look was intended to show tremendous surprise.

"The trouble is," he went on, "the secret—if one can call it that—isn't altogether my own. What you can rely on, though—still strictly between ourselves—is that Superintendent Wharton will almost certainly be told in due course."

Then he was giving me his most charming of smiles and apologising for being so mysterious, and after that what could I do? As for the second happening, it occurred after Wharton had telephoned a second time. The first had been at six o'clock to say he wouldn't be in to dinner. The next time he telephoned was at nine o'clock, half an hour before he appeared again in person. The message was for me and merely an announcement that we were taking over the case.

CHAPTER VII
ENQUIRY BEGINS

WE HAD a friendly argument on that Friday night. George was making the Roebuck his headquarters, and I naturally proposed to go there, too. As I told Bernard, it was little more than impudence to make use of him and his house. I'd come down for a holiday and the holiday had abruptly ended. Very well, then; I'd go to the Roebuck with George, and maybe at some later and convenient season Bernard would permit the holiday to be resumed.

Bernard wouldn't agree. Meals out by all means, but why couldn't I go on sleeping in the house? When I said I might be in and out at all hours, he said I could have a key, and the room would be there. Wharton agreed with him. The arrangement he proposed was just the kind of thing I should have expected. Far better for me to stay on at The Pleasance, he said, because that would give me a kind of foot in both camps, and there I knew he was thinking specially in terms of Truebent. One of my jobs, I gathered, would be to induce Truebent to talk to me as a friend, and it was a job that I didn't particularly like. That was one of the reasons why I insisted for once on having my own way.

Immediately after breakfast, then, I was in Wharton's car and on my way to the Roebuck and also to see two women about whom I knew no more than Wharton knew himself. The more important was Drew's daughter. Umberson had already seen her in connection with her father's disappearance and then in connection with his death, and he'd been unable to get just the information he needed, and that information was vital as determining to within a few minutes the time of that death. Once more let me explain.

As a result of the post-mortem Hadcote and a colleague were certain of two things. Firstly, death had taken place on the Wednesday night and at about half-past eight, with an allowance of half an hour or so each way. But it was the stomach content that would determine a time that was more exact. There Drew's daughter should have helped, but owing to an unfortunate combination of circumstances neither she nor Drew's housekeeper had been able to state with certainty the time of his last meal. Wharton was hoping to succeed where Umberson had failed.

The second point on which the doctors were agreed was that Drew had lived no more than half an hour after receiving that blow on the head. Judging from the extent of the cerebral haemorrhage he had never recovered consciousness. In other words, then, and by way of summary, Drew might have been struck on the head as early as half-past seven and died at eight o'clock, or he might have been struck as late as half-past eight and have died half an hour later. That hour was very definitely the vital thing. Somehow or other it would have to be whittled down; if not, the checking up on alibis was little more than a farce.

"Where's Umberson fitting in from now on?" I asked George.

Umberson would have plenty on his hands, I gathered. His main and immediate job was to check up on Drew's movements from the moment he left his house on that Wednesday night. Someone surely must have seen him on his way to Stepford. He had gone neither by bus nor by hired car, of that much Umberson was certain, and his own car was now locked in his garage. But Drew was wiry enough for all his scragginess, and that walk to Stepford—he could have anticipated catching a bus home—would have been easily within his powers. And Umberson, so Wharton confided, was of the opinion that Drew had for reasons of his own gone out that night to Stepford for the purpose of snooping round the woodyard, and, if so, he might have wished to keep secret his means of getting there.

There was another thing that Umberson and his men were well fitted to do: to keep ears open in pubs and places where the town's knowing ones congregated and to collect every idea about the nature of the disclosures which Drew had threatened to make at the council meeting. Sergeant Matthews had a roving commission of something of the same nature, and, not being a local, might perhaps hear the more.

One other small piece of evidence had emerged from the inquest: that Drew had been wearing his hat when he was struck, but as it was a flimsy felt affair it would have helped very little to soften the blow. The thing that had struck him had had a rounded head and it must have had considerable weight. It hardly looked therefore as if it had been a chance piece of timber of the kind with which the whole of that woodyard was strewn, for even the shortest bit of waste would probably have had at least one sawn edge. Nor did the fact that Drew had been struck while wearing his hat prove in the least that he had been struck while out of doors, though that had seemed to Umberson a kind of clue.

Just as we were passing the bungalow suburb the first drops of rain spattered the windscreen. Luckily we had dressed accordingly, for the weather report had promised more wet. There we were, well into February and after the wettest January for sixty years, and the rain still coming down. George said it was beginning to get on his nerves. I remembered Truebent's job of draining that gravel pit. If it was a contract job he was certain to lose money.

Bernard had pointed out Stanley Corbit's house to me, and Wharton drew the car up outside. A woman—obviously Mrs. Corbit—opened the door. She was short, dumpy, wispy-haired and stolid looking. Wharton assumed his best paterfamilias manner.

"Mrs. Corbit, isn't it?"

"Yes," she said, and her eyes went from him to me.

"Is your son at home, Mrs. Corbit?"

"No. He's not at home. He's away."

It was a quick, disjointed sort of answer.

"Can you tell me where I can find him?"

"He doesn't always tell us his business," she said. "He's away. That's all we know."

"He took a bag with him?"

He got the question in and no more. She had shielded herself behind the door and now it was almost closed. Wharton's hand went to it and he had a foot inside.

"We're from the police, Mrs. Corbit. Perhaps we'd better talk somewhere inside."

"But the police have been here already."

It was a feeble protest, for she was backing down the passage, and then she was opening a door. It was the living-room, and the three of us went in. She didn't ask us to sit.

Wharton said we were there to help. There had been the disappearance of Mr. Drew, who had just been found dead. Now it was said that her son was missing. If so, it was the duty of the police to help. She insisted that he wasn't missing. He'd often been away like that before.

"Like what?"

"Well, without leaving word."

"And when did you see him last?"

"At breakfast on Wednesday," she said. "He went off in the car. He didn't tell either of us where."

"He brought the car back?"

"Oh yes, because his father—"

She stopped as suddenly as that. The eyes opened wider and the tongue gave a quick lick to the lips. She had let something slip, and she knew it. Wharton seemed not to notice.

"You mean because your husband found the car in the garage when he came home."

"Yes," she said, and far too quickly. "My husband did find the car."

"And what time was that?"

"When he got home?"

"That's it. When he got home here from the shop."

"At about six," she said. "He always comes home about six—except on Thursdays. That's early closing."

"And he was in all night?"

"Oh yes. He never stirred out all night."

Everything shrieked at us that it was a lie. And she was edging towards the door as if desperately anxious for us to go.

"Your son took a bag with him?"

"I expect so," she said. "He doesn't like us looking in his room."

"But you look in his room when you make his bed?"

"But that's different. I mean looking at his things and interfering."

"I see," Wharton told her, and appeared to understand. "And just one last question, Mrs. Corbit, before we go. Has anyone rung you here to enquire about your son?"

"Oh no. No one's rung."

The answer was too quick and too certain.

"No one of the name of Reuben Goldberg, for instance?"

She shook her head. "I don't know anyone of that name."

"That's that then," said Wharton resignedly. He hooked off his ancient spectacles and slowly put them in their antiquated case.

"A good son, was he? I only ask because I'm a father myself."

"Yes, he was a good boy. Always a good boy to his mother."

"Glad to hear it," Wharton told her, and then turned puzzledly to me. "That's the kind of thing that ought to worry us. A good boy to his mother, and been away since Wednesday morning and never a ring or a postcard or anything."

"Nelson wasn't one for writing," she told us quickly, and was opening the door to let us through.

"Well, thank you, Mrs. Corbit," Wharton told her at the front door. "As soon as you do hear from your son I'm sure you'll let us know."

You'd have expected her to make some comment, but she didn't. So anxious was she to put a question of her own that she and Wharton were talking at the same time.

"What was your name, please? My husband will be sure to want to know."

"Wharton. Superintendent Wharton. I'll write it down for you. Here's a card, though. A private card."

He thanked her again, and as we moved the car on there was a quick glimpse of her at the window of the room which we had just left.

"Very interesting," George said. "Very interesting indeed. She's scared to death of something and I don't think it's about little Nelson. Or is it?"

"It looked as if her husband was definitely out on the Wednesday night," I said. "And as if there'd been rehearsals of everything she'd have to say if the police happened to call. And why should she be so anxious to have your name?"

"Plenty of time," George told me and with that Colosseum look again. "Which is the way to that back road to Corbit's shop?"

We were just passing it. But the road was clear and George backed a few yards and turned left. One or two vans were in that narrowish road and we had to wriggle a way along. I had been told to look out for the back of Corbit's shop. A private car was drawn up by it and facing north. It was an Austin 12 with a black saloon body. Wharton moved his own car carefully past.

"That like the car you saw at Blifield church that afternoon?"

I could only say that it was certainly like it, though I couldn't guarantee it was the same. Things had happened far too quickly in the swirling dust of that Blifield lane.

We stopped for a minute or two at the police station while Wharton made certain that Drew's daughter was in, and then we moved on up the hill to the Ipswich Road. Corbit's house had been a little detached villa of the three-rooms-up-three-down type, and small rooms at that. Drew's house was a detached one, too, but Corbit's could have gone inside it without making a bulge. It was brick-built and slated, Victorian and solid, lawned and shrubberied with as nice a balance of this and that as the ornaments on a Victorian mantelpiece. In the teeming rain it reminded one of mausoleums and graves and epitaphs, but it was well enough tended. Solid and dull and eminently respectable was how it looked, and when the door opened to our knock I was giving a sniff as if I'd expected to smell the roasting of some vast joint of beef.

"I believe we're expected," Wharton told the housekeeper, and at once she was ushering us into a room off the hall. It was a room that had in it a lot of money in spite of a lack of taste in arrangement—two superb Morland prints, for instance, and hung between them a quite trivial mirror. The pictures looked especially good. And the room had comfort. A good fire was burning brightly, the thick-piled carpet was luxurious to the tread, and the easy chairs were large and comfortably cushioned.

A woman came in, and I was seeing Drew's daughter for the first time. She was a brunette of about thirty, tallish and with an attractive figure. On her face was never a sign of grief. It was, in fact, a hard face, and the lips had a kind of cynical twist.

"You are Mr. Wharton?"

"Yes," said Wharton and gave a little bow. "This is my colleague, Mr. Travers."

"How do you do. And won't you sit down?"

There had been complete self-possession. The voice was the least bit unpleasant. It had a kind of hardness, like the face.

"What are we to call you?" Wharton asked apologetically. "Miss Drew or Mrs. Corbit. . . ."

The question tactfully lingered.

"*Mrs.* Drew," she told him. "I can't very well be Miss."

"And you're not anxious to retain the name of Corbit?"

I thought the question a bit too pointed. She didn't turn a hair. "Should I be?"

"Well"—George was knocked slightly off his perch—"I suppose not. Not that we want to enquire into your private business."

"Does it matter?" she told him. "After all, everyone in Helmsbury knows my history. I married Nelson Corbit and I divorced him. That's all there is to it."

"You wouldn't care to tell us—strictly between ourselves—why you divorced him? I ask you that because it may tie up with certain of his activities which we'd rather like to question him about."

That seemed to amuse her.

"I don't think you'd be interested in that—I mean, why I divorced him. I just knew he was fooling around with another woman and I had him watched. That's all."

"Exactly," Wharton said lamely. "You knew, by the way, that he was missing?"

That interested her.

"You mean he's disappeared? Like my father?"

"He seems suddenly to have left the town, and since Wednesday night."

"I see." Her eyes suddenly narrowed. "You're not suggesting that he—"

"Not in the least," he told her virtuously. "Purely coincidence perhaps. I mean—well, what possible reason might he have for harming your father?"

"I don't know," she said, and was looking away. "I oughtn't to say it because it makes me out a fool, but he was a nasty piece of work. As plausible as they make them. Butter wouldn't melt in his mouth."

"Ah, well," said Wharton. "Maybe he'll turn up. But about this dreadful business of your father. We're here to help you, and we know you want to help us. You've been questioned already—we know that. All we want to do is to approach things just once more and from a new angle."

"You'd like a drink?" she was suddenly saying.

"Rather too early," Wharton said. "Very good of you, all the same."

"Some coffee?"

We didn't refuse, and she went to the door and called to the housekeeper. Betty, the name seemed to be. Then Wharton got her to tell us about the last time she had seen her father alive. It had been at just before half-past one on the Wednesday afternoon. Lunch had been early because the women were going to the Embassy for the first performance of *Gone With The Wind*. He had been asked if he wanted tea left for him, and he had said he didn't know. When they went out, however, they told him there was food on a tray in the kitchen and tea in the pot. Since the stove was an Aga he had only to put the kettle on for a minute or two and his tea would be ready.

There was a tap at the door and the middle-aged house-keeper was bringing in the coffee.

"Where shall I put it, Miss Margaret?"

"Bring that table up, Betty," she was impatiently told. "And while you're here, tell these gentlemen what happened when we got back from the cinema."

There was nothing really to tell. They got back at exactly a quarter-past seven, for they'd gone in the car and had left it during the performance in the Embassy car park. Mr. Drew had had his tea, and in the kitchen, and apparently he'd gone out. No note, however, had been left, and that was the last that had been known about him.

"You washed up?" Wharton asked her.

She said she had. And she'd handled the tea-pot.

"How warm did it feel?" Wharton asked her. "Think back. Try hard to remember."

"It was still warm."

But she hadn't sounded any too sure. Wharton asked if something might be done. Might tea be made in the same pot and then the pot stood on the kitchen table. The housekeeper said she'd do it at once, and long before we'd drunk our coffee she was calling that the tea was made.

"This council-meeting quarrel between your father and Mr. Truebent," Wharton asked Margaret Drew. "Did your father tell you anything about it?"

She said he hadn't. She'd pulled his leg about it, but he'd been quite touchy. She knew, in fact, no more than was in the local paper.

"He never discussed his private business?"

"I wouldn't say that," she said, "but he just didn't feel inclined to discuss this."

There was something she was remembering. She gave a faint smile, then shook her head.

"Thought of something?" prompted Wharton.

"Not about that," she said. "It was just a hint he threw out. About my dear late husband."

"Yes?" said Wharton, and waited.

"It was on the Wednesday," she said. "It was just before lunch. Someone rang him and he was looking ever so pleased. I

said, 'What's happened. Dad? Come into a fortune?' and he said
. . . what did he say?"

She frowned in thought, then said she couldn't guarantee the
exact words. But it was something about having Nelson Corbit
just where he wanted him. Wharton's eyebrows lifted.

"And naturally you asked him what he meant."

"I was going to, but Betty called to me to help bring in lunch.
I remember I intended to ask him about it when I got home
from the cinema."

"Perhaps you'll remember exactly what it was he did say,"
Wharton told her, and then he was getting to his feet. "Might we
go to the kitchen and test the warmth of the tea-pot." When we
got there, Betty said the tea-pot was still hot. Wharton felt it and
said we might as well wait for it to cool.

"You've been living in town, I believe," he asked Margaret
Drew.

She said she was a receptionist-secretary at an hotel. Perhaps we knew it—the Burford, just off Kensington High Street.
We talked about that, and Betty had another test. The tea-pot
was still too warm.

"And what now?" Wharton asked. "You think you'll go on
living here?"

"I'd hate it," she said. "All this happening, after what happened before. You're a Londoner yourself. Would you like to be
cooped up down here?"

Wharton grimaced as if it was the last thing he wanted.

"By the way, what was your father doing in London before
you came down here, Mrs. Drew?"

"He was in the furniture business," she said. "He and my
late father-in-law were in partnership. I think there were five
shops when the war came. They sold out to one of the combines, you know."

Wharton was asking for another test of the tea-pot. Betty
said it was just about right—she thought.

"Thirty-five minutes," Wharton said. "That means roughly
that he had his tea at half-past six. A bit late, wasn't it?"

It depended, as Margaret Drew said. Perhaps he'd been out and had got home late. All the same, she seemed surprised. Her father usually had his tea at about five o'clock. But tea wasn't what she'd call one of his meals. All he'd eaten, as she'd already told the police, had been one paste sandwich and one piece of cake.

I felt that tea-pot again and it still seemed to me to be warm. The Betty woman said that that was how it might have felt on Wednesday night, and Wharton said it looked as if we might be there all morning, and with that he was looking at his watch.

Margaret Drew saw us to the door. Wharton said he doubted if she'd be troubled again, and when the funeral was over he didn't think there'd be anything except her private affairs to keep her in Helmsbury. The rain was still teeming down and that made our exit far from dignified.

"None too satisfactory, that test," I said.

"We've got to start somewhere," George said. "I think we should compromise and make his tea-time six o'clock. If my calculations are right, that would mean he was hit on the head at half-past eight."

"And where was Truebent at half-past eight?"

"Says he was at home working on accounts. Got so interested—so he told Umberson—that it was a regular shock when he saw it was half-past eight. He played bridge afterwards at that other antique dealer's place, didn't he?"

"If he was at home, can't his alibi be confirmed?"

"That's just his misfortune," Wharton told me. "They've a daily maid and she'd gone home at five as usual."

"What about his wife? He's married, isn't he?"

"Another one that went with the wind," he told me wryly. "She had tea with a friend and then they both went to the second house at the Embassy."

CHAPTER VIII
STANLEY CORBIT

A MURDER ENQUIRY, at least in my experience, would often seem to the uninitiated a far too leisurely thing. Take the initial stages, for instance, which are generally something of an absorbing of atmosphere—getting the feel of a case as George calls it—and a quick appraisal of this person and that. All the time, too, there's a listening and a looking for the unusual or the contradictory, and only when that general survey and assessing is complete is it usual for Wharton to begin his process of eliminating suspects.

Even I, who, as I have said, had already seen each likely suspect, had profited by the morning's work, and Wharton, in one bound, so to speak, had caught up with me. Already he could feel the furtive, hostile undercurrents that moved beneath the surface lives of a small group of people in what some might have thought a sleepy, amiable country town. There was old Drew burrowing mole-like as in the case of that land project which Bernard had helped to foil. Truebent was doubtless another mole, with his nominees or agents in this racket and that, and himself in the background to take a due share of the spoils. The interests of Drew and Truebent had conflicted. Somewhere underground the two had met head on, and the result had been the open quarrel at the council meeting and the threat of disclosures. In old Drew's mind there had been something else hidden—his hatred of the Corbits and his patient biding of his time, and yet that, as I pointed out to George, had not ended in trouble for the Corbits, but in the death of Drew himself. Had the Corbits then felt a sort of closing in? Was Drew's killing a blow in defence?

Those were some of the things George and I were talking about over our early lunch at the Roebuck, or shall I say that George was in one of his pedagogic moods and was driving home the lessons of the morning as if it was twenty years before and I at my first case.

"Remember what I told Umberson?" he said. "No panic, no hurry. Take your time and use your eyes and ears. He was all bursting to get to work on Truebent. In about five minutes he was going to have the whole case over."

"Do you think Truebent was bluffing when he said Drew couldn't substantiate those threats at the council meeting?" I asked him.

"Why should he have been? Drew was a fool. He gave him too much warning. Whatever Truebent's been up to, you can bet he's covered his tracks—or thinks he has."

"And that eliminates his motive."

"He's not out of our net yet," George told me grimly. "Wait till we're satisfied about his alibi."

I said that Truebent might have put in some time in fixing that, too, but not because he was guilty. The lack of an alibi might make him *look* guilty, and that was enough to scare any man. We'd met that kind of thing before: people who lied because they were too scared to tell the comparatively harmless truth.

"What about Mrs. Corbit?" I asked him. "Why's she lying? What's she frightened of?"

George's attitude was the very opposite of what I'd expected. "Both she and her husband have every reason to be scared," was what he said. "Everyone in the town knew about the bad blood between Corbit and Drew. And you can bet that Corbit knew a great deal about what his son was up to, even if he wasn't in it himself up to the neck. And the son had done a twelve months' stretch, if you remember. That'd make his mother scared at the sight of the police."

"You think she knows where Nelson is?"

It was a question that wasn't answered, for a waiter was telling me that I was wanted on the telephone. It was Bernard, and ringing, he said, from Frosbeck's shop. There was something which he and Frosbeck thought Wharton should know. I said we'd be over at once, and I was told to use the side stairs.

The two were waiting for us in the living-room, and the first thing I noticed was that Zurbaran lying face upwards on a side table. I think George saw it, too, even if he was busy shaking hands with Frosbeck.

"You've had lunch?" Frosbeck was asking us.

George said we'd practically finished when the telephone message had come.

"You'll join us in coffee? We're just about to have some ourselves."

His woman seemed to have been forewarned, for she brought in four cups. While Frosbeck poured out, Bernard began telling us what it was all about.

"I'm afraid Superintendent Wharton is going to think me guilty of a certain amount of duplicity—about that stolen picture, I mean. The fact is, of course, that Frosbeck here wasn't able to tell me all he knew, and the little I did know or guess was his secret and not mine."

Wharton was disclaiming any such thoughts.

"Whatever you did, Mr. Ampling, I'm sure it was right. I don't know a lot yet about Mr. Frosbeck," and he gave an ersatz chuckle. "I haven't run my police rule over him yet. But if he's a friend of yours, then I'm sure whatever he did was right enough, too."

"That's very handsomely spoken," Frosbeck said. "I had to be very cautious myself. But for Mr. Drew's death I should still be cautious. A man who's in business, Superintendent, has to respect the confidences of his clients. And he mustn't be mixed up in local politics or scandal."

Wharton nodded patiently, though his eyes had strayed once or twice towards that picture.

"However," Frosbeck was going on, "Mr. Ampling and I have talked things over—chiefly at his instigation, I might say—and we think you ought to know the facts."

He fetched the picture and gave it to Wharton.

"This is the one that was stolen from Hickford?" I asked him.

"We think there's no doubt of it," Bernard said.

Frosbeck took up the tale. Not more than a few days after that snippet in the Press about a stolen Zurbaran Drew came into the shop. He removed the brown paper from a parcel and showed Frosbeck a picture and asked what he thought of it. A dealer has often to temporise. Frosbeck asked where he had got it. Drew said he wasn't in a position to say. What he wanted was Frosbeck's opinion on it, and he was told that it was hard to give an opinion straight away, but for what the immediate opinion was worth it was not particularly valuable. It was definitely Spanish and probably early eighteenth century. The frame was contemporary.

"Mind you," Frosbeck added. "I hadn't the least notion at the time that the picture was the stolen one. The idea never occurred to me. Not even when Drew did what he did. He asked me, in fact, to find out everything I could about the picture, and to keep the matter confidential, and I said I'd do what I could."

But Frosbeck more or less forgot about it and when Drew came in a fortnight later, he had to prevaricate. Then he consulted his own books and learned nothing, and finally he showed the picture confidentially to Bernard. Bernard found it very interesting and asked if he might take it home. There he examined it carefully, but reached no satisfactory conclusions. But in the meanwhile Drew was harrying Frosbeck again and Frosbeck told him the picture was in the hands of an expert and he was hoping for a report in the very near future.

"It's a bit of a muddle from now on," Frosbeck said. "Everything overlaps, but I think you'll see what happened. Mr. Ampling did send the picture away for an expert opinion and it took some little time before it came back. The opinion was that the picture was by the Spanish eighteenth-century painter Pedro Milonos and of no great value. Mr. Ampling has the actual report."

"It was not by Zurbaran."

"I never thought it was," Bernard said. "I certainly never suspected it was the one stolen from Hickford. Sorry, Frosbeck. You carry on."

Frosbeck said it was necessary to go back a bit. Drew came into the shop again and he was cock-a-hoop with a tremendous secret. He hinted, in fact, that the picture had been unlawfully acquired by the one from whom he had bought it, and that the Corbits were involved. He hinted at more, and at what he said more openly to his daughter—that he had Nelson Corbit just where he wanted him.

Frosbeck had to temporise once more. It didn't do for him to take sides in the Drew-Corbit feud, and Stanley Corbit was a brother dealer. And Drew was talking pretty libellous stuff. But Frosbeck's very reticence made Drew all the more talkative. He said he knew the picture had been stolen from a church. He'd had his suspicions and had paid a visit to the very village, and then he produced a copy of the handbook with its photograph of the picture. But he kept the handbook in his hand and Frosbeck couldn't see the name of the village. All the same, he remembered the paragraph in the newspaper and wondered if the picture was the supposed Zurbaran missing from Hickford church. Naturally he didn't confide his suspicions to Drew or to Bernard.

"So it was Drew who paid that visit to the vicar of Hickford," Wharton told me, and then explained to the room.

But there was more to it, Frosbeck was going on. Drew was in full spate about the Corbits and he thought he had something else on Nelson. He'd been going to town one morning in December and Nelson Corbit had boarded the same train, and he had been carrying a very large and uncommonly heavy suitcase. At Liverpool Street he had taken a taxi, and Drew had taken another and followed him. The pursuit ended at Green Street, off Aldgate, where Nelson Corbit entered a pawnbroker's shop. Drew dismissed his own taxi and went to a tea-shop almost opposite and kept the pawnshop under his eye. He had to linger on for nearly half an hour, and then Nelson came out from a passage at the side of the shop and he no longer had even the suitcase.

"Just a minute," Wharton said. "Let me write the address of that pawnshop down."

He took the particulars again and was waiting for Frosbeck to resume. But there was nothing else to say, except that Bernard had had the picture back and had returned it on the Wednesday night—the night Drew was killed. Frosbeck had intended to return it to Drew on the Thursday morning. In fact he had rung Drew's house and was told that Drew wasn't in. Then came the news of Drew's disappearance and, still later, of his death.

"A very interesting story," Wharton said, "and I'm very grateful to you, and to you, Mr. Ampling. I think I may say you both acted for the best."

"If anything should arise out of it you'll be able to keep my name out of it?" Frosbeck said. "It mightn't do my name much good if I was to give evidence against a fellow dealer."

Wharton was sure the question wouldn't arise. What he suggested was sealing the picture and putting our signatures on the wax, and then locking it in Frosbeck's safe. Then he'd get in touch with the vicar of Hickford and explain the situation.

Then he was giving another chuckle.

"I don't know that we ought to tell him it isn't a Zurbaran after all. What do you say?"

Bernard chuckled, too, and agreed. Where ignorance was bliss it was folly to put the vicar wise. And that was that. The picture was locked in Frosbeck's upper safe. Wharton remembered something as we prepared to go.

"That Wednesday night when you took Mr. Ampling and Mr. Travers home—"

"Plus one mirror," added Bernard gravely.

Wharton's nod showed that the point had been seen.

"Plus one mirror," he said. "I know you saw nothing unusual on your way there, or Travers would have mentioned it. But what about coming back?"

"Nothing whatever," Frosbeck said. "I passed—that is to say met—two cars and otherwise I didn't see a soul."

"Just one other thing," Wharton said. "This is highly confidential, but we're all men of honour. So tell me, Mr. Frosbeck: have you the least idea how Drew guessed that picture had been stolen by one of the Corbits?"

"I haven't," Frosbeck said. "But he hated the Corbits. It was almost frightening the way he spoke of them. In fact, if it had been either of them who'd been killed I couldn't have helped but think he'd had something to do with it."

Wharton grunted. Then he was asking if old Drew knew anything about pictures. Frosbeck said he was a very good judge indeed. He had had quite a lot to do with the trade and was something of a collector.

"If you should happen to go into his house," he said, "you'll probably spot a Constable and a Gainsborough. Not the best work, perhaps, but pretty valuable. And there's a lot more very good stuff. I had a standing order to let him have the first look at anything I got myself. He was known in the town as a collector. I believe he'd hinted at bequeathing a lot of stuff to the local museum."

"Yes," cut in Bernard amusedly, "but that was when he was putting up for the council. I wouldn't mind betting there's no mention of it in his will."

Bernard walked to the Roebuck with us, and just before he left us he said there was something he thought he ought to mention. I wondered what it could be, for he was most apologetic about it. This detective business, and practically on his own doorstep, he said, had set his own thoughts stirring in new channels. And being mixed up with that picture business had given him a detecting itch.

"It's about Mrs. Turbey," he said. "She's the wife of the man who found Drew's body. I don't think you saw her, but she comes in three mornings a week to help Ellen, and she's a most rabid gossip. Practically everything that happens in Stepford reaches me through her and Ellen. But the really funny thing is—even Ellen noticed it, or else I'd never have known it—that Mrs. Turbey wouldn't discuss that Drew business. Ellen's very much of a gossip herself and naturally she wanted to know what there was to know, but Mrs. Turbey was a regular clam. Ellen couldn't get a word out of her after the original news reached us."

Wharton nodded meaningly.

"Doesn't her husband work for Stanley Corbit?"

"Yes," Bernard said, and looked enquiringly. Wharton merely nodded meaningly again.

"Maybe we'll be seeing Mrs. Turbey," he said, and that of course brought Bernard in again. Help in the house was a problem, and if Mrs. Turbey had the least suspicion . . .

"You leave it to me," Wharton told him reassuringly, and that, in fact, was how it had to be left. The rain had ceased, but it was a muggy afternoon, and George left his overcoat in the hotel and then we moved on to the police station, where I waited while George did his telephoning. Umberson was out, but had left a message that he'd like to see Wharton at five o'clock, if convenient.

It was after four o'clock when George appeared again, and out to the High Street we went. I thought he was bound for the Roebuck, and tea, and over it perhaps a discussion on the next best move. But George had that move all planned, and it was Corbit's shop that we made for.

"Just a week ago when I was in his shop," I said. "Wonder if he'll remember me."

"You needn't worry," George told me. "It's fifty to one his wife rang up and gave him our descriptions as soon as we were out of the house this morning. It's up to him to do the worrying."

At the ring of the shop bell Corbit at once came through from a back room. There was a pause as his eyes met us. And he didn't use his stock phrase and ask us in what we were specially interested.

"You're Mr. Stanley Corbit?" Wharton asked him. Corbit said he was, and George was showing him the warrant card. In Corbit's eyes was a most curious look. It was somehow pathetic: the look of a dog asking not to be beaten.

"Where can we talk?" Wharton wanted to know, and without a word Corbit was leading the way through to the back room. In it were a few pieces of furniture, but most of it was an office.

"Just a formality," began Wharton, "and everything's in strict confidence—at the moment. We're checking up on Mr. Drew's death. I believe he was a friend of yours at one time. And a business associate."

"Yes, he was."

He wanted to elaborate, but evidently the words wouldn't come. George cut in again.

"I don't know the ins and outs of the quarrel between you, but you'll appreciate the fact that everybody regarded you and him as being on pretty bad terms. That's why we'd like you to tell us where you were on Wednesday night last, say from seven till nine."

"I was in my house." Corbit told him, his voice so matter-of-fact as to be almost devoid of expression.

"Any evidence, beyond that of your wife?"

"But how could there be if I was indoors?"

"No callers? No telephone calls?"

There'd been nothing at all. Corbit had simply gone home and stayed there, as he did most nights.

"That's all right then," Wharton told him amiably. "You realise, of course, that you might have to give evidence on oath to that effect?"

"But look," said Corbit, a new note of apprehensive defiance now in his tone, "why should I have anything to do with his death? People quarrel. They always quarrel. But they don't kill each other. Why should I kill him and get myself hanged?"

"Why indeed?" Wharton told him. "But about this bad blood between you and Drew. Tell us confidentially how it all started. How'd you meet him in the first place?"

Corbit seemed glad to talk. Drew had had two furniture shops, he said, and dealt in both modern furniture and the antique; the latter, of course, of second or third-rate quality, as suited that particular trade. Any good stuff he acquired would be placed privately. Corbit, who had a small factory in Bethnal Green, supplied Drew with much of his modern furniture. Out of that emerged a partnership. Drew put money into the factory to enlarge it and Corbit and he acquired three more shops to handle the expanded output. Corbit's share was a two-sevenths one.

In 1939 the firm of Drew and Corbit received a very good offer from one of the smaller furniture combines—Homeland Furnishings Limited. Business had been none too good that year, and the partners sold out, factory and all. Drew's wife was a Helmsbury woman and he had an interest in the Ritz cinema, and Helmsbury was therefore where he retired. Corbit came there, too, not only because the two wives were friendly, but because Drew had said there were plenty of ways in Helmsbury to use one's money.

But Corbit soon found out that the last thing Drew intended was to put him in the way of making money. There was unpleasantness, too, over his daughter and Corbit's son. Drew had big ideas for his daughter, so Corbit said.

"Just what was your son doing?" Wharton asked.

Corbit gave a quick look. Wharton's poker face told nothing, and Corbit decided to tell the truth—if necessary.

"You know about my son, Superintendent?"

"I know what happened to him, if that's what you mean."

Corbit sighed.

"He had his business in Fulham and most of my money was in it. Then he thought he could make easy money for himself, and you know what happened. Almost everything was gone. At my age I had to sell my house and begin all over again. And it was not my fault. How could I know what was going on?"

Wharton put it more directly. If Corbit had known, then he'd have been in the dock with his son. Drew always disliked Nelson Corbit, though not till the two families came to Helmsbury had he been so openly hostile. Then when Margaret Drew ran off and married Nelson, Corbit knew he had an even more bitter enemy.

"Still in confidence," Wharton said, "just what was it he said to you that made you strike him?"

Corbit half-turned away, and he was shaking his head as if he hated to remember.

"He said we were dirty crooks, my son and me. I forgot myself, and I hit him. Afterwards I was sorry, but what could I do?"

"Yes," said Wharton heavily. "A bad business all round. Would you say that Drew's attitude was simply an example of professional jealousy, or what?"

Corbit shot him another look.

"It boiled down to that, yes."

"Business rivalries can be nasty," Wharton said casually, and then Corbit was looking in a drawer of the desk. He found the paper he wanted and gave it to Wharton. It was the firm's bill-head and gave a list of the five shops.

"North-west London," Wharton said, and suddenly frowned. "This one in Hampden. I think I remember it. Quite a big shop, next door to a chemist's." Then before Corbit could speak, "Not that I want to talk about that. What I was particularly wanting to speak to you about was the present whereabouts of your son."

Like a flash the pleasure had gone from Corbit's face. He knew nothing of his son's present whereabouts. The last time he had seen him had been on the Wednesday morning at breakfast when he talked of going to Ipswich in the car.

"What for?"

"He would see various dealers," Corbit said, "or perhaps there was something in a private house that he wanted to see. He used to get me most of my stock. If there was a sale, perhaps I would go or he might go. It depended."

"He was your employee in this business or your partner?"

Corbit said he was neither. He preferred to work on a commission basis. In fact Corbit said he didn't know how his son used all his time. He believed he still had interests in London, but he resented questioning, even from his mother.

"Where'd he bank?"

Corbit said he didn't think he had a banking account, at least not locally.

"I see," said Wharton. "And after breakfast on the Wednesday morning you didn't clap eyes on him again?"

"All I did was to find the car," Corbit said. "Maybe he called to me in the shop and I didn't hear, but when I came out to lock up, the car was there at the back."

Nothing of Nelson's had been in it, so he drove the car home and garaged it. When his son didn't appear that night he wasn't unduly concerned, even if he usually said something to his mother when he was going to be away. And that seemed to be all that he could tell us. Where his son stayed in London he had no idea. As he said, Nelson was a man of over thirty. You couldn't question him as you would a child.

"Well, we're grateful to you, Mr. Corbit," Wharton said. "When your son turns up I'd like a word with him. Nothing for you to worry about. Just to put him in the clear."

Corbit showed us out the back way and he seemed so genuinely grateful—heaven knew why—that I'm sure I could have bought anything in the shop for a song.

"Curious chap," Wharton said as we made our way along Back Street. "I don't know why, but I almost like him."

"That's just what I was thinking myself," I said. "The first time I saw him I thought he was just an oily sort of specimen. Now I'm like you. I think that underneath he may not be such a bad chap after all. And he's certainly taken a knock or two in his time."

We took the passage-way through to the High Street and I could have said quite a lot more about Stanley Corbit. But I didn't, for Wharton hasn't a lot of use for what he'd have called the poetic. All the same, there'd been that hurt look in Corbit's eyes; the look of a man who, whatever his weaknesses, had suffered deeply. The experience had not had an ennobling effect, perhaps; he was cowed by authority, but there was a curious dignity in his very submissiveness.

There was no time for even a cup of tea and we made our way to the police station. Umberson was waiting for us, and he had something at last. Nelson had had a kind of high tea that Wednesday night at a little café in the Market Square. He had entered at about half-past six and had left just before seven.

"Then where the devil could he have gone after that?" Wharton asked himself. "Wherever it was he couldn't have gone by car—if his father's telling the truth."

"He didn't go anywhere by train or by bus," Umberson said. "We've checked up everywhere. That's what's kept me."

"He couldn't have helped himself to a car?"

"None missing that we've heard about," Umberson said.

And so to the second piece of news. The conductor on the eight-thirty from Helmsbury through Stepford saw a man leaning over a gate just beyond the woodyard, and a little farther on there was a car drawn up at the roadside. Now the conductor came to think of it, it had almost looked as if the man didn't want to be seen, or else why should he have had his back to the road and been looking over a gate on a pitch-black night.

"Wouldn't that be just short of the chapel?" Wharton asked.

Umberson said it was. He'd been along there himself to see if tyre marks had been left, but the road was too hard and there'd been too much traffic for that.

"What was the man like?" Wharton wanted to know.

"He couldn't say, sir. Just a man wearing a waterproof. A bigger man than Drew, though."

"Drew hadn't a car," Wharton said. "His daughter was using it that night."

It was then that there was a tap at the door. One of Umberson's men came in, and he was carrying a small attaché case.

"Got something?" asked Umberson.

The case was opened and there was something like a double-ended brass club. It was just about a foot long.

"Where'd you find it?"

"Just happened to look along the road inside the meadow," the man said. "It was lying in the meadow about twenty yards back, as if it'd been thrown there. I've got the spot marked."

"What is it exactly?" Wharton was asking, and was lifting it with a gloved hand.

"It looks to me like a pestle," I said. "It must have been a pretty big mortar, though."

"That's it for a fiver," Wharton said. "I've got a much smaller one at home like it." Then he was giving us a queer sort of look. "Isn't this the kind of thing you only get at an antique shop?"

<h1 style="text-align:center">Chapter IX</h1>

<h1 style="text-align:center">SABBATH MORN</h1>

WE DUSTED that pestle for prints, and it was quite a time before we could make head or tail of what we found. Minute traces of prints were blurred, and only one fairly clear thumb impression was left. But that was queerly placed. Imagine that pestle as a heavy foot-long club. Had it been grasped by an ungloved hand prints should have been wrapped, as it were, round one end. Then there should have been the prints where the same hand grasped it to throw it across the meadow, but it was at those ends that there was blurring, as if the *gloved* hand that had grasped it had eliminated prints already there. As for the thumb print, that was *down* the pestle and not round it, and it was fairly near the middle. It was, we thought, as if someone at some far from recent date had lifted it by its middle. The thumb would have been in advance of the fingers, and whereas the finger-prints had been blurred or removed by the later gloved hand, the thumb print, being in the middle, had remained.

Hadcote had been sent for, and while we were waiting for him to arrive Wharton had an idea. In Corbit's shop his hands had been gloved, and now with a gloved hand he brought out that sheet of trade notepaper of the former firm of Drew and Corbit. Corbit's prints came out clear, especially the thumb.

"Now, let's have a look," Wharton said, and with no great faith.

Then he was gaping. He was looking round at me. Those two thumb prints were identical.

"What about it, sir?" Umberson said. "Shall we ask him to step in?"

"Not for the moment," Wharton said. "Let the doctor see it first. Then get everything photographed." He looked at his watch. "What time will Corbit close his shop?"

Just short of six o'clock, Umberson thought.

"Then ask him to be so good as to come along here when he's closed," Wharton said. Then he was cocking an ear. Hadcote was coming in.

"How's this for your blunt instrument?" Wharton asked him.

Hadcote's eyes popped as he saw it. He took out a pocket rule and measured the knobs at each end. He borrowed Wharton's glass and looked at the knobs through that.

"No blood or hairs," Wharton reminded him. "Drew had his hat on when it struck him—if this was it."

Hadcote said he was wondering about felt or fibre from the hat, and Wharton doubted if there'd be any. That pestle had far too smooth a surface. Not that it'd do any harm to put it under a microscope.

"Well, it certainly looks like what we've been looking for," Hadcote said. "Everything tallies as far as I'm concerned."

So much for that. It was about a quarter to six, and Wharton and I had a cup of tea while the photographing was being done. Corbit arrived sooner than we expected, and he had to be kept waiting till the pestle was brought back.

"Sorry to bother you, Mr. Corbit," Wharton told him, "but there's something you can do for us. This object here. Have you ever seen it before?"

Corbit spotted it at once. And he was looking the most surprised man in the world.

"It looks like the one I had!"

"Really? The same one, you think? I mean, there couldn't be another exactly like it?"

"It's mine," he said. "I missed it about a week ago. It belonged to a mortar, and I went to show it to a customer and the pestle wasn't there." He shrugged his shoulders. "Naturally the customer didn't want the mortar without the pestle. It's still in the shop."

"It could have been missing for more than a week?"

"Perhaps," said Corbit and did some quick thinking. "A fortnight perhaps. But no more."

"How'd you acquire it?"

"At a sale here in the town. It's got the lot number still on it."

"Just look here a bit more closely," Wharton told him. "See that print? That's your thumb."

Corbit smiled.

"You see," he said, and smiled disarmingly. "I told you it was my pestle."

"Yes," said Wharton and nodded. "All the same, we'll have to keep it for a day or two before you get it back."

"That's all right, sir."

"But just another little matter. Who could have stolen it from your shop?"

Corbit shrugged his shoulders.

"From what I'm told, the mortar was an unusual size," Wharton went on.

Corbit agreed. If anything, it was too unusual; far too large for the average buyer. It was, in fact, the largest one in brass or bronze or gun-metal that he'd ever had.

"There we are then," Wharton said. "If what I might call a customer stole it it could only be because he or she had a similar mortar without a pestle. What about the man who works for you? No reason, is there, why he should have taken it?"

Corbit said there was no reason at all. He had in fact asked Turbey about it, and Turbey knew nothing.

"Ah, well," said Wharton resignedly. "Another one of life's little mysteries. Much obliged to you, Mr. Corbit, and sorry we've had to trouble you."

Out went Corbit. Umberson was looking a bit puzzled.

"Well?" said Wharton amusedly. "What's on your mind?"

"Nothing at all, sir," Umberson told him. "Except perhaps I just wondered why you didn't pin him down about that thumb print."

"Where was the point?" Wharton asked him, and still amiably. "It was in his shop and he handled it from time to time. That doesn't prove whose gloved hand it was that eliminated the rest of the prints. Admittedly it might have been his. He might have thought he'd rubbed every print off, if and when he struck Drew on the head. But how're we going to prove it?"

"Then we're back where we were, sir."

"Not necessarily," Wharton told him. "Who else had the run of that shop?"

"Why, Nelson Corbit."

"And where's he now?"

"You're asking me, sir," Umberson told him with a grin.

"Exactly," and Wharton wasn't grinning. "That's why an SOS is going out for Nelson Corbit."

And he wasted no time. It wasn't quite an SOS that he wanted, for that might have led to false assumptions. *In connection with the death of Alfred Drew, the police are anxious to interview . . .*—that was the wording, that fitted the case, and he was asking the Yard to rush it through for the Sunday Press and Radio. Then just as we were going to call it a day, the telephone went for him. Another department of the Yard was on the line. I moved on to the hotel, and it was quite a time before he joined me there, and he was looking quite pleased.

The message had been about that East End pawnshop. The owner, Harry Markson by name, had sworn that he knew no one of the name of Corbit. Neither he nor his assistant knew of anyone resembling the description of Nelson Corbit and carrying a heavy suit-case. But the interesting thing was that that shop had been under Yard surveillance for some time. Markson had wriggled out of trouble once before.

"I wonder what was in that suit-case?" I said.

"Maybe a couple of rugs," Wharton said. "Those oriental rugs fold up pretty small."

Then I was wondering why Nelson Corbit hadn't gone up to London by car. Wharton said he'd talked that over with Umberson and, guardedly, with Frosbeck. Frosbeck's petrol had been cut, and there wasn't the additional private basic. Frosbeck could manage fairly comfortably, since his car was scarcely used at all. Corbit's, on the other hand, was used quite a lot. A journey to London and back would use over four gallons, and black-market petrol was hard to come by.

And, if he'd been stopped, Nelson Corbit could hardly have found justification for using the car when the train was available.

Over our belated meal I was asking for the next day's programme. Wharton had it all arranged. At half-past nine we were seeing Truebent at his house. Soon after eleven, and when her husband had left for the chapel, we were seeing Mrs. Turbey.

It was half-past nine to the minute when we drew up outside Truebent's front door on that Sunday morning. It was a good-class modern house on the Newmarket Road, and there was a moneyed air about it, from the newly-painted greenhouse to the stretches of well-kept gardens. Truebent himself let us in, and he didn't seem too surprised to see me with Wharton. Doubtless he now knew all about me, and, if anything, he looked quite pleased.

It was the room that he called his office that we went to. Wharton insisted that the call was largely a formal one; merely in fact a final elimination of Truebent from any possible suspicions in the matter of Drew's death. Not that such suspicions were in any way official, George was plausibly adding. It was local suspicion and gossip that might be the annoying thing.

"You tell us, and I hope for the last time, just what you did on that Wednesday night, Mr. Truebent. Starting at seven o'clock, shall we say."

Truebent hooked his thumbs in the armpits of the pullover and leaned back in his swivel chair.

"At seven o'clock I was in here, going over some accounts with a—well, I suppose you'd call him a business associate, though he's not that really. He left just before eight o'clock, and then I checked up on what we'd been talking over, and then I got so absorbed that I was perfectly horrified to find it was half-past. I'd just time to dash upstairs for a quick wash and change my collar and so on, and nip off down to Frosbeck's place in my car. I had intended to be there soon after eight."

He gave me a look, but I was saying nothing. My policy was to be little more than an ornamental appendage to Wharton.

"Yes," said Wharton, and frowned, and then he, too, was giving me a look. "Of course we'll have to see this business associate of yours. Just for a cross-check. Your word's good enough for us, but you know what red-tape's like."

His note-book was out and he was waiting.

"What's his name?"

Truebent cleared his throat.

"As a matter of fact I'd rather not tell you his name."

Wharton looked flabbergasted.

"Not tell us! But why?"

Truebent shrugged his shoulders.

"Sorry, but that's how it is."

"But this is ridiculous," Wharton told him. "Your alibi depends on it. More than that. You've got, by your own admission, no alibi at all from eight o'clock till the time you appeared at Mr. Frosbeck's flat. I wouldn't mind that; I could get over it, in fact, if you could prove the alibi up till eight o'clock."

"Look, Superintendent," Truebent said, and leaned forward in his chair. "I didn't kill Drew. I know I didn't kill Drew. I doubt if any amount of faking in the world could make a case for me killing Drew. I'll give a thousand pounds to any charity you care to nominate if you can find a living soul who saw me anywhere near the woodyard on that Wednesday night."

"Yes?"

"And I'll swear in any court you like that I spent my time on that Wednesday night as I've told you." He shrugged his shoulders again. "I'm sorry, but that's how it goes."

"Ah, well," said Wharton resignedly. "I suppose I'll have to use the few wits I was born with. Just let's suppose for a minute. On that Friday when his body was found Drew had threatened to make certain damaging disclosures about yourself. I imagine he was pretty sure of himself, or he wouldn't have said so. Let's imagine, then, that you'd stepped just over the line and he'd discovered it. Let's say you'd made an error of judgment."

Truebent nodded, and his look was as quizzical as Wharton's own.

"Obviously everything was to do with the council," Wharton went on. "The administration of public funds, perhaps, or the matter of a contract. Whatever it was, a third party seems to be indicated—a business associate, shall we say? And naturally you'd want to square matters with that associate. Very well then. On the Wednesday night you two arranged everything to your satisfaction. As you told us on the Friday morning, Drew had nothing on you. You had an answer all ready to anything he might say." He smiled. "Well, how far am I out?"

Truebent looked up at the ceiling and he was frowning in thought. His lip drooped as if something was suddenly amusing him.

"Is what we're talking about confidential?"

"At the moment most certainly so," Wharton assured him.

"Then let *me* do a little supposing. Suppose everything was as you say. Suppose I had made what you called an error of judgment. I'll go further. I'll lay some cards on the table. I'll suppose I'd fixed things with this so-called business associate so as to spike old Drew's guns. But that wouldn't be the end of it."

"Why not?"

"This is still confidential?"

"Most certainly," Wharton assured him again.

"Then haven't you heard of the existence of the Commissioners of Inland Revenue?"

"Ah!" said Wharton. "Now we're getting somewhere. Not only would the Commissioners be asking you awkward questions; they'd be after this business associate as well."

"Yes," said Truebent. "It's all supposition, of course, but that's how it would look to me. If it were so, wouldn't it be compounding a felony, or whatever they call it, if you knew all about it and kept your mouth shut?"

"Well," said Wharton slowly, and as slowly got to his feet, "that requires a bit of thought." Then he was giving a grim sort of smile. "Still, you've helped us a lot. You've as good as told us who that business associate was."

Truebent's eyes narrowed.

"I don't think so. I work with, and for, scores of people in this town."

"Maybe," Wharton said. "All the same, if I were a betting man I wouldn't mind risking quite a small sum."

Then he was holding out his hand.

"Much obliged to you for seeing us. Some time tomorrow we may be seeing you again."

"Any time you like," Truebent told him, and his tone had the least bit of an edge, or was it a challenge?

Wharton drove at his full thirty miles an hour back to the police station. It was Sergeant Matthews we wanted, but Umberson was button-holing Wharton straight away.

"I've got a bus driver here, sir, if you'd like to see him. He says he saw Mr. Drew on Wednesday evening."

That was important news and Wharton hurried in. The bus driver was on the Helmsbury-Ipswich route and he claimed to have seen Drew at about a quarter to six on the Wednesday evening. The bus, going towards Ipswich, met him just at the Helmsbury side of the gravel pit.

"Getting a bit dark, wasn't it?" Wharton said.

Not that evening, the driver told him. That was one of the few fine days we'd had.

"And why could you be sure it was Mr. Drew? You must have passed him pretty quickly?"

"Well, for one thing, sir, we always slow down there to take the bend. And I ought to know Mr. Drew when I see him. I drove one of his lorries before I got the job with the bus company."

When we came to assess the value of all that, it didn't look so important. As Umberson said, it looked as if Drew was taking a walk after being indoors all the afternoon, and the Ipswich Road would be the natural way for him to take. But the point was whether Drew had taken that walk before tea or after. Wharton was inclined to think the walk came first, and he was basing his theory on the warmth of a certain tea-pot.

"Nothing gleaned yet about those revelations that Drew was going to make at the council meeting?" he asked Umberson.

Umberson said there was nothing but conflicting gossip.

"Let's see if we can get a bit further forward on our own account," Wharton said. "What are Truebent's principal interests?"

"Well, there's the woodyard, and that's his own. Then there's Parton and Webb. They're general engineers and he's a director. His wife was a Miss Parton."

"Are they the firm who're supplying the pumping plant at the gravel pit?" I asked.

"That's it, sir. They're doing some drainage work for Fred Sheffield."

"Any significance in Drew's taking a walk that way on the Wednesday evening?"

Umberson didn't think so. And when I pointed out that work at the gravel pit would have ceased and therefore any snooping on Drew's part wouldn't be noticed, he still didn't think there was anything in it. If Drew wanted a walk—well, he just stepped out of his front gate and along the Ipswich Road.

"Any other interests?" Wharton asked, a bit impatiently.

"Lemming's garage in Upper Street," Umberson said. "He's interested in the Ritz cinema."

"And what else?"

"Well, there's Drew and Mason, the coal business. That's his. Then there's a sort of building combine, and he's in that."

That seemed to be all, and the problem was where the interests of Drew and Truebent seemed to conflict. And to that there seemed no answer. As far as the town council was concerned there could be no conflict of interest, for the very simple reason that each man, as a councillor, was debarred from tendering for any council work or supplies. Even if he merely had a monetary interest, however small, in a firm, that firm could not tender.

Wharton waved the whole argument impatiently away.

"I'd better try my own short cut," he said. "Mr. Travers and I have just made Truebent a bit nervous. I hope we've bluffed him into thinking we know far more than we do. He may be doing some telephoning at this very minute, but I don't think he'll risk seeing anybody before dark. I'd like my Sergeant Matthews put on his tail, say from half-past five on. He doesn't know Matthews."

Then he was changing our plans and Umberson had to ring up Drew's solicitors for an immediate appointment. As Wharton said, the quickest way to all of Drew's interests was to know just what he had left, and maybe to whom he had left it. Then when the appointment was fixed, I was deputed to see Mrs. Turbey, and as George said his business with the solicitor might take quite a long time I rang Bernard and asked if it would be convenient for me to drop in to lunch. He said he'd be delighted, so I made a rendezvous at the church for soon after twelve.

There was plenty of time, so I walked to Stepford. The final bell had ceased well before I got to Endover Lane, but I waited for the duration of a pipe before I walked on to Turbey's cottage. It was a fine morning, and in the sheltered spot where I had waited the sun had been quite warm.

In my young days a cottage front door was chiefly ornament and rarely opened from one year's end to another. Even on that Sunday morning I felt it seemly somehow to go round to the back. And that door was open as I neared it, for it had shot open as I passed the window of the kitchen.

"It's you, sir," said Mrs. Turbey. "You give me quite a turn."

Her face was red and perspiring, and her hair all wispy. Her hands were covered with flour and there was the smell of apples.

"You're making an apple tart," I said.

"Turbey's very partial to apple pie," she told me. "Did you want to see him? Because he's at chapel. You could catch him when they come out."

"I don't think it matters," I said. "I would like a glass of water, though. Perhaps I might sit down for a minute. I love kitchens, especially when they're as spotless as yours is bound to be."

She drew back to let me in, but I didn't feel welcome for all that. Even when she made me a cup of tea it wasn't because she had asked if I'd like it. What she'd said was that she supposed I wouldn't like it. But over it I told her I'd walked from Helmsbury and was having lunch at The Pleasance. I added that I mustn't disturb her, and I'd love to see her making her pie.

Then it was she who began asking the questions.

"How're they getting on with finding out about poor Mr. Drew?"

"Not very fast," I said. "These things always take time."

"Then they don't know who done it?"

"Not yet," I said. "All the same, I think they've got some useful information already."

She shot me a quick look at that, and one that I pretended not to see, and in just the same way I was pretending not to know that she knew that the *they* included myself. A polite fiction that, and an amusing one.

"Well, we don't know anything," she said. "We was both indoors all night. Never saw nor heard a thing, we didn't—neither of us. You could have knocked me down with a feather when I knew what'd happened."

I said I wasn't surprised. What I had no intention of saying was, "Just why did you tell me that when I hadn't even hinted at your knowing anything? And why the emphasis on *both* of you?"

Then she was changing the topic and talking about Bernard, and The Pleasance, and so to my holiday, and then round to Wharton.

"What a fine-looking gentleman that was who was staying there with you! Reminds me rather of Turbey's father. Just such a big, stout man, he was. They tell me he's a Londoner."

I said that he was—in a way. And he wasn't so pleasant as he looked, at least when he was investigating anything like murder. He'd quite an uncanny way of knowing when people were telling him lies.

A bit crude, perhaps, and yet it seemed to be effective, for Mrs. Turbey was suddenly leaving her scalloping of the edges of her pie and was looking at the oven. She made quite a show of it.

"I can't stand lies myself," she told me. "Speak the truth, as my mother used to say, and shame the devil."

"And a very good motto, too," I told her as I put my cup on the draining-board. "Sorry I missed your husband, Mrs. Turbey, and thank you very much for an excellent cup of tea."

She was actually smiling as she showed me off through the door. The smile went when I added something else—that I had an idea that Superintendent Wharton might want a word with Turbey in the very near future.

Chapter X

SABBATH WELL SPENT

As I passed the chapel there was the sound of singing and what I imagined was the final hymn. The Coach and Horses was open, so it had just gone twelve. I lingered out my walk, and it was not till the first worshippers were leaving the church that I made my way there. Bernard appeared almost at once, and Ethelberta Langdon was with him.

There was a word or two of general greeting, and when we moved on Ethelberta was going with us. Bernard had suggested the usual Sunday-morning walk, and it appeared that she was paying a quick visit to an old lady who lived in Endover Lane, two cottages beyond the Turbeys'.

"Mr. Ampling tells me you're engaged on trying to find out who killed that poor Mr. Drew," she said. "Such a horrible business. I do hope you catch him."

I mumbled that the whole thing was *sub judice*, or something like that, and Bernard backed me up by telling her that even if I knew anything, I wasn't allowed to talk. But that didn't stop Ethelberta Langdon.

"But fancy him being there a whole day before they found his body! When I think of it, it absolutely gives me the shivers."

"A guilty conscience?" Bernard asked amusedly.

"Of course not." Then she turned to me. "It *was* on the Wednesday night he was killed, wasn't it?"

There was no harm in telling her what everyone else knew—that it certainly was.

"That's it," she said to Bernard. "And to think it might almost have been me."

"But you weren't at the woodyard on Wednesday night?"

"Not *at* it," she said, "but very near it. In fact I went past it. I had to if I had to see Borcombe."

I stopped in my tracks. The others didn't seem to notice, so I moved hurriedly on.

"Do I gather that you actually went past the woodyard on Wednesday night, Miss Langdon?"

"Yes," she said. "I went to see Borcombe. About his wife, you know. He was having difficulty in getting anyone to sit up with her at night."

"And what time would it be, Miss Langdon?"

"Let me see," she said. "It was about half-past eight when I got there and I didn't stay more than a few minutes. That's right. It was just short of nine when I got home again. I remember that because I turned on the nine-o'clock news."

"And you didn't see a soul?"

"Not a soul," she said. "Except when I was coming back. That was that antique dealer. You know—the one this end of the High Street."

It was to Bernard she had spoken, but it was I who asked if she meant Corbit.

"That's the man," she said. "I think he must have been to see Turbey about something. Turbey works for him, you know."

"You mean he was coming from that way?"

"Yes," she said. "He was just in front of me all the way to the chapel. I wondered who it was, and then I recognised him when he got into his car."

I didn't want to go further than that. I said that naturally he'd been to see Turbey, and then I began talking about something else. Not that there was much time to talk about anything. We had passed Turbey's cottage, with never a glimpse of him or his wife, and in a moment or two Ethelberta was saying a temporary goodbye—"Bernard," she added, "must bring me to tea sometime"—and after those amiabilities we moved on down the lane.

"Awkward for Corbit, isn't it?" Bernard said.

Years of association with Wharton have made me a fluent liar in a righteous cause. I said we'd had a shrewd idea already that Corbit had been in the vicinity of the woodyard on that Wednesday night, and for a sufficiently good reason. But after that I could hardly use the telephone at The Pleasance for reporting the morning's discovery to George. But I did take the early bus back to Helmsbury instead of spending a comfortable afternoon.

I did something else during that lunch. I won't say that I'd been feeling rather ashamed of those suspicions I'd had about Bernard and that stolen picture, for it would be truer to say that with a small amount of shame there'd been the crestfallen realisation that I'd committed, and not for the first time, the crime of jumping too easily to conclusions. But as I couldn't apologise, I got the matter off my conscience in my own way.

"Wouldn't it have been rather awkward," I said, "if I'd happened to see that supposed Zurbaran in your possession?"

"I was taking pretty good care of that," he told me. "You can't be too wily when you've a sleuth in the house." Then he was giving one of his little ironical smiles. "Mind you, I'm not setting up to be more honest than my fellow collectors. I haven't had the temptation yet, but I tremble to think what might happen if I saw something lying too carelessly about."

"That reminds me," I said. "Weren't you going to tell me about these two rugs?"

"These two?" he said, and the smile was now one of pure amusement. "But my dear fellow, I *have* told you."

"I assure you you haven't."

"Oh yes," he said. "I've told you the facts. It's up to you to put them together."

But when I began telling him just what he *had* told me, he refused to listen. He said he'd always wanted to see me in action, and now he had his chance.

I had no time that afternoon to think about rugs. George was back at the hotel soon after I arrived, and he'd lunched apparently with the solicitor. I asked no questions, for I was telling him about the morning's discoveries. As we agreed, that identification by Ethelberta Langdon was virtually proved by the behaviour of at least two other people. That slip which Mrs. Corbit had made was now proof that Corbit had gone out in the car, and the fluency of her story showed that it had been rehearsed. Then there was Mrs. Turbey's volunteered and emphasised statement that neither she nor her husband had seen a soul that Wednesday night. As an extra there was the statement of the bus conductor who had seen a man—a bigger man than Drew—leaning over a gate, with a car drawn up just beyond him.

George was pursing his lips and saying he couldn't make it out.

"If Corbit killed Drew, why was he such a fool as to let Turbey know he'd been near the woodyard?"

"I think you're working on the wrong assumption for once," I told him. "You're assuming that Drew was killed *before* Corbit saw Turbey—supposing, that is, that Corbit did the killing. But suppose Corbit had a reason for seeing Turbey and then saw Drew afterwards and quarrelled with him and struck him. The Friday morning, when Turbey reported for work and told Corbit about Drew's body, Corbit would get him to keep his mouth shut about the Wednesday visit."

"There's something fishy somewhere," George said. "That line of argument's about as straight as a donkey's hind leg. Why should Drew be at the woodyard?"

"Spying on Truebent."

"Truebent offered to bet a thousand pounds he wasn't there. And what about the pestle? Why should Corbit have it with him? And who was Corbit waiting for at the chapel?"

"Maybe Turbey," I said. "Turbey didn't arrive on time, so Corbit went to find him at his cottage."

"But if his business was legitimate, why a rendezvous at the chapel? Why not drive his car down the lane to Turbey's cottage?" Then he was giving a snort. "No use theorising. We want facts, not theories. What we'll do is have a friendly chat with your friend Turbey."

"Now?"

"Oh no," he told me. "The morning'll do. We'll let him spin us his own yarn and then we'll have him and Corbit together. The shop's the place for that."

Then he was telling me about Drew's will. It was a voluminous document that had revealed very little more than Umberson had indicated. The estate might amount to as much as seventy thousand pounds, and the trustees included his bank. Everything was left to his daughter, with sole control after five years. There was a proviso that any association of hers with Nelson Corbit, her former husband, would mean a forfeit of the estate which was then to go to a list of specified charities.

"So he took his vindictiveness to the grave," George said. "Not that it tells us anything. There was no confliction of interests with Truebent's as far as we could see."

"And what now?" I said.

George said he was taking things easy, or so he hoped, till dusk, and then something might happen at Truebent's house. I said that if that was so, then I'd have a breather, too, and I was thinking that I'd rather like to put in an hour with Frosbeck. When I rang him, he was in, and he told me to come right over. His housekeeper was out, but she'd left the tea ready, and he thought there'd be plenty for two.

It was indeed a treat to be in that snug, pleasant room of Frosbeck's again and talking nineteen to the dozen, as George would say, about antiques. There was a cold wind whistling outside, but we had a cheerful fire and a couple of easy chairs, and most of the time I was priming Frosbeck to spin yet more yarns connected with his trade. There was one celebrated fraud about which he knew a considerable deal, and there was an experience he had had himself with a couple of confidence men. I'd had an experience of much the same sort, and it was when I'd just finished telling him about it that he caught sight of the clock.

"Half-past four," he said. "I don't know about you, but I feel like tea."

I said I'd help get it, but he said there was nothing to do but wait till the kettle boiled. So as soon as he was in the kitchen, I made for the books.

I had no particular book in mind. I glanced at Hornby's *Spanish Painters* and its couple of Zurbaran reproductions, and then I was attracted by the older and almost moth-eaten volumes on the lowest shelf. One or two seemed to have been bought in a job lot and the three or four I looked at bore either no name at all or that of some unknown owner. There were some novels, too, and I recognised an old friend of mine, Glaister's *Medical Jurisprudence and Toxicology*. But it was from a volume with a torn and faded back—*Numismatology* by a G.H. Tame—that the paper fell out. It was a folded bill-head and on it were some pencilled notes.

W. FARMER

ANTIQUE AND MODERN FURNITURE. WORKS
OF ART

Upholstery. Loose Covers. Bedding remade.

That was the heading, and the address was 29 Main Parade, Hampden. That was amazing in itself, but still more strange was the fact that those pencilled notes on that bill-head were Frosbeck's. There was no mistaking it, for I had seen his writing on that receipt and guarantee he had given me for the mirror. It was an old-fashioned copper-plate and almost vertical, and as I was staring at it, in he came with the tray.

"I've been looking at your books," I said, "and this just happened to fall out. It's a perfectly staggering coincidence."

He set down the tray and I gave him the paper. I was replacing the book, and when I turned round again he was still frowning at that paper.

"It *is* staggering," he said. "I never knew I had it. Perhaps I should have told you before. . . . And yet I don't know."

I had the feeling that I had intruded on some privacy.

"I'm sorry," I said. "It was unpardonable curiosity on my part."

"Oh no," he told me quickly. "But why should *you* find it staggering?"

"Well, in strict confidence, we were making some enquiries of Corbit yesterday and he produced one of the bill-heads of the firm of Drew and Corbit. I'm pretty sure that one of their shops was 25-29 Main Parade, Hampden."

"Yes," he said slowly. "I think that's perhaps what I should have told you or Superintendent Wharton. If it had been Corbit who'd been killed perhaps I would have done. In the case of Drew, it didn't so much matter."

"But how does it affect you?" I asked him, and I must have been looking even more bewildered.

He smiled for the first time since he'd seen that paper. It was a quiet sort of smile, and a slow shake of the head accompanied it.

"It affects me," he said, *"because I was Walter Farmer."*

We sat down to tea, and he was telling me all about it.

"I expect I looked as if I had seen a ghost," he said. "Perhaps I had. . . . Two ghosts."

If I give you my version of his story, it is because it is more compact and perhaps more strictly in order of happenings.

Frosbeck was the son of an antique dealer, and he himself had worked as a young man for a firm in Liverpool, and it was there that he married and there that his son was born. Then his father died and he inherited the Hampden shop. Business had been in none too good a state—the depression was in full blast for one thing—and Frosbeck repented having taken it over. However, the change which he effected in the nature of the business—the introduction of modern stuff—improved things considerably. Then in 1938 the adjoining premises—numbers twenty-five and twenty-seven—were opened by Drew and Corbit. They could sell at cut rates and Frosbeck realised that his number, so to speak, was up. He ultimately sold out to Drew and Corbit and, considering everything, he made quite a fair bargain and one that he didn't regret.

For one thing he didn't care for the neighbourhood, and also there was the matter of his wife. She had had a severe operation and was due for another, and he couldn't keep his mind on his business. While the actual sale was going through, his wife died. No sooner was it sold than Frosbeck had a nervous breakdown. Then his only son was killed at Dunkirk.

"I'll show you," he said, and was getting to his feet.

In his bedroom were two enlarged, framed photographs: one of a sweet-faced and quite young-looking woman, and the other of a young man in the khaki battledress of a sergeant of infantry. He was a fine looking boy, and his father again to the life.

What could I say, except that I was sorry.

"Nothing to be sorry about," he told me as we went back to the fire and the last remnants of tea. "It brought things back with a bit of a jolt—that's all." Then he was smiling quietly again. "But you're wondering why I changed my name. It was after my boy died. I was ill, and one day I saw myself unshaved. That was how the idea came to me. I thought I'd start life all over again, and I did. The time even came when I could hang those two photographs in my bedroom. A sort of dual existence. Wiping out the past and then being able to live with it after all."

"Amazing that you should come here," I said.

"Not really," he said. "I'd known Tidman when he had the business and I'd always liked Helmsbury. As a matter of fact I happened to learn from Tidman that Drew was living here, and Corbit." He smiled. "Between ourselves, that rather intrigued me. There seemed something almost adventurous in the idea of Drew not recognising me. Perhaps you wouldn't understand that sort of feeling."

"But I would," I said. "It's just the kind of thing I'd have felt myself. But, tell me: did Drew recognise you?"

"Not for some considerable time," he said. "He'd begun to look at me in a puzzled sort of way, and then one day—it wasn't actually till about a year or so ago—he remembered, and he challenged me."

"And Corbit?"

"I'd never met Corbit," Frosbeck said. "I'd heard about him, mind you, and during the negotiations for the sale Drew always quoted him to me as the partner who wanted the pound of flesh."

"A sort of Codlin and Short business."

"That's just it. Drew made grudging concessions from time to time after he'd induced his partner to agree to them. So he said. Now I know, of course, that Corbit was only a bogey to scare me into concluding the deal. All the same, I didn't feel too good about Corbit. That's why I said that if Corbit had been killed—not Drew—I should have felt a bit uneasy in my mind."

"But why, my dear fellow?"

"Well, he was a fellow dealer. What you people might call a trade rival. And he'd been concerned with buying my business in Hampden. You might have thought I'd been squeezed out. That wouldn't have looked too good."

"We'd probably have checked up," I said, "but I don't think we'd have made mistakes like that. Besides, it wasn't Corbit who was killed. It was Drew. How did you get on with him, by the way?"

He shrugged his shoulders.

"As well, I suppose, as most people got on with him. I didn't altogether trust him, perhaps."

"Do you think he ever told Corbit who you were?"

"I'm sure he didn't," he said. "He and Corbit were a long way from even speaking terms well before he discovered who I was."

What could I say for the final summing up, except that I was sorry, in a way, that he had had to tell me about things that maybe he would rather have kept in the background of memory, and no more.

"I think it's done me good," he said. "I've kept all this to myself far too long. Mine's a fairly lonely life, you know, Mr. Travers. That's why I'm so pleased to have an occasional game of bridge, and to have the friendship—if I may say so—of people like your cousin. Before that I was getting far too introspective. I might even have been heading for another breakdown."

"You like Bernard Ampling?"

"Very much, indeed. I admire him and respect him."

"Then tell me something," I said, and smiled. "You did him a very good turn over those miniatures, but strictly between ourselves, did you have more than a shrewd idea what they were?"

"Well"—there was a twinkle in his eye—"maybe I did, and maybe I didn't. Suit yourself."

"Well, a little ground-bait's very useful," I said.

He shrugged his shoulders amusedly.

"Perhaps I might do something in the same line for you, too, if you did something in return."

"And what's that?"

"I think the police should be made to watch Corbit night and day," he told me. "After what I've been telling you this afternoon it might be very uncomfortable for me if anything was to happen."

I told him to leave all that to me.

Dusk was in the sky when I got back to the hotel, and George had left a message that he had gone to the police station. I had a look at the popular Press—I'd seen the soberer sort at Bernard's—and in two of the papers was that police notice about Nelson Corbit. I thought of the buzz of gossip there'd be in Helmsbury, and I wondered how Stanley Corbit and his wife would be taking it.

Then inevitably I was leaning back in my chair and thinking about Frosbeck and the story he had told me that afternoon. I tried to twist that story to make it have some bearing on the relationships between Drew and Stanley Corbit, but there seemed to be none. Even if it had always been Drew's policy during the partnership to instance Corbit as the harsh and implacable bargainer, that had been no reason for enmity, for the cheaper a property could be bought the better for Corbit himself. Then I was thinking again of what I had pointed out to Wharton—that the wrong man had been killed. Drew, it still seemed to me, had come to hate Corbit far more than Corbit had hated Drew. Even Frosbeck had talked about Corbit being killed and not Drew.

I was puzzling my wits about all that when I was called to the telephone. Wharton was asking me to come round for a minute or two, and when I got to the police station he was with Umberson and Sergeant Matthews.

"My hunch was right," Wharton told me. "Truebent nipped out on foot just after six o'clock and Matthews followed him. Where do you think he went to?"

George didn't look in the mood for flippancy or I'd have said to church.

"No idea," I said.

"To see that chap Sheffield who owns the gravel pit."

I was rather disappointed.

"Well, why shouldn't he?" I said. "After all, it's Truebent's firm's plant that's draining the gravel pit."

"There's more in it than that," he said. "You tell him, Umberson."

Umberson said that Sheffield's was the very name they'd been looking for. For the last three years he'd secured a very lucrative contract from the council for the supply of sand, gravel and hardcore in connection with the town's building programme. What seemed likely was that Truebent had had an undisclosed partnership with Sheffield, and Drew had got wind of it.

"Maybe that was why Drew was prowling round the gravel pit on the Wednesday night," I said. "But suppose you're right. Suppose Drew had made charges and substantiated them at last Friday's council meeting. What would have happened to Truebent?"

"He'd have lost his seat on the council, for one thing, and there'd probably have been an action against him for fraud. Maybe the income-tax people would have been after him, too."

There was certainly a motive for giving Drew a crack on the skull. Truebent was a big noise in the town's business circles, and while people are apt far too soon to forget a matter of graft, they wouldn't so easily forget a matter of twelve months' imprisonment for fraud.

"Even so, I don't like it," I said to George. "Sheffield—we'll suppose it was he—was with Truebent on that Wednesday evening, and you can bet they were cooking the books. On the Friday morning Truebent boasted to Umberson that Drew's threats were all hot air. Then if that was so, where's the motive?"

Umberson said it might have been Truebent who was talking the hot air.

"Let's get back to Truebent's alibi," Wharton said. "He daren't mention Sheffield as having been with him on the Wednesday night because that would have connected him with Sheffield—the last thing he wanted. All the same, I think we can now get him in the mood to say whether it was Sheffield or not. We might see him again in the morning. And Sheffield, too."

"What about the period from eight o'clock to nine?" I asked. "Didn't any of his neighbours hear or see Truebent's car at a quarter to, when he left for Frosbeck's place?"

"There's one neighbour who says she heard a car at about that time," Umberson said.

George and I went back to the hotel, and George was giving me his last-minute views. Something was telling him, he said, that Truebent was a case for the income-tax people, not for us. We'd do better for the moment to concentrate on the two Corbits. He was harping on that again that night after we'd listened to the nine-o'clock news, and the police request in the matter of Nelson Corbit.

Talking and talking and getting nowhere is far too much like chess for my liking, so I managed to steer the conversation round to Frosbeck. George seemed very interested, and, as was not unusual, he was wise enough after the event.

"Something told me about that chap that he'd had a pretty thin time in life," he said. "He was so quiet in his manner, as if all the time he was thinking about himself. Losing your wife and your only son is a pretty nasty jar."

It was half-past nine and he said he'd be going up Wooden Hill, and he gave me a look as if that was what I ought to be doing, too. A full day in front of us, he said. The inquest on Drew in the morning and the funeral in the afternoon, though neither would be much concern of ours. But we'd have to see Turbey and Stanley Corbit, and maybe the man Sheffield, and probably Truebent again. And after the newspaper notices and the broadcast, there might be news of Nelson Corbit, and that might mean a quick visit to town.

I finished a crossword puzzle and followed George up the stairs. I thought, like him, that we'd have a busy Monday, and it might be well to have a little sleep in hand. But naturally I'd no idea just how busy it was going to be. I very much doubted if Nelson Corbit would turn up, but I was to be wrong. There was also to be the little matter of a cable from Bernice.

CHAPTER XI

THE SECOND BODY

WHARTON IS one of those extraordinary people who cannot lie on in bed after a certain hour; in his case seven o'clock. He boasts that he wakes up regularly as clockwork just before that time, and then he simply has to get up. When we've been staying at hotels I've known him come down on winter mornings and, if it was wet, huddle in a deserted lounge to the annoyance of the cleaners. When it was fine he usually went for a walk.

That Monday morning it was fine and I gathered that he'd gone out for a walk, for he couldn't be found when he was wanted on the telephone. I slipped on a dressing-gown and went downstairs. It was then about ten minutes to eight and the maid had just brought my cup of tea.

"The Superintendent there, sir?" The voice was Umberson's and it seemed to have an urgency.

"He's certain to be in at any second now," I said. "Can I take a message?"

"It's about Corbit," he said. "Will you tell him that they've just found his body."

In the flash of a second I was thinking about Frosbeck, and a remark which he couldn't possibly have meant me to take at all seriously. "Awkward for me if anything happens to Corbit," was what he'd said.

"Stanley Corbit, you mean?"

"No sir, no!" he told me impatiently. "Nelson Corbit."

"Nelson Corbit," I said. "Where'd they find him? And who's *they*?"

"Drowned in that water in Sheffield's gravel pit. Truebent's men found him when they went to work this morning. I've only just this minute heard."

"You'd better get along there yourself," I said. "We'll follow as soon as we possibly can."

Then I was remembering half a dozen other things. I supposed the doctor had been warned, and Truebent. Nothing ought to be done about Stanley Corbit till Wharton made a decision. And Sergeant Matthews had better bring our car round to the Roebuck. I didn't think Sheffield would be of any use to us, but he might be warned, just in case.

I asked the girl at the desk to get Wharton to come up to my room the minute he came in, and then I sprinted back upstairs to shave and dress. I was practically ready to go down again when George walked in. He looked as if he could hardly believe his ears.

"Drowned?" he said. "What the devil did he mean by drowned? What was he doing in a place like that?"

Then he was wanting to know what I'd told Umberson, and I was hoping there was nothing I'd left out. He was graciously pleased to say that I couldn't have done better, and then he was rushing me downstairs for a quick meal, for heaven knew when we should get another. In any case there was no tremendous hurry, and when we did get there Umberson should have finished the preliminaries.

"About the last thing I expected," George said as he waded into his scrambled egg on toast. "Wonder how long he's been there. If it's been since last Wednesday night, then we're up against something far different from what we thought."

"Curious that Drew should have been seen in the neighbourhood of that gravel pit last Wednesday evening," I said. "There may be no significance, of course, but it's odd all the same."

I've no great use for soggy toast and dried egg and I'd finished my meal first.

"Just ring up Stanley Corbit," Wharton told me. "Use your own judgment what you tell him, except that we don't want him at that gravel pit."

It was Mrs. Corbit who answered the telephone. I gave her my name and asked to speak to her husband, and I heard her calling to him up the stairs, and I heard each step as he came down.

"Mr. Corbit," I said, "I don't think you'd better let your wife hear what I've got to tell you. It's about your son. He's just been found—drowned."

"No," he said, and "No."

I could hear his wife's voice.

"We can't give you any more particulars at the moment," I said, "but the minute we can we'll let you know. Perhaps you'll be at the shop."

"At the shop," he said, and it was like an echo that had come from nowhere at all.

I gulped down a second cup of coffee and then we were off. Inside five minutes Matthews was drawing the car up. Ahead of us were three other cars and an ambulance. Through the entrance gap we could see a small group of people standing by the water's edge below the far gravelled face of the pit. Wharton was still in no hurry, for in spite of some hours of fine weather the tracks were little more than mud, and as he drew near I could see him making a quick survey of the waiting group. Truebent was there and what looked like two of his men. The doctor was there and Umberson with him, and three of Umberson's men were standing by. On the wet sand by the water's edge lay a body. Wharton gave it a quick look, then drew back.

"Morning, doctor. Nasty job of work for you."

Then he appeared to catch sight of Truebent.

"Morning, Mr. Truebent. Not too nice a job of work for you either."

"How do you mean?" Truebent asked him.

"Well, either someone's got a grudge against you, or else you're being very unlucky. Was it your men who found him?"

Truebent motioned them forward. One was the foreman and the other operated the pumping engine, and it appeared that they'd seen the body at the same time. A something peculiar had been floating half-way between the water's edge and the face of the pit, so the foreman had found a broken rail in the hedge and had manoeuvred the body ashore.

"You knew who it was?"

Both of them had known. Nelson Corbit was a reasonably familiar figure in the town, and maybe that radio police message had sharpened remembrance.

"It's Nelson Corbit all right, sir," Umberson said.

"What about you, doctor?" Wharton asked. "Have you had a look at him yet?"

"Only a superficial look," Hadcote said, but there was a hint of something in his tone. Wharton drew him aside.

"Something you've found?"

"Depends what you mean," Hadcote said, "If you mean the cause of death, then I think it was manual strangulation. Whether he was actually dead when he got in here I can't say at the moment."

"Right," said Wharton, and grunted, "Keep it to yourself for a bit. You'd like to get him away?"

"No great hurry," Hadcote said. "As soon as you're ready will suit me."

But there was nothing particular that Wharton had to do. Since the body had been floating, there was no point in marking the spot where it had first been seen, Wharton called True-bent over.

"How deep's the water at the face?"

"About six feet," Truebent told him. "It was much deeper than that before we got it away."

"And it must have reached nearly up to the main road?"

"It wasn't far short," Truebent said. "But what's worrying me is how the devil Corbit could have got in. What was he doing here?"

"That's what I'd rather like to talk with you about," Wharton told him. "Whose land is that up there?"

Truebent said it was Sheffield's land, and by land he meant the rough pasture that still ran upwards above the face of the pit. A row of decrepit railings made a kind of guard, and every-where were clumps of thorn and straggling briars.

"If you can spare the time we'll go up there in a minute or two," Wharton told him, and then was going back to the body. There was no point in taking a photograph, as he told Umber-son. Where the body was then was nothing to do with where it had been found, just as where it had been found was no indica-tion at all of where it had originally entered the water.

The body was on its side, face towards the water. Whar-ton turned it over on its back, and then was hastily putting a hand-kerchief to his mouth and nose. Over his bent shoulders I could see a puffy and swollen face that bore little likeness to the face of the man I had seen in the lane by Blifield church.

Two buttons of the raincoat were fastened. Wharton undid them and then undid the jacket. His hand went inside to the inner breast pocket. He gave a grunt.

"No wallet," he said, and opened the pocket wide. His fingers went to the fob pocket and he was bringing out a small bunch of keys. He passed them up to me, then felt the trousers pockets. A shake of the head and he was getting to his feet.

"No use keeping him here any longer," he told Hadcote. "But you might be so good as to send his clothes to the police station and make an inventory of anything you happen to find."

Truebent's men fetched a couple of planks and the body was moved off to the ambulance.

"Stand by for a minute, Umberson," Wharton said, and was making for Truebent again. Then his eye caught a movement. A man—a stranger to us—was coming along the entrance track.

"Who's that, Mr. Truebent?"

"That's Sheffield," Truebent said. "This is his gravel pit."

Sheffield was a tall, loose-limbed man of about fifty, and a worker by the look of him, for he was wearing dungarees, and his Wellingtons were daubed to the tops with mud.

"Glad to meet you, Mr. Sheffield," Wharton said when Truebent introduced him. "You've just missed seeing a very unpleasant sight."

"Nelson Corbit, so they tell me," Sheffield said. "You could have knocked me down with a feather when I heard."

"You weren't the only one," Wharton told him, and then his look was curiously benign. "I very nearly came to see you last night, by the way."

"Me, sir?"

"Yes," Wharton said. "About quite a different matter, of course. In fact I would have come to see you if I hadn't thought you'd done quite enough talking for one night." He beamed amiably on Truebent. "With our friend Truebent, here."

Truebent's mouth suddenly gaped. Sheffield looked startled, too. Wharton apparently didn't notice.

"Still, that's neither here nor there. That's your land up there, Mr. Sheffield, I believe."

Sheffield said it was. He was a farmer as well as owner of the gravel pit.

"Perhaps you and Mr. Truebent wouldn't mind coming with us," Wharton said, and was telling Umberson to bring his men.

On that main Ipswich Road, just beyond the railings that made a crude boundary for the gravel pit, was a field gate. Beyond us to the left some bullocks were grazing. Sheffield said they were his.

"How long have they been there?" Wharton wanted to know.

"I shifted them out of another field last Friday," Sheffield said. "They've been here since."

The gate opened easily and we all went inside. The grass was pitted deep with the hoof-marks of the bullocks.

"Scout round from here all along the top of the pit," Wharton told Umberson. "See if you can find a hat. And there might be some footprints."

We watched the men move off. Truebent whispered to me if it was Corbit's hat that was meant. I said it was.

"These railings don't look any too strong," Wharton said to Sheffield.

Sheffield said a bit sheepishly that he'd intended to get them put right, but somehow he hadn't found time.

"I know you farmers," Wharton told him roguishly. "I'm a countryman myself. Still, they're your own bullocks."

"If I may say so," cut in Truebent, "Corbit couldn't possibly have fallen in. The rails are too far back from the edge. Besides, what business had he got here in any case?"

"Just what I was thinking," Wharton told him. "All the same, he might have been carried there."

"Good God!" said Truebent, and gaped. "You don't mean like old Drew's body was dumped in my woodyard?"

"A possibility," Wharton said. "But for these bullock marks we might have seen some footprints. I don't think he weighed much more than nine stone, but if someone carried him that person's heels would have gone in pretty deep."

He shrugged his shoulders.

"Still, Umberson may find something. But while you gentlemen are here we might as well kill another bird with the same stone. Is there anywhere we can talk?"

Inside the pit there was a rough shed and we made our way there. An unlit stove stood in the corner, and a kettle on it. A couple of boxes did for chairs, and on the rough table was pinned a blue print of the new drainage system.

"Now we're all here," Wharton began, "there's one little matter I'd like settled."

He took out his spectacle-case and slowly adjusted the antiquated spectacles. He peered at me over their tops.

"I don't think there's any need for us to tell these two gentlemen what we've discovered. Perhaps we'd better keep it a private matter between the four of us. Murder's my job, not parish politics. All I'm interested in, for his own sake, is where Mr. Truebent actually was last Wednesday night between seven o'clock, say, and nine. You were with him for some part of that time, Mr. Sheffield?"

Sheffield shot a look at Truebent. Truebent was biting his lip.

"Come on, come on," said Wharton with a humorous impatience. "Either you were or you weren't."

"Well then, I was."

"From seven o'clock till eight?"

"About that," Sheffield said.

"All so simple," Wharton told me. "All these two gentlemen have to do is make a formal statement and we needn't bother them again. No time like the present. What about running down to the police station in my car. Five minutes or so and we'll bring you back again."

It took a bit longer than that, but the statements were duly signed. Both said that from seven o'clock till eight they'd been discussing the gravel pit drainage in Truebent's house, and Wharton never batted an eyelid as he read it. Truebent's added what he had told us before. I added a confirmation that he had arrived at Frosbeck's flat at about ten minutes to nine.

"Just one little word," Wharton said when the stenographer had gone. "You two gentlemen have given me a considerable amount of trouble. I'll tell you here to your face that you thought you could shuffle your way out of certain things. So you may have done for all I know—or care. But let me tell you this. Drew's inquest is at eleven o'clock this morning. If you hadn't signed these statements I'd have had you both there to answer certain awkward questions in a public court."

He let that sink in while he put his spectacles away.

"The next time the law asks you questions answer them. For instance, is there anything whatever about Drew's death that either of you know and haven't mentioned?"

Truebent said he'd told everything he knew, and that was nothing at all. Then he thought of something.

"What was that, Fred, about you seeing Drew along the Ipswich Road on Wednesday evening?"

"Oh, that," Sheffield said. "That wasn't nothing, really. I'd been up to that gravel pit meadow to see what it was like in case I wanted to put them bullocks in, and old Drew went past. About a quarter to six it'd be. Just getting dusk."

"You didn't speak?"

Sheffield said he hadn't spoken. Drew was a surly old devil who generally gave only a grunt when you did speak.

That seemed to be all, and we went out to the car again. Sheffield asked to be dropped well short of the gravel pit. Truebent left us in his own car. Umberson had caught sight of us and was calling us to come.

The hat—a brown felt one—had been found caught in some briars between the railings and the pit edge. So decrepit were those railings that when Wharton put a foot to one it came away from its shaky nails. But there was no need to make more gaps. In at least two places the top rail had gone altogether and it was easy to step across. Opposite one of those gaps was Umberson's second discovery. Between gap and edge were three sets of footmarks, and all facing towards the pit. Wharton got down on his hands and knees and had a good look at each.

"What do you make of them?" he asked Umberson.

Umberson said it looked to him as if someone had been carrying Corbit's body. There was where he had stepped across with one foot sideways. A yard on was where he had halted and braced himself, and then two deeply blurred prints where he literally heaved the body over the edge.

"That's how I read it," Wharton said. "You haven't a lot of time before the inquest, but you'd better get these prints photographed and take some casts. What size boots do you think they are at a rough guess?"

Umberson thought they were about tens, like his own, but he'd know more when he'd taken the casts.

As the car moved off towards the town Wharton was consulting his note-book. I asked where we were bound for next, and he said that café-restaurant where Nelson Corbit had had a meal on the Wednesday night. When we got out there, he was telling Matthews to stand by at the police station with the car.

The owner of the café wasn't there, and it was to the manageress that Wharton had to speak. All he wanted, he said, was a private word with Miss Gandle. The manageress called down the stairs to a Doris, and we all went into a back room that was not yet open for trade.

Doris was quite a pretty girl, though she looked a bit scared. Wharton told the news about Nelson Corbit, but without a mention of the gravel pit.

"He often had meals in here?"

It was the manageress who said he did.

"And to think he's dead!" she said. "And the police wanted him on the wireless."

"Well, he's dead enough," Wharton said. "And I wouldn't be surprised if it was Miss Gandle who saw him last. That's why we want to check up again on that meal he had here on the Wednesday evening. What time, for instance, was it when he came in?"

Doris said it was just after half-past six and when he left it was about ten to seven. Asked why she was so certain, she said it was only natural to keep an eye on customers who came in after half-past six. The café closed at seven sharp, and if customers came late that made the staff late, too.

On a sheet of café notepaper Wharton wrote those times down. It was added that he had eaten the usual tenpenny portion of spaghetti in tomato sauce on toast, followed by two pastries. With the meal he had had a pot of tea.

The statement was signed and Wharton was saying that that was fine. But there was just one other little matter. Did Doris notice him take any money out of his pocket to pay the bill? A wad of notes, for instance, or just a wallet?

The manageress cut in again. A customer wouldn't pay the waitress. The waitress would give him his bill and then he'd pay at the desk as he went out. But Doris was bursting to say something.

"I don't know what he had that night," she said, "but he did have ever such a lot of notes. A bundle of them, just like this."

"You saw them?"

"Freda and I both saw them."

Freda was sent for. She and Doris, she said, had been standing by the counter between orders. Nelson Corbit had been having lunch and at the end of it he pulled a wad of notes out of an inner pocket and held it below the table while he picked out a note—perhaps to pay his bill. It was because the two girls had had a sideways view that they had happened to see.

So much for that. Wharton said he was most grateful, and out we went. What he now wanted was to get the details of Nelson Corbit's meal to Hadcote.

"I think I'll see him personally after he's given his evidence at the inquest," he told me. "I don't think there's any need for you to come."

I said I might get myself a cup of coffee, and we agreed to meet at the police station twenty minutes later. Which just goes to show how the tiniest happening may turn the whole course of events. Had I gone with Wharton to the police station and kicked my heels there while he was talking with Hadcote I'd never have been told about Drew's last meal. *Drew's* mind you. Not Nelson Corbit's.

It was a fine morning, but the wind was keen. I was telling myself I hadn't had enough breakfast to set the bloodstream working; at any rate I was feeling decidedly cold, and a cup of coffee seemed an excellent idea. But the only place I knew was the one to which Bernard and I had gone on my first Saturday, so I made my way there. Then as I was passing Frosbeck's shop Frosbeck himself looked out. There were smiles and good mornings.

"Anything new?" I said.

"Yes," he said, and drew back for me to enter.

"Sorry, but I'm just off to have a cup of coffee," I said. "I may be able to slip along later."

"But have some with me," he said. "I'm just going to have some myself."

He called to Tom Potter, who seemed to be working somewhere at the back, and the two conferred.

"Right," he told me. "Let's go up and have this coffee. And I might as well bring this with me."

When we got to the lounge it seemed to be a tea-pot he was unwrapping.

"There we are," he said. "Came in only this morning. A really nice piece of Queen Anne."

It was nice, and I said so, but of no use to me. I said there were more unlikely things than the Traverses might be in the market as sellers. My wife had a Queen Anne set and I'd inherited a George the First one, now at the bank.

Frosbeck laughed and asked if I'd give him the first offer. Then the coffee was coming in, and there was a curious association of ideas. I was sipping hot coffee, and on the table was that silver tea-pot. Drew's last meal had included tea, but made in an earthenware pot.

"I wonder which holds the heat longer," I said. "A silver pot or an earthenware one."

"I'd say undoubtedly the earthenware one," he told me. "I'm no great shakes as a physicist, but surely a smooth metal surface would dissipate the heat?" He smiled. "Why this sudden interest?"

"This is confidential," I said, "but it largely determines the exact time of Drew's death. His daughter was out and tea was left for him. Whether he had it at five, or whether he had it at six, we don't know with any degree of confidence. What we do know and from two distinct sources is that he took a walk along the Ipswich Road and probably got home about six. Did he have his tea then? Or did he have it before he went out?"

"But this is extraordinary!" he said. "You say that you know he'd been for a walk along the Ipswich Road and he got home at about six?"

"That's what I said."

"But I saw him! I saw him just before he got home. *I think I can tell you when he had his tea.*"

What had happened was this. Frosbeck had closed the shop at half-past five, for there had been little doing. He had had his tea as usual in the office and he'd also been trying to arrange that four for bridge. Then he thought he'd slip along to the Grammar School and see Falkner personally. It was only an eight-minute walk and it was just as he passed Drew's house that he saw Drew himself. He would have liked to dodge him, and on account of that picture about which Drew would be sure to make enquiries. But there was no avoiding him, and enquire about the picture was just what Drew did. Frosbeck said he hoped to have news at any moment.

"Well, I must get on," Drew said. "I haven't had my tea yet."

Frosbeck wouldn't swear that those were the very words, but that was the substance. Then he asked where Frosbeck was going. Frosbeck said he was going to the Grammar School to see Mr. Falkner, whereat Drew said he thought he'd seen Falkner going Ipswich way in his car. But Frosbeck didn't want to get entangled in more talk about that picture, so instead of walking back with Drew he said he'd go on to the Grammar School in any case. What he actually did was cross the road and take a side street that brought him home again.

"But this is terrific," I said. "It means that you were probably the last person to see Drew alive. The last person of whom we know, of course. A pity we didn't know it before."

He was looking quite perturbed.

"Have I done anything wrong? I mean, should I have told you or Superintendent Wharton before?"

"Not a bit of it," I said. "Why should anyone ask *you* if you'd seen Drew on that particular night?"

"The fact of the matter is," he said, and gave a wry shake of the head, "I always seem out of things somehow. The shop seems so much my whole existence that I sort of wake up sometimes and realise that something's going on outside it."

I caught a glimpse of the clock, verified it by my watch and got to my feet. I was five minutes late and Wharton might be fuming.

"You sure he isn't going to be annoyed with me?" Frosbeck asked as we went down the stairs.

I said it'd probably be just the other way about, and Wharton would be giving him a medal.

Chapter XII
CORBIT TELLS THE TRUTH

As it so happened, it was I who had to wait for Wharton, and when he did turn up Umberson was with him. We went along to Umberson's room, where the two had some tea. I told them at once what I'd just learned from Frosbeck. Wharton was all cock-a-hoop and was telling Umberson about that experiment we'd made with the tea-pot at Drew's house. I didn't say that I'd thought that experiment just a bit footling and—however much events now seemed to justify and confirm it—wholly unreliable. For that kitchen of Drew's had been quite warm on the Saturday morning when we had made the experiments, even though a window had been open. Consider then the evening when Drew had his tea there. The door and the windows were shut and the Aga stove made a pleasant heat. That was why he had been told to have his tea there. Ignore the time at which he had had his tea, and even then one fact seemed to be clear. Before his daughter's return that pot would have lost much of its heat, but what it would have done was to retain some warmth consistent with the almost stuffy atmosphere of the room. When the housekeeper handled it—and she would probably have come in with cold hands—the tea-pot would have felt warmer than it actually was.

But all's well that ends well. We had had a stroke of luck in Frosbeck, even if George wasn't quite so sure how to profit by it.

"Half-past eight's now the approximate time Drew was hit on the head," Umberson said. "That doesn't put Truebent any more in the clear, sir. His real alibi's only up to eight o'clock."

"Don't I know it?" Wharton told him. "But how was Truebent to come into contact with Drew that night? The two were at daggers drawn."

"I wouldn't trust either Truebent or Sheffield," Umberson said obstinately. "Why shouldn't they have got hold of Drew and suggested some sort of compromise? They might even have bought him off."

"Let's get down to brass tacks," Wharton told him. "You're suggesting in so many words that they lured Drew to Truebent's house and then did him in. Say, if you like, there was a quarrel and Drew got struck on the head. If so, what about the body? If you tell me that Truebent ran it up to the woodyard in his car and dumped it in the sawdust, then the only answer is that he must have been several kinds of a fool. Who'd kill a man and dump him in his own property?"

"He might have buried it there a bit too quickly," Umberson said. "It'd have to be a hurried job in the dark. Next day he was proposing to get rid of it permanently."

"Then why didn't he?"

Umberson had no answer. Wharton grunted.

"I know men," he said. "I've run my rule over Truebent and Sheffield, and I'll lay any amount of money they never had a hand in murder. Soon as I blew the gaff this morning and as good as told them I knew all about that rigged-up ownership of the gravel pit they both sort of heaved a sigh of relief." He whipped round on me. "No hesitation about making statements, was there? Of course there wasn't. And because they hadn't anything else on their minds."

"Then what did happen?" Umberson was asking. Wharton's incipient glare ended in a shrug of his shoulders. "That's what we've got to find out. All we know is that Drew left his house again after he returned from that walk. Somehow or other he went to Stepford woodyard. He walked about there—snooping, probably—and then got hit on the head, and at about half-past eight. The only person who was near the spot was Stanley Corbit. Which reminds me. Does he close during the dinner-hour?"

Umberson said the lunch-time closing of shops was staggered. Some shut down from one to two and some from half-past twelve to half-past one, and he thought Corbit's was the latter.

"Get hold of him on the phone," Wharton said. "Tell him we'll pick him up at whatever time it is he closes."

I told George I thought he was being a little hard on Umberson. If ideas weren't put forward then they couldn't be exhausted, and if they were put forward then sooner or later there'd be one that was more than worth while. George took the tactful reprimand uncommonly well. The fact was, he said, that he'd never known a more cock-eyed case. Before he could say just why, Umberson was back. Corbit closed, he said, at half-past twelve and he'd be waiting outside the shop.

"Do you know how he took the news about his son?" Wharton asked him.

"I don't know about him, sir," Umberson said, "but his wife has had a sort of breakdown. They've had a doctor there, and a neighbour in helping."

It was ten past twelve and so we had a twenty minutes' wait. That was what I was thinking as I looked up at the clock.

"I wonder," Wharton was saying, and he was frowning in thought and pursing his lips till the walrus moustache splayed out like a toy umbrella.

"Wonder what?" I said.

It was a kind of psychological problem, he said. There were vital questions that Corbit must be asked, and the problem was how he would react. Would this blow about his son make him open his mouth? Or would it have a numbing effect and make him persist in the lies he'd already told? If so, it mightn't look so good if he was brought to the police station for concentrated questioning. A shrewd counsel might subsequently say that Corbit had made a statement under both stress and duress.

"Why not let things work themselves out as we go along?" I said. "You know all the tricks of the trade, George. Just get him talking and then ease him along."

That little bit of flattery did the trick. That was what we'd have to do, George said. All the same, it was a pity we shouldn't be able to talk to the mother as well. There were one or two things she'd have to be asked to explain.

"Anything from Hadcote yet?" I asked.

"Not a lot," he said. "Except that he's already of the opinion that he's been dead since last Wednesday night."

So that was why Wharton had said it was a cock-eyed case. Two men, in some ways closely connected, disappearing, as it were, into thin air on the same night, and both to be later found murdered. And yet, on the face of it, no possible connection between the murders. Drew had a possible motive for killing Nelson Corbit just as Corbit might have had a motive for killing Drew, but who on earth could have a motive for killing them both?

That's what I told Wharton, but there was no time to begin arguing things out. A minute or two later and we were in the car and drawing up outside Corbit's shop.

Corbit was looking shockingly ill: his face pale and his eyes heavy, and in the eyes was something of that spaniel look he had given Wharton once before. There was misery in it, and an unspoken appeal.

I was sitting in the front with Matthews. Wharton's voice in the back had never sounded more genuine.

"A dreadful business, Mr. Corbit. Bad for you and worse for your wife. How is she, by the way?"

Corbit said the doctor had given a sleeping draught and the last he had heard was that she was still asleep. A neighbour was in the house at the moment.

Wharton's voice lowered and I could faintly hear him breaking the news of just what had happened to his son, and then the car was at the house. Corbit let us in with his key and switched on the electric fire in the living-room. The neighbour looked in but drew back when she caught sight of Wharton and me. Wharton called to her to come in but all she had to tell us was that Mrs. Corbit was still sleeping.

"Well, that's good news at any rate," Wharton said as he helped himself to a chair. "Pardon me telling you to make yourself at home in your own house, Mr. Corbit, but we may have quite a lot of things to talk about. A friendly talk, I hope. After all, we're both interested in the same thing. We're out to get the man who killed your son."

Corbit looked to me to be pretty near a breakdown. I passed my cigarette-case and held the lighter, and the very first puff seemed to steady his nerves. In so suddenly unstable a world even a cigarette made a something to cling to.

"About last Wednesday," Wharton said. "I wonder if you'd mind going very carefully over the day again. Believe me, it's important."

There was never a variation from what we'd been told before. But two things seemed to need elucidation.

"This business of your son calling on various dealers," Wharton said. "I wonder if you'd mind explaining all that."

The explanation had in it a lot of what Bernard Ampling had insisted to me—that a dealer couldn't be omniscient. Dealers bought things from each other and in most instances things they could place at once. Every dealer had on his books customers or collectors interested in this and that.

"And what about the likelihood of his calling on some private person?"

Corbit said he ran an advertisement not only in the local paper but in neighbouring ones as well, offering high prices for various kinds of antiques. When letters came in it wasn't always convenient to see the writer that same day and in that case a letter would be sent in return making an appointment. Such an appointment might have to fit in with others because it was necessary to economise on petrol. That particular side of the business was Nelson's. He handled the correspondence and called on the sellers.

"I get you," Wharton said. "And he got a commission on the various things he bought. But one other little matter, and don't think it's a trap. I'm not trying to find out if any transactions didn't appear in the books. I dare say they didn't, but that's no business of mine. What I want to know is if your son was in the habit of carrying about with him a considerable sum in notes."

"He did carry a lot of money," Corbit said. "I told him it was foolish. So did his mother."

"And did your son handle any money of your own?"

Corbit said he did. He often had to draw cheques on the local bank to pay various customers.

"Don't be hurt by this question then," Wharton went on. "In his dealings with you, was your son scrupulously honest?"

"Always," Corbit said, and his hands quivered with the intensity of what he felt. "Never did he rob me of a penny, and he was good to his mother."

"You think he was trying to make up, shall we say, for having been responsible for losing your money in that cosmetics business?"

"I think yes," Corbit said. "When he came back here he was queer in his ways. He resented being spoken to for his own good, even by his mother."

"He was secretive, shall we say? He kept himself to himself?"

That was it, Corbit said. Sometimes he'd be away for a day or so, but he'd never say where. Then he was giving a sigh of resignation. That was how it was, he said. Your children grew up and ceased to be your children at all. All you became was a kind of convenience.

"I know," Wharton said, and was getting to his feet. "I wonder now if we might go up to his room. I have his keys in case any of his things are locked."

We went quietly up the stairs and into a room on the left of the landing. The bed was made and the room itself was spotlessly clean and perfectly tidy. There were two chests of drawers, but only one had a locked drawer. And it seemed to be full of oddments of clothing.

"Some of his summer clothes, I think," Corbit said.

Wharton said we'd have a look, just in case, and began taking out shirts and vests. Then he must have felt something different, for his hand went underneath and it was coming out with a thick white package. He slipped off the stout rubber band and the package revealed itself as a wad of notes—and five-pound notes by the look of them.

"We'll count them together," Wharton said, and began telling them carefully out. Then we counted them a second time, and the total was definitely a hundred and forty-five.

"That means seven hundred and twenty-five pounds if my arithmetic's right," Wharton said. "Afraid I must take it with me, but I'll give you a receipt. Now let's have a look at the unlocked drawers."

Nothing else was found. Nelson Corbit must have been secretive indeed, or possessed of an excellent memory, for there was never a letter or note or paper.

"He carried his correspondence on him?" Wharton asked.

Corbit shrugged his shoulders. All he knew was that Nelson would sometimes take various papers from his wallet—business papers—to refer to perhaps in the shop. That was all he had ever seen.

"And how did he spend his evenings?"

It varied, Corbit said. He was a good billiards player for one thing and sometimes played at the Crown. Perhaps he was indoors no more than two nights a week, and then he'd either play patience or read a book. Detective stories were what he liked. Occasionally he went to the pictures and when there was anything she might specially like he would take his mother.

We went back to the living-room and Corbit found note-paper for Wharton to write the receipt. Corbit was looking both relieved and expectant, as if he hardly hoped that would be all. And it wasn't all.

"We shan't keep you much longer," Wharton told him, "but we might as well be comfortable while we're here."

I offered Corbit another cigarette. Wharton was drawing his own chair nearer the fire. Something was coming, and I wondered just what.

"Once more I don't want to hurt your feelings, Mr. Corbit," was how he began, "but there's a question which has to be asked some time or other, so why not now? You've told us your son led his own life, so to speak. He resented having what he regarded as his private affairs enquired into. *But tell us this.* Did you have any suspicions at any time that he might have been engaged in something that wasn't strictly within the law?"

Corbit looked away. His hands rose, and fell.

"Well, I think we might take that for an answer," Wharton told me.

"After all," I said, "he had got into trouble before. Mr. Corbit has told us he was an embittered man. Perhaps he had the idea it was some sort of revenge on the law if he indulged in—what shall we say—black-market operations."

"Exactly," Wharton said. "And if we knew the people he was operating with we'd be pretty close to the one who killed him. That's all we're trying to get at, Mr. Corbit. And remember that everything we're talking about is strictly confidential. There'll be no need for his mother to know, for instance. Nothing'll get farther than this room."

"It was his mother who was worrying," Corbit said. "She'd happened to see him with that money. The money we found upstairs."

"There was more money than that," Wharton told him, "and I tell you that because his wallet and everything was taken when he was killed. What we found was his savings, so to speak. He had to have working capital as well."

Corbit's body went suddenly limp. In the slow movement of his hands was a misery that made me wrinkle up my eyes.

"Everything has been like it was a curse," he told us. "Ever since we came here, nothing but trouble."

"Yes," Wharton told him gravely. "That's how things go sometimes. People call it bad luck, but I don't know. But it's you we're worrying about now—not your son."

Corbit looked at him. Wharton leaned forward. His voice had a tremendous regret.

"Why did you lie to us about last Wednesday night? Was it because you thought you were shielding your son? Or was it to shield yourself?"

Corbit's lips moved, but no words came. It was to me that Wharton spoke.

"There's you and me, always thinking it can't possibly happen again. And then it does happen. People thinking they can get away with lies. And all the time they've nothing to fear if they'll only tell the truth."

He shifted in his chair till he was even closer.

"The truth, that's all we want. Just why you were waiting in your car near Stepford chapel last Wednesday night?"

There's nothing more distressing than to see a man cry. Wharton got to his feet and he was shaking his head as he looked down at the sobbing man. He patted him on the shoulder, and waited. A long minute, perhaps, and Corbit was wiping his eyes.

"Now you'll feel better," Wharton told him. "It doesn't do to keep things to yourself too long. There are times when most of us have wished we could sit down and have a good cry."

"Perhaps it might help," I said, "if I told Mr. Corbit why he was at Stepford on Wednesday night. It was because he was expecting to meet someone there. But that someone didn't turn up and he was worried. That's why he went to Turbey's house and asked if Turbey had seen or heard anybody. Oh no," I said at his sudden look, "Turbey didn't tell us that. He did what you asked him. He swore he hadn't had a caller that night. So did his wife."

"Let's leave it to Mr. Corbit himself," Wharton told me with a kind of gentle reprimand. "Let him tell us about it in his own way."

There had to be more prompting before the story was told. It began on the Wednesday evening at about a quarter-past seven. The telephone went and Corbit answered it. He thought it was Nelson, ringing from somewhere in the town. But it wasn't. It was a strange voice, and what that voice said was a tremendous shock. Corbit couldn't remember the exact words, but the message was roughly this.

"You're Mr. Stanley Corbit? This is Police-Inspector Brewer. I'd like to see you with reference to something to do with your son. There'll be no necessity for me to come right into Helmsbury. Meet me at half-past eight at Stepford chapel and we can talk over the matter there. I don't guarantee to be strictly on time, but if I'm not there by nine o'clock you'll know I've gone straight through to Helmsbury."

"What was the voice like?" Wharton asked.

Just a man's voice, Corbit said. Rather high, but what he'd call a grown man's voice. And so he'd gone to Stepford, he said, and he'd waited till well after nine o'clock. Then he'd gone back home and his wife said there'd been no callers. That alarmed him and his wife had seen it. He'd had to confide in her and the two had waited up till past midnight. Then they'd gone to bed.

"I see," Wharton said, and nodded to himself. "So you and your wife accepted this Inspector for what he said he was. In fact, you weren't all that surprised to learn that your son was in trouble with the police."

"There's a verification of all this," I said. "Not that we doubt Mr. Corbit's word. But when you and I called here, if you remember, Mrs. Corbit was most anxious to get your name right. I think she was expecting you to be the Inspector Brewer who'd rung on the Wednesday night. And, of course, in his wish to protect his son, Mr. Corbit had stressed the importance of her telling us that he hadn't been out all night. And, again, there was the business of Drew's body being found near where Mr. Corbit himself had been at the time."

"Well, we're not upbraiding anyone for that," Wharton said. "Once we've got the truth we can let bygones be bygones. But now just one other little matter, Mr. Corbit, and we've finished. Your son is beyond the law. No point now in smirching his name. We don't want to make more trouble for you or your wife. We want the man who killed him. So tell us, and as man to man. Did you or did you not know what reason there was for this Inspector Brewer to want to question your son?"

Corbit swore he hadn't known. It was just a feeling that he and his wife had had that his son was mixed up with something in London. Something of the sort that had landed him in trouble before.

Wharton got to his feet and he was holding out his hand. There were thanks for what Corbit had told us, another word of sympathy, and finally a guarded threat.

"Let this morning be a lesson to you, Mr. Corbit. In the long run it's only the truth that pays and the law is something mighty unpleasant to be up against. If we have to question you again I'm sure you'll bear that in mind. And now are you staying on here, or shall we take you back to the shop?"

Corbit was staying and we left at once. Wharton was giving a jaunty nod of the head as we settled ourselves in the car.

"Well, daylight at last. All we've got to do now is prove the non-existence of this Inspector Brewer."

"You're dead sure Corbit couldn't have made him up?"

He gave me a look of infinite pity.

"What's suddenly happened to you that you can't see further than your nose end? Can't you tell the truth when you hear it? It's fifty to one there never was an Inspector Brewer. Corbit was framed. What we've got to do is find out where the call came from."

I snapped back and maybe because I was feeling none too warm and most devilishly hungry.

"I realised all that," I said. "I wanted to know what *you* were thinking. Even a fool like me could tell Corbit was speaking the truth."

Wharton clicked his tongue.

"A bit touchy all of a sudden, aren't you? Of course he was telling the truth. What's worrying me is how long it'll be before the truth's any good to us."

It was well after two o'clock when we got back to the hotel and a meal. At the police station Umberson had been given a priority job—to trace that call on the Wednesday night. After that would be enquiries of Chief Constables over a wide local area for a possible Inspector Brewer on a strength. But for his own pangs of hunger I think George would have seen Hadcote as well, but, as I said, we went back to the hotel.

The meal was almost over when the waiter brought me a telegram. In that usual first flurry that accompanies a telegram I wondered what it could be, and then I saw it was from Bernice. I read it, and passed it to George.

Positively identified. Am writing. Love.

George's eyebrows lifted enquiringly.

"It's something fairly obvious now," I told him. "I expect you've had it in your mind for quite a time. About Turbey. If it was Nelson Corbit who did the robberies, then the fat look-out man must have been Turbey."

George said he'd had ideas, but he still didn't understand the wording of the telegram.

"Turbey's daughter got married last year," I said, "and the local paper was supplied with the usual photographed group. I sent Bernice a copy. She saw the look-out man. I didn't."

"We'll find out," George said, and disappeared in the direction of the telephone. When he came back he was looking quite pleased. Corbit had just told him that sometimes Turbey had gone out with Nelson in the car. Turbey was a good judge of furniture and was useful for making examinations from a tradesman's angle—condition of wood, existence of worm, faking and repairs, and so on. Sometimes the two had brought stuff home in the car and sometimes not. After all, it was Nelson's job and he'd have resented questioning.

"What's for this afternoon?" I said. "A little call on Turbey?"

"Oh no," George said, and he had that Colosseum smile again. "He's there when we want him."

Then he was all of a hurry to be gone. Umberson ought to have checked on that telephone call. Everything depended on that, he said, and what Hadcote could tell us about the time of death. And it was to be what Hadcote told us that was to prove a shock.

CHAPTER XIII
ANOTHER DAY

THE POST-MORTEM was over and Hadcote was due in a minute or two. He'd rather see Wharton personally, he said, than give a report over the telephone. Umberson had finished his enquiries, too. Incoming calls were naturally difficult to trace, but there had been no distance call for Corbit on that Wednesday night. It was almost certain, in fact, that the call had been local.

"Well, get that Chief Constable circular going," Wharton told him. "I know it's a waste of time, but there's just a possible chance. And if we don't do it, somebody's bound to ask us why."

I felt just as Wharton did, that Brewer was a myth. Someone had rung Corbit to induce him to appear at the woodyard at a very definite time. And I had ideas who it might have been. Hadcote's arrival stopped my putting them to Wharton.

"What about time of death?" Wharton was firing at once.

"It's an open-and-shut case," Hadcote said. "A Home Office pathologist wouldn't thank you for calling him in. In fact he'd think I was a fool if I advised you to. Corbit was killed on that Wednesday night. And within twenty minutes or so of when he had that meal."

Wharton's eyes bulged.

"There's just a million-to-one chance against it," Hadcote went on. "But for the stomach content it'd have been difficult to place the time of death as on the Wednesday or up to twenty-four hours later. The question is then, did he have an absolutely identical meal some time during those twenty-four hours?"

"He digested the first meal and then had another exactly like it," Wharton said, and pursed his lips. "But he didn't—not at that café."

Hadcote said the chances against death on the Wednesday night might be disregarded. He'd mentioned them only because everything—however fantastic—ought to be considered. As for the cause of death, that had been manual strangulation. Corbit had received a blow on the back of the skull and had then been strangled.

"The same weapon?"

"Impossible to state," Hadcote told him. "He'd a thicker skull than Drew. No skin broken and no bleeding."

We had a look at the photographs. To me they conveyed little, and Wharton could only shrug his shoulders and put one final, comprehensive question.

"No use keeping a dog and barking yourself," he said. "The whole thing boils down to this. I'm safe in working on the assumption that he was killed somewhere between ten to seven and ten minutes past on the Wednesday night?"

"Most decidedly," Hadcote told him. "To my mind there's no reasonable doubt."

As soon as he'd gone Wharton was letting out a breath.

"Now we know where we are," he told me.

"And where's that?" I said.

"A damn sight further off than we were before. Everything's blown sky-high. Where's the connection now between Drew's murder and Corbit's?"

"What are you going to do then? Assume Corbit was murdered solely for the sake of that wad of notes he showed a bit indiscreetly sometimes?"

"Whoever killed him would take the notes," he told me testily. "He'd have to take them, just to give the impression it'd been that kind of killing."

"Let's look at it that way then," I said. "Let's assume the taking of his wallet was camouflage. Let's explore the original tie-up between the Corbits and the Drews."

George agreed, if not too graciously. But we did at least make ourselves comfortable and get our pipes going, even if our notebooks had precious little in them after the best part of an hour of talk. Umberson was in for most of it.

Nelson Corbit did not kill Drew. That was the basis of all argument. For the killing of Drew, Corbit was an unquestioned elimination, and even the knowledge of that gave a feeling that we might get somewhere. But the next and obvious question was vastly different. *Did Drew kill Nelson Corbit?

Could Drew have killed him? The answer was yes. Drew was wiry enough to have cracked an unsuspecting man on the head and knocked him out, and then the strangling would have been easy. Very well then; Drew might have killed Nelson Corbit, and the time of that killing was seven o'clock or shortly after. And so to the question of *where* the killing was done. The logical answer, indeed the only answer, was at or in the immediate neighbourhood of Drew's house. A continuity stared us in the face. Corbit left the café and went, say, along the Ipswich Road. Drew's house was in the Ipswich Road, and still further along was the gravel pit where the body was found. A straight line, so to speak, between café and gravel pit, and a murder somewhere in between. And that in-between place could only have been Drew's house, for there couldn't have been time for Corbit to walk as far as the gravel pit. And why should he have gone to the gravel pit in any case? He'd nothing on Truebent and Sheffield. In any fight between Drew and Truebent he'd have been on Truebent's side if he'd had any feelings in the matter at all, and that was an extremely unlikely thing.

So far, so reasonable. But *why* should Nelson Corbit go to Drew's house? Two answers presented themselves: to have some sort of a final showdown with his ex-father-in-law, or to talk with his ex-wife. Of those two possible reasons the latter seemed the more likely. What it was he wanted to discuss with her was of no great consequence. Even if we questioned her, she'd almost certainly have no idea herself. Or might she?

"It's the funeral this afternoon," Umberson said. "She's bound to be in tonight, though."

"No hurry," Wharton told him. "Let's get this thing argued out before we talk about seeing people."

We'd got Nelson Corbit at Drew's house. There he was expecting to see his ex-wife, but it was Drew who opened the door. Thereafter everything had to be conjecture. Did Drew admit him? Was there a violent quarrel? If so, it must have flared up absolutely at once, or Corbit couldn't have been dead by ten-past seven.

"I hate to throw a spanner into the works," I said, "but aren't we up against another of those paradoxes we've noticed all through this case? Nelson Corbit should have killed Drew. Drew had boasted that he had Corbit where he wanted him. It's almost a certainty that Drew acquired that picture indirectly from Corbit. If Drew pinned the theft on to him it'd have meant a term of imprisonment for him. You see what I mean? We've an excellent reason for Nelson Corbit going to Drew's house. Drew had opened his mouth too wide and Corbit had an idea what he was in for. He had to stop Drew dead in his tracks. But he didn't! It was Drew, by assumption, who killed Corbit."

Wharton refused to see it, or perhaps he saw it another way. All I'd done, he said, was give the best of all reasons for Nelson Corbit to go to Drew's house. Then there'd naturally been an immediate quarrel. The wrong man had got killed. And why not? All that had happened was that Drew had struck first.

"Let's accept that," I said. "We've got Nelson Corbit dead at Drew's house. Now what about disposal of the body?"

I never knew an argument collapse so quickly. From that moment the talk was talk for the sake of it. It had no heart. That disposal of the body was like coming suddenly to some impossible cul de sac. There we were, and there was nothing to do but go back. And if we went back it meant an abandoning of the whole idea.

But take some of the theories that seemed for a moment to show a way out. Did Drew hide the body, intending to dispose of it later? If so, who found it, and who disposed of it? The only answer was that Margaret Drew disposed of it. She took it to the gravel pit in the car, either on her return that Wednesday night or on the following night. But she could never have carried the body up the slope of that rough meadow to the edge of the gravel pit. If she'd somehow dragged it, there must have been signs left of the dragging. The same test applied when Umberson suggested that Margaret Drew might have killed her ex-husband, and there was the additional matter of the time. She and the housekeeper had not returned home till a quarter-past seven. Or might that have been a false statement? After all, if the doors for the second house at the cinema opened at seven the first house would be out well before. That was the one thing of which Wharton made a note.

But to go back to that moment when Drew had supposedly killed Corbit. Had it been Drew who had then rung Stanley

Corbit? One fact certainly stood clear. *Whoever* it was that rang Stanley Corbit knew that Nelson Corbit was dead. If not Stanley Corbit could have questioned his son about the supposed Inspector Brewer. But whoever it was that rang knew for a certainty that Corbit couldn't question his son. The fake Inspector Brewer had been created only because of that certainty. And why then had Drew lured Stanley Corbit to the woodyard? Where he should have lured him was to where the body was. And even then, what was the point in luring Stanley Corbit to the woodyard, even if Drew had intended to take the body there? Surely Corbit could never have been suspected, however skilful the framing, of killing his own son! If Drew had intended to put Nelson's body in the woodyard it could only have been to frame Truebent. And what possible connection could there be between Truebent and Nelson Corbit?

The whole thing was fantastic, and momentarily we gave it up in despair. Umberson had a pot of tea brought in, and after it the argument revived for a minute or two and then gave a last kick and expired.

It was Drew on whom we concentrated, and ignoring altogether the question of Nelson Corbit's death. Drew had very definitely gone to the woodyard that Wednesday night, and the problem was why? And then came the new tangle. Who could have killed him if not Stanley Corbit? And yet Corbit's story rang true. I'd have bet fifty pounds to a dead match that Corbit had had no hand in Drew's death. I could see Corbit's face as he talked to Wharton and me. A curse on him ever since he'd set foot in Helmsbury, he'd said, and nothing but trouble after trouble. Would such a man invite more trouble? A trouble that might end in final extinction on the gallows?

It was then that I had a sudden idea.

"Isn't there someone we're overlooking, George?"

"Who?" he said, and glared.

"Turbey," I said.

"Yes," he said slowly. "There's Turbey."

That meant explanation to Umberson, and what it all came to was this. Although Turbey worked for Stanley Corbit and might therefore have been expected to bring solely to his employer's notice anything in the antique line of which he might happen to hear, yet he was a slippery customer who sold in the best market for himself whatever he happened to acquire. Apparently he offered things to Bernard Ampling, and so why shouldn't it have been he who offered that picture to a well-known collector like Drew? That Drew and Stanley Corbit were enemies wouldn't count with Turbey. All Turbey wanted was the best market. What he put in Stanley Corbit's way brought only a possible commission, but what he sold himself brought him the whole profit.

"We've got something there," Wharton said. "Let's think it out a bit more. Turbey *could* have taken that picture. He could have slipped it under his coat as a kind of private perquisite. He could have sold it to Drew." He frowned for a moment, then gave a grunt. "Drew was cocksure. I'll bet a fiver he had the evidence all written down. We'll see his daughter. Kill two birds with one stone. Something might be found among Drew's papers."

So there we were—on to something at last. To say it looked promising was an understatement. Now apparently we knew why Drew had gone to the woodyard, and the reason was that he hadn't gone to the woodyard at all. *He'd* gone to see Turbey. He'd got Turbey in worse than a cleft stick. Turbey would simply have to spill all the beans. Turbey, through threats or bribery, would give the last bit of needed evidence that would land Nelson Corbit in jail. But Turbey hadn't trusted Drew. Turbey saw only one safe way out—to get rid of him. Turbey had had access to the pestle. Turbey had killed Drew and had dumped the body in the sawdust.

"Then why did he discover the body?" Umberson asked guilelessly.

Wharton jumped right down his throat. Why cloud things up? And hadn't we had enough of argument? Time enough for all that when we'd found definite proof that Turbey had handled the picture.

"Five o'clock," he said. "Get hold of Drew's daughter for me and ask when it'll be convenient for us to call. Say we shan't keep her long."

While we waited for Umberson we left the case alone. How Wharton was feeling I could only guess, but my head was swimming after that two hours session of concentrated thought. In fact I was sorry when I foresaw even more talk in store, for Umberson came back with the news that Margaret Drew would see us whenever we liked.

Wharton rang the bell and it was Margaret Drew herself who let us in. She was still in her funeral black, and a very smart black it was. The air, too, was still heavy with the scent of flowers.

We went into that room where we had been before. Wharton had hooked on his antiquated spectacles to lend a colour to his fatherly air.

"I'm sorry we couldn't do any more than inform you officially of your late husband's death, Mrs. Drew," was how he began.

"Won't you have a drink?" she was asking us, and as if he hadn't spoken at all. "What shall it be? Whisky? Sherry?"

"Nothing at all if you don't mind," Wharton told her and just a bit out of his stride. "We're not supposed to drink when on duty, you know."

She smiled. She had lovely teeth and they showed up somehow against the scarlet of the mouth. The scarlet went with the black of the high-backed frock. Maybe she was setting herself out to kill, and I was wondering why.

"But aren't we all friends?"

"I hope so," Wharton told her. "In fact I'm sure we are. That's why we're paying this sort of informal visit in connection with the death of your late husband."

She paused in the act of pouring herself a sherry. The smile was ugly now. It was almost a sneer.

"Well, what do you expect me to do? Cry down your neck?"

Wharton grunted.

"You didn't like him."

"I hated the sight of him."

"But not always."

She brought her drink to the chair. I drew a small table alongside and she gave me a special smile. It went as quickly when she looked at Wharton.

"Look," she said. "Let's get this straight. He meant nothing to me. He's dead and—well, what of it? I don't know who killed him and I don't care. He was a rat. A lying, treacherous little rat." She gave a little grunt, and then something of a smile came again. "Now I've got that off my mind, won't you have a drink after all?"

"It's good of you, but no," Wharton told her. "All the same, I don't think you're as hard-bitten as you'd like us to believe. Not that that matters. What I'd like to put up to you is another point of view. *His* point of view. You may have come to hate the sight of him, but did he hate the sight of you?"

"Believe me, yes," she told him, and the words were a sneering drawl.

"He'd never have attempted to see you here?"

"To see me!" She laughed. "I was the last person in the world he'd have tried to see. I knew too much about him."

Wharton changed his tactics. He told her, in fact, about the time of death and how we'd had an idea that Nelson might have come to the house.

"Just a minute," she said, and her eyes narrowed. "Are you suggesting he might have killed my father?"

"Impossible," Wharton said. "Your father was alive and left this house long after Nelson Corbit was dead. He was dead before you got back here yourself that night. Let me see now. That was at about a quarter-past seven."

"A quarter-past seven to the minute," she said. "That's a chiming clock and it struck the quarter just as we came in." Then she was asking just the question that Wharton must have been praying for.

"Who do you think killed him?"

"Nelson Corbit? That's what we were hoping you'd help us with perhaps," Wharton told her. "From what you were telling us, he must have had enemies."

"Enemies?" She laughed. "He was a twister. He just couldn't do anything on the level."

"Frankly, that's becoming our impression. But I wonder if you'd tell us something, strictly in confidence. Just what did he do for a living during the time you were with him?" She shrugged her shoulders.

"I don't know. After the honeymoon most of my time was spent in the flat. All I know is he used to be out at all hours, and all sorts of people used to ring up. All I could get out of him was that he was in business." She smiled to herself. "So he was. Keeping two homes going was part of it."

"But you must have had suspicions of what sort of business he was in?"

"Perhaps I did," she said, "but I'm keeping my mouth shut. I've had quite enough publicity in this town already."

And that was all she would say, and there we had to leave it. The fact that one of her ex-husband's London associates might have murdered him didn't interest her in the least. What did interest her was dissociating herself from the name of Corbit. She'd made a fool of herself and she'd paid for it. It was an episode, and it was over, and she was taking good care that it *was* over.

"I wonder if you'd give us permission to have a quick look through your father's papers," Wharton said. "There's a certain private transaction we've run across which might have a bearing on his death."

"You're just in time," she said. "Everything's going to the executors tomorrow."

She took us through to the room her father had used as an office. It was a room I'd have liked myself. Even the desk was a knee-hole Queen Anne, and there was a tall clock in a walnut case that made my mouth water.

"Your father was a pretty shrewd collector," I told her.

"Antiques were his real business," she said. "The modern stuff was only a stand-by. Plenty of money in it, though."

"And you're not staying on here?"

"Not on your life," she told me. "Everything's being sold."

"Going into the hotel business yourself? In town, I mean?"

"I wouldn't be surprised."

There'd been something roguish or provocative in the very snappiness of the answer. I ventured further.

"Getting married again, perhaps?"

"I might," she said, and the smile was quite girlish. I rather liked her like that. It was better than that pose of hardness; the straining to show that she was as tough as the man who'd made a fool of her. Perhaps, I thought, there'd been a straining, too, to make him out far worse than he'd really been.

She had given Wharton the keys and he was going over the contents of the first locked drawer. The open papers didn't interest him; there were so many that a looking through them might take half the night. What he'd do about them, he said, was to get the executors to pass on anything that might seem to have a bearing on that private business which he'd mentioned.

The second drawer of the desk was opened. It was a boring business watching Wharton looking for no more, perhaps, than a chance piece of paper, and she was soon tired of it, and she gave us a nod and said she'd be back in a minute. The minute turned out to be ten, but it was lucky for us. It was just before she came back that Wharton found something. I didn't see what it was. All I saw was his hand going into his breast pocket, and then he was nodding to himself and re-locking the drawer.

"Why not have some coffee?" she was asking us, "and then go on again, if you want to. It's all ready in the drawing-room."

Wharton said maybe we would. A despairing hand was waved round the room. Far too big a job, he said, as he gave back the keys. Much better leave it to the executors after all.

We adjourned to the drawing-room, but not for long. Wharton was reminding me of an important engagement. Margaret Drew looked quite disappointed. In those few minutes she'd enjoyed being hostess and displaying herself at what she knew her best. We must come again, she said, but unofficially the next time. I said she must certainly give us a ring.

"A smart woman," George told me as the car moved off. "Been mixed up with a pretty tough set all her life, too. She'd probably have drunk both of us under the table if she'd a mind to."

"Yes," I said. "I expect she gave old Drew a few anxious moments in her time. But she didn't kill Nelson Corbit."

"I think you're right," he said. "Irrespective of the alibi, there's the personal angle. If Nelson Corbit was thriving and prosperous, for instance, and she'd come down to nothing, then there'd be a motive. But the boot was on the other foot. It was she who had the laugh on him. I'll wager she wouldn't be sorry if Nelson Corbit was still alive, just so she could flaunt her money in his face. Show him what he'd missed."

"Which brings us back to the same old paradoxes," I said. "She wishes Nelson were still alive. The same with her father. His interest was in keeping Nelson alive. What's the good of having an enemy just where you want him and then he goes and gets murdered on you and you're robbed of all your satisfaction."

Umberson was waiting for us at the police station and he was reminding George about enquiries at the Crown, in case by any chance Nelson Corbit had looked in on the Wednesday night. George said that while he was there he ought to ask any of the billiard-room habitués if they had seen him flash a wad of notes.

As soon as the door closed on Umberson, George was producing a sheet of notepaper on which were written, as far as I could see, a series of notes. Pinned to it were two things: that page—torn from the Hickford church handbook—that described the supposed Zurbaran, and a newspaper paragraph mentioning the theft. The notes scribbled in Drew's sprawling hand were merely odd words, or phrases, but they were roughly in chronological order. As for the why and wherefore of the notes, it rather looked as if Drew had jotted down the first one and had then added from time to time as occasion arose. He'd be sitting at the desk at some business or other, perhaps, and then he'd remember the Corbit affair, and out would come that sheet of paper, and he would contemplate it while he thought out the next move.

The notes themselves were these—

Paid him cash. Cheque (that word was heavily underlined). Why rugs?

See F.
V. of H.
F. (underlined).
M? No.
Ipswich Enquiry Agency (scored through)
    31 Vintner Street,
        Ipswich
F. (heavily underlined).
See U.

The story we read into them was this. The *him* of the first note was Turbey, and the cash was paid for the picture. The word cheque—an obviously later addition—was underlined because of the exasperated realisation that if Turbey had been paid by cheque then there'd have been tangible evidence of the transaction. The query about rugs was a wonder why Turbey had mentioned them. Turbey, we guessed, had brought the picture to Drew's house at dark. If Drew had taken him to the office there was an oriental rug there, and if to the drawing-room then Turbey would have seen two really fine ones. I could see Turbey in my mind's eye and hear his broad Suffolk.

"Rare nice rug you've got here, sir?"

And so to a sounding if Drew would be interested in rugs. But not, of course, for such rugs as Nelson Corbit might acquire, but those that Turbey himself might be able to offer as a result of private enterprise.

The references to F(rosbeck) were understandable enough, since Frosbeck had told us all about them, and the underlining represented merely a growing impatience for a report on the picture. M? seemed to suggest that he had wondered if he should tell his daughter what was in the wind, and had decided against it. Time enough to astonish her with the news when the mine had been set off. Then after the last call on Frosbeck, when he had been assured that the report was due at any moment, Drew was already anticipating seeing Umberson to set the law in motion.

But it was the address of an Ipswich Private Enquiry Agency that was the most intriguing thing, even if the scoring through seemed to show that nothing had come of the idea to have Nelson Corbit—or Turbey—watched. Probably Drew had thought of that after the morning when he had followed Nelson Corbit to that pawnshop. As for the note V. of H. (Vicar of Hickford), that was scribbled somewhere at the side, but Frosbeck's story enabled us to insert it where it belonged.

"First thing in the morning I'll ring this Ipswich firm," George said, "and if they've got anything to tell me I'll slip along."

"Then we'd better postpone our call on Turbey," I said, and George agreed. It was getting on for nine o'clock in any case and a fairish while since we'd had a meal. And before we could see Turbey we had to be sure that he hadn't been paid by cheque after all. In fact there seemed every good reason for calling it a day.

CHAPTER XIV

IN VAIN IS THE NET

IT WAS ten o'clock before George could get hold of one of the principals of that Ipswich firm. Drew, it appeared, had definitely put up a proposition, but the firm preferred not to discuss it over the telephone, so at half-past ten George left for Ipswich in the car. He'd lunch there, he said, and but for one or two jobs which I myself had in mind I was free till the late afternoon.

I thought the occasion a good one for ringing Bernard Ampling and apologising for an apparent neglect. He said he quite understood how busy I'd been, but when I suggested he should lunch with me at the Roebuck he was mentioning a hare that was going to be jugged, and I didn't hesitate about promising to lunch at The Pleasance instead, especially as the main dish at the hotel looked to me like a rissole under some high-sounding name.

Umberson, by the way, had told us that Nelson Corbit had definitely not looked in at the Crown after leaving the café that

Wednesday night. As for his wad of notes, it seemed to be an understood thing that he carried one, and that was all.

"There's more than one who frequent the Crown that carry a wad," Umberson told us. "I don't say we've got the real London type of spiv here in Helmsbury, but we've got plenty who could pay cash down for a hundred or two. Real bright lads some of them are."

"And what's the opinion of the bright lads about Nelson Corbit?" I asked him.

"He wasn't popular," Umberson said. "He was a clever trader, and cleverness isn't well liked in a country town like this. Also I think he was a bit too tight-lipped. He never used to let a word drop about his business."

That was when I learned something else. Originally, George informed me, Stanley Corbit's name had been Samuel Corbitz. When he had gone into partnership with Drew he changed it, and at the same time Nathan had become Nelson. This news seemed to shed considerable light on a good many things, though I rather disliked recognizing the fact. In any case, it was something to bear in mind. Maybe I've far too sympathetic and romantic a mind, but I couldn't help thinking that a birthright had been sold for less than a mess of pottage. I couldn't help wondering just how Corbit felt about it now.

Well, Wharton left for Ipswich and I went to the bank to see the manager. I was out again in five minutes, for Drew had drawn no cheque in favour of Turbey. Then I thought I'd see Frosbeck and ask if Drew had ever discussed with him the theft of rugs. Frosbeck was in his office and he looked, as ever, quite pleased to see me.

"How are things going?" he asked me. "Making any headway?"

I said it was a question of slow and sure—I hoped. And I was asking if he'd been surprised to hear about Nelson Corbit.

"Surely one's always surprised at murder," he said, "especially in a town like this."

"Did you run across him much?"

"Not more than two or three times," he said. "I sold him a bureau not so long ago."

"What'd you think of him?"

He looked surprised at the question.

"To me he was just a customer," he said. "I found him quite reasonable to deal with. I don't say he was the sort of man I'd ever like."

"He never tried to sell you a rug?"

I'd smiled, and he didn't take that question seriously.

"As a matter of fact," he said, "he never tried to sell me anything. I've bought one or two things off his father, but never from him."

"We've been wondering about Drew," I said. "Did he ever give you the impression that he had an idea that Nelson Corbit was concerned in those thefts of rugs?"

"Rugs—no," he said. "I think I told you what he hinted to me about having the Corbits where he wanted them, but there was no specific mention of rugs. As a customer it was pictures that interested him—and fine furniture."

"Sorry to go on with the catechism," I said, "but what about Turbey? Did he ever try to sell you anything?"

"Me personally—no," he said. "Though Tom Polter—yes. Tom and he are friends of a kind. But nothing of any real value. What I'd call cottage or farmhouse oddments, that's all."

"Well, that's that," I said, and then before I could go on he was mentioning Nelson Corbit again.

"It's a pity about Nelson Corbit," he said. "He'd been a bit of a bad egg, I know, but it's his mother I'm thinking about. I know what it is to lose an only son."

There was nothing I could say that wouldn't seem an intrusion on a private grief. I did ask if there was anything new in the shop, and after a quick look round I was leaving him. When all this business was over, I said, I hoped we'd be able to have some more bridge.

I treated myself to a morning coffee and then had another idea. A bus was leaving for Stepford and I caught it. It was early yet for Bernard, but I hoped that Truebent might be at the woodyard. Not that I had any particular object in view in seeing him; it was just the hope, perhaps, that something might by chance emerge.

As it happened he was in his office, and alone. I'd expected a cool reception, but he seemed rather glad at the sight of me. He even asked me if I'd like a drink.

"Well, as this isn't an official visit, I rather think I would," I said. "Beer, if you have it."

He brought out a couple of bottles and we drank each other's health.

"Wasn't it a bit of a shock to you seeing me with Superintendent Wharton?" I asked him.

Not too much of a one, he said. Bernard Ampling had told him before I came on holiday what my job was.

"If you mean, was I scared, then I'll tell you straight that I never was," he told me. "When you know you haven't done a thing, why should you be scared?"

He gave a nod at his beer, then took another swig.

"What did scare, mind you, was finding Corbit in that gravel pit—on top of finding Drew, I mean. It still worries me. Doesn't it look to you as if someone'd been trying to frame me?"

"Unofficially and confidentially," I said, "I'm damned if I know. By the way, have you any enemies?"

I didn't put the question too seriously, but he took it seriously enough. Probably he had plenty, he said. And he'd gone over every possible one in his mind and there wasn't one who'd do anything so fantastic as to murder old Drew for the sake of incriminating Donald Truebent. As for killing Nelson Corbit, the whole thing didn't make sense.

We talked about that for a bit, and then I was asking him if he'd tell me, in very strict confidence, just how he had got at loggerheads with Drew. I was a man with an insatiable curiosity, I said, and I'd like to know, and that was my only motive.

"I thought you'd have worked that one out for yourself," he said, and then proceeded to explain. It was a beautiful tale of graft. Drew had a big interest in certain building firms in the town, and these firms worked a racket. They rigged their tenders for public works and they had friends on the necessary committees. And Drew had seen the advantage of having an interest in Sheffield's quarry, since it was the only one within a reasonable distance of the town, and so he had made a private offer. Sheffield had turned the offer down, whereupon Drew had tried a little blackmail. Unless Sheffield agreed to terms, he'd expose the fact that Truebent had an interest in that quarry. Sheffield hold him to expose and be damned.

I think I looked a bit too interested in that last remark. Truebent's smile was what I'd call dry and cautionary.

"I shouldn't get ideas about Fred Sheffield, if I were you," he told me. "He didn't give a Shinwell for old Drew. Besides, as soon as he left me that night he went straight home. And he didn't stir out again. And he can prove it."

I told him he'd got me all wrong, and in any case we'd never been interested in Sheffield. And by that time I'd finished my beer and the moment seemed propitious for departure. Maybe, I said as I'd said to Frosbeck, we might get some more bridge when all the unpleasantness was over. He seemed quite pleased at the idea—or was it its implications?—and offered to run me to The Pleasance in his car. I pleaded the want of exercise and walked.

I had an excellent lunch with Bernard, but nothing happened that had the slightest bearing on the case. Then I caught the early afternoon bus and by half-past two was waiting for Wharton at the police station. Umberson, who'd had his second inquest in two days, told me that nothing had happened about those enquiries for an Inspector Brewer. That meant that nothing was likely to happen since a telephoned reply had been requested in the case of a positive result.

It was after three o'clock when Wharton got back, and he had very little to report.

Drew had, however, called on that firm of enquiry agents about three weeks before his death. His opening insistency had been for secrecy and he was duly assured. But when he outlined what he wished the firm to do there were difficulties which he apparently hadn't anticipated, and the more he revealed of what was in his mind the less the firm liked the job.

What he said was that he was practically certain that a Nelson Corbit was responsible for the robberies from churches, and he wanted him watched. Asked for his grounds for suspicion, he said he preferred at the moment to keep them to himself, but he could produce a reliable witness who was of the same opinion as himself.

"Who could that have been?" I asked George. "It couldn't have been Frosbeck. Frosbeck hadn't given an opinion on that picture three weeks before Drew was killed. And he told me only this morning that he and Drew had never mentioned the subject of rugs."

"That's what's been worrying me," George said. "But maybe Drew was putting up a bluff."

Whether that were so or not, the firm didn't undertake the job. To watch a man in Helmsbury and follow his every movement would mean using two men, and a special car, and for that they hadn't the petrol. And if they had, then the minimum charge per day would be at least six pounds and a retaining fee of fifty. But, as Drew was frankly told, the firm preferred not to handle the matter it all, and Drew was strongly advised to take his suspicions to the police. It was, in fact, a job for the police and no one else.

"How did Drew take it?" I asked.

"Quite well, I believe. He said the cost didn't worry him provided he got the information he was after. It was that matter of the petrol that showed him he hadn't really thought things out."

"Going back to that witness that Drew said he could produce," I said. "Could it have been Turbey?"

George shrugged his shoulder.

"Drew could have offered Turbey a better job and have paid him well," I said. "Turbey's the kind who wouldn't be disinclined to sell any pass provided he saw immunity for himself and some cash as well."

That was the moment when George produced the damper about Turbey. Drew, as I soon was realising, wasn't the only one who wanted to act before he'd properly planned.

"You seem to be thinking we've got Turbey in a cleft stick," George told me. "Have we?"

I looked surprised.

"But he sold Drew that picture!"

"Did he? Who says so? Did Drew ever tell anybody so?"

"Well, no," I said. "He certainly didn't tell Frosbeck. But what about Drew's housekeeper? She might have let Turbey in that night he called."

"Nothing like finding out," George said, and was asking at once to be put through to the Drew number.

"Ah, good afternoon, Mrs. Drew. This is Superintendent Wharton troubling you again. . . . Oh no. Only a trifling matter. . . ."

We hadn't more than a minute or two to wait. That house-keeper had never known Turbey come to the house and she had never heard Mr. Drew mention him. She herself knew Turbey by sight and name and no more.

"There we are then," George told me. "Those notes that Drew scribbled on that sheet of paper aren't worth a cuss as far as convicting Turbey is concerned." A hand went up to check my reply. "I know what you're going to say—that Bernice is prepared to swear it was Turbey she saw at Blifield church. But what if she does? Was anything stolen from Blifield church?"

"I suppose you're right," I said. "We might prove highly suspicious conduct, but that's no good to us."

Then I must have gaped a bit.

"You're not telling me that we're not seeing Turbey after all?"

"To tell the truth, I haven't made up my mind," George said. "Is it better for the moment to let him think he's got away with everything?"

"If we're going to wait for real evidence," I said, "where's it going to come from? Drew can't talk. Nelson Corbit can't talk. Frosbeck knows no more than he originally told us. And so, what?"

"I know, I know," he told me testily. "But all this picture and rug business must be tied up with the murders. I can't see any way round it."

"Well, we've got nothing on Turbey but theories," I said. "He had a motive for killing Nelson Corbit; if, that is, he thought Nelson might give the show away somehow. He had the same motive in the case of Drew. But what can we prove? Presumably he came home from work as usual. He was certainly at home when Stanley Corbit called. And we can't get away from the fact that it was Turbey who found Drew's body. If he'd killed Drew he could have hidden the body five fathoms deep long before that Friday morning."

We talked around it and about, and then George at last made a decision.

"We'll see him," he said. "Plenty of things we can put up to him, and he might panic and own up. Even if he doesn't, he might let something slip."

We gave Turbey plenty of time for his tea, and it was nicely dark when we left the car at the end of the lane and walked on towards his cottage. There was no light visible at the front, and the Turbeys, we thought, were in the kitchen. Then we saw a faint light from Turbey's workshop, and we made our way quietly along the path. What turned out to be old army blankets had been tacked over the windows, and through a chink we could see him at work, and he seemed to be sharpening a chisel. He was humming to himself as that chisel went to and fro along the oilstone. Wharton gave a quick rap or two at the door, then looked in.

"Ah, there you are, Turbey. Just the man we want to see."

"Indeed, sir?"

Turbey was shooting a look at both of us. He wiped the chisel on some shavings, and again on the palm of his hand. Neither Wharton nor I had said a further word. Wharton was casting a not unfriendly eye round the workshop.

"And what can I do for you two gentlemen?"

"Just give us a little information," George told him offhandedly. "Mending a bureau, are you? Looks a nice job of work, too."

"Just sort of patchin' up an old wreck I bought kinda cheap," Turbey told him, and he was also giving me a quick questioning look.

"And what'll it be worth when it's finished?"

"To you, sir—fifteen quid."

"I know," Wharton said, and produced an ersatz chuckle. "And ten quid to anyone else. No wonder you're a wealthy man."

"Me, sir!"

"You own this property, don't you?"

"Well, yes, sir, and no." He fingered his fat, stubbly cheeks. "Bowt through the buildin' society this property was, and it ain't all paid for yet."

Wharton seemed to have forgotten the matter. He was looking at that framed portrait of Charles Haddon Spurgeon.

"You're a Baptist, are you?"

"Me, sir? No, I'm a Methodist. One o' the real old Primitives."

"What's that?" Wharton asked jocularly. "A sort of Praise-God-Barebones?"

That was well above Turbey's head. He gave me another quick look, but George was going on.

"Well, I suppose there're rascals among Methodists just as there are everywhere else. Reminds me of something an old country police sergeant once told me. He'd been sent to collect a certain man and when he got to the village this man was at a week-night chapel meeting. He was actually in the pulpit, so this sergeant marched up to a front pew and sat down. I believe they'd just sung the first hymn and the preacher was about to offer up a prayer."

"That's right, sir. That's how we do it."

"From what I gathered," Wharton went on, "he included nearly everyone in his prayer. He even said, 'God bless and protect our policemen.'"

"Did he indeed, sir."

"He did," Wharton said. "But the old sergeant told me it didn't make any difference. He waited outside when the service was over and he clapped his hand on his shoulder—like this!"

Turbey's eyes bulged. Wharton's grip tightened.

"'I had him, sir,' that's what the old sergeant told me," Wharton said grimly, and then the grip relaxed. He smiled. "Must be a funny sort of feeling, Turbey, to have the law put its hand on your shoulder."

"You're right, sir," Turbey said, and wriggled his shoulder and licked his lips. "But what was it he was wanted for?"

"Robbery, or embezzlement, I forget which," Wharton said indifferently. And then he pulled himself together. "But we mustn't stand here wasting Turbey's valuable time," he told me. "And I'm afraid it's going to be a bit of a shock."

He took out his note-book, looked at nothing in particular and put it slowly back. His eyes lifted as slowly to Turbey's.

"Would it surprise you, Turbey, to learn that if Nelson Corbit hadn't died when he did he'd probably have been arrested for various robberies?"

"You don't say, sir!"

There had been something not quite natural about Turbey's gape. Wharton's eyes narrowed.

"And the curious thing is, you yourself would have been an important witness."

"Me, sir!" Turbey looked as if he couldn't believe his ears.

"Taking rugs and things from lonely churches," Wharton went on. "You used to go with him in his car, didn't you?"

Turbey licked his lips. He was shaking his head as he reached for his jacket and began putting it on over his carpenter's apron.

"So that's what he was up to," he said and shook his head again.

"Are you seriously telling us that you didn't know? You were the look-out man, weren't you? We know you were. We've got a witness to prove it."

"God's my witness—"

"Better keep Him out of it," Wharton told him curtly. "Tell us about it instead."

"Well, as far as I was concerned, sir, I thought it was just that he was interested in churches. Nice old stuff in some of 'em, sir, and I reckoned he wanted to have a good look in case he could do a deal. Some o' them church parsons are regular hard-up, you know, sir."

Wharton smiled grimly.

"And what did you think when he came out with a carpet or a rug?"

"I never see him with no carpets or rugs."

"And why were you supposed to warn him if anybody came?"

Turbey shrugged his shoulders.

"That weren't no business of mine, sir, and he didn't tell me. As far as I was concerned it was a real good outin' or two. We'd look over a sale, it might be, or call on some dealer or other, and then we'd be passin' a village and he'd say, 'Turbey,' he'd say, 'that looks a nice little church. Might as well have a look in. Give me the tip,' he'd say, 'if anyone comes.' And as far as I was concerned, sir, that's all it was. Weren't no business o' mine what he did inside them churches."

"And it never occurred to you that he might be up to something crooked?"

"Never for a minute, sir."

"You certainly did your job very efficiently," I told him. "There was that day at Blifield church when you told a certain lady she couldn't get into the church by the porch door and you sent her on a fool's errand while you warned Corbit. Remember that?"

"Can't say as I do, sir." He frowned for a moment or two, then gave a Whartonian chuckle. "I think I do remember something now, sir. Just a little joke, that's all it was. I always was one for a joke."

Wharton let out a breath.

"What are you, Turbey? Fool, or knave?"

"I don't reckon I'm altogether neither," Turbey told him with a sudden assumption of dignity. "My motto is, keep your nose out of what don't concern you. Nelson Corbit was my boss and it didn't cost me nothin' to do what he said. Ask no questions and you'll hear no lies. That's true enough, ain't it, sir?"

"In your case—yes," Wharton told him. "There was that lie you told us about the Wednesday night. You'd never seen a living soul. I suppose you forgot about Stanley Corbit?"

"Well, that, sir." Turbey shuffled a bit. "Mr. Corbit told me he'd explained all that to you, sir." His face lighted. "Just what I was tellin' you, sir. Do as you're told and ask no questions."

"Maybe," Wharton told him curtly. "But you saw Stanley Corbit that night. So tell me this. What time was it when you saw Drew? Before or after Corbit came?"

"Drew, sir?" He shook his head. "God's my witness I never saw Drew—not till I see him layin' on that sawdust on the Friday morning."

"We'll take your word for it—God knows why." He grunted. "But another piece of information you ought to be able to give us. I want you to think back very carefully. You remember a certain night when you took a picture to Mr. Drew at his house?"

"A picture, sir?"

Wharton smiled wearily.

"Don't tell us you don't remember that. A picture. An oil-painting in a gilt frame. A crucifixion scene."

"I know nothing about no picture, sir."

Wharton's hands rose, and fell.

"I see. And you never were at Hickford church."

"Hickford, sir. Where might that be?"

George's lips clamped down tight. It was a moment or two before he trusted himself to speak.

"Well, Turbey, that's all—for the present. If your memory should happen to come back, you might let me know. And don't go taking any holidays or anything like that. I'd like to know you're in Helmsbury for the next few days."

"You needn't worry about me, sir—"

"I'm not," Wharton told him. "You're the one who's got to do the worrying. Don't trouble to come out. We can find our way all right."

There was a young moon that night, and when I looked back from the gate Turbey was watching us from the workshop door, and to see, no doubt, if we were going to the cottage. But we went on up the lane. George said never a word.

"In vain is the net spread in the sight of any bird," I told him. "We left Turbey alone too long. He had it all figured out."

CHAPTER XV
THE MIRROR

I HAPPENED to be up early the following morning, and by that I mean that instead of just getting down to breakfast at eight o'clock I was down some minutes before. It was a cold but remarkably fine morning, and just when I was thinking of taking a brisk ten minutes' walk I was called to the telephone. Wharton was saying that there was something at the police station in which I might be interested.

The something turned out to be Stanley Corbit. The post that morning had brought him a small package, and when he opened it there was his son's wallet. And in the wallet were notes to the value of a hundred and eighteen pounds. There was also the identity card. Corbit had at once got into his car and taken the package to the police station. He was apologising to me because he hadn't had time to dress properly or shave.

A note accompanied the wallet. The paper was of a cheap, white, unruled type, and the writing was bad but legible. It looked as if the writer had used a sharp, spluttery nib, for here and there it had plucked the paper and the glass showed small spatterings of the blue-black ink.

This is what it said:

Stepford,
Febuary 10.

DEAR SIR,

My little boy found this in the ditch and I am sending it on as it looks as it might be your sons what was found dead.

A FRIEND

"Who wrote it, man or woman?" Wharton asked me.

I said I thought the writing was a woman's, as was the general impression, so to speak. Wharton said that he and Umberson were of the same opinion.

"Prints?" I said.

"Quite a nice set," Wharton said, so I asked him what was the trouble then.

Apparently it was something he wasn't anxious for Corbit to hear. At any rate he was giving Corbit a receipt and telling him we'd let him know if anything emerged.

"It's this Stepford address and postmark," he told me as soon as Corbit had gone. "The letter implies that the wallet was found at Stepford. What was it doing there? Nelson Corbit couldn't ever have been near Stepford."

"What about the ditch?" I said.

"Ditches everywhere," Umberson told me. "There's hardly a road anywhere outside the town that hasn't got ditches each side. And they'd all be running with water."

"You mean the contents of the wallet were soaked?"

He showed me. Wharton pointed out that the notes in the middle of the wad were still wet. From the puckering leather of the wallet it looked as if the sender had tried to dry it before the fire or in an oven.

"Well, there's two choices," Wharton said, "if we're going to find where that wallet was found. We can make an appeal in Stepford with a loud-speaker van, or we can try house-to-house interviews."

Umberson was in favour of the latter. Stepford was a small village and it ought to be easy to check up on the households that had a "little boy". The village schoolmaster might also be asked to question the boys in the school. A boy wouldn't find a wallet and keep the finding to himself, whatever his mother might have told him.

"Take some slips of paper with you," Wharton told him, "and if you have any suspicions any particular woman is lying, get her prints. And before you go, see Nelson Corbit's clothes and belongings are brought in here. After breakfast we'll have a look at them."

Umberson said he'd get his men on the Stepford job at once. I was asking Wharton if the post office shouldn't be questioned.

"No need to go into the post office to post a. little packet like this," he said. "Besides, there's something else that makes the whole thing look fishy. We checked up on the weight and there's a penny stamp too much. The post office would have weighed it and put the right amount on. And look at the stamps themselves. Two at twopence and three at a halfpenny. Would the sort of woman who's supposed to have written that letter have had twopenny stamps lying about? She might have had an odd twopenny-halfpenny or so, but I doubt if she'd have twopennies."

"True enough," I said. "And would such a woman have the faintest idea how much postage was required for a packet like this? I think if everything was what it's supposed to be she'd have gone to the post office."

We adjourned for breakfast. It was half-past nine when we got back and Umberson had already managed to send a message. The girl in the post office shop remembered the little packet and she had actually put it on the scales and checked its weight before applying the official stamp. As Wharton had said, it had been a penny overweight. And considering what had been happening in Helmsbury, she'd been interested in the address. She'd wondered, too, for a moment if *Mr. Stanley Corbit, Helmsbury* was a sufficient address, and, considering the publicity, had decided it was.

Wharton said we'd know more before the morning had gone, though he'd be prepared to bet any reasonable sum that Umberson would never find the sender of that wallet. When I asked if he meant that in his opinion Nelson Corbit's killer had sent it as a blind, he wouldn't be drawn into argument. What he was more interested in at the moment was Nelson Corbit's clothes.

"Are those two murders connected or are they not?" was what he wanted me to say.

I said I thought there wasn't any doubt. Irrespective of the relationship between the two men, there'd been their deaths on the same night, and by the same method of killing. Each had been stunned and each would have been strangled if in the case of Drew an abnormally thin skull hadn't made the strangling unnecessary.

If that was so, and we'd argued the point before, then the killer had had a busy night. First he'd killed Nelson Corbit somewhere in the neighbourhood of the gravel pit and then he'd killed old Drew more than three miles away. He'd disposed of Drew's body to the extent of putting it on the sawdust pile, and previous to all that he'd had to lure Stanley Corbit out to Stepford chapel. Quite a busy night, in fact. But was there anything that he needn't have done that night? The answer surely was that he needn't have dumped Nelson Corbit's body in the gravel pit. He could have kept it till the following night in what Wharton gruesomely called cold storage.

The clothes had been dried and no more, and we spent a good hour on them, and there was nothing to give the least indication of where the body might have been kept for a night. Wharton returned them to their paper bag and then we had a look at the shoes. It was in the patent rubber of one of the heels that Wharton saw something unusual. Something was wedged tightly in the groove of the pattern and the glass showed what I can only call the remains of a smear.

Wharton found a pin under his lapel and felt the something wedged in the groove. He sniffed the pin and he put a match to the black stuff that adhered to it.

"Tar," he said. "There isn't a shadow of a doubt about that."

Tar it almost certainly was. At some time on that Wednesday night Nelson Corbit had stepped on some tar, and the chances were that it had been *after* he left the café. Had it been earlier, then there'd have been no trace worth mentioning outside the groove, for even a short walk on a pavement or road would have worn it away.

"That's it," Wharton said. "There's been road repairs or something and he stepped on a tarred patch. Or where somebody had spilled some tar."

Then he was ruling that last suggestion out. "Couldn't have been ordinary tar. This is thicker, like bitumen. He stepped on it or his heel just caught it. It pressed into this groove and stayed there. What stayed outside it got practically worn away."

Five minutes later we had gone round to the town hall and were in the surveyor's office. We had to wait for quite a time before he could see us.

"No road tarring," he told us. "Nothing of that sort anywhere near last Wednesday."

"What about ordinary patching?" Wharton said. "Filling up little pot-holes. Was anybody doing anything of that?"

Apparently that was too insignificant a job to have come under the notice of the surveyor himself. He had to get in touch with his assistant, and, as Wharton whispered to me after twenty minutes' wait, maybe the assistant would have to ask the foreman. But the wait was worth while. The surveyor came back to announce that there'd been some patching done at two different places on the Wednesday—in Clare Street, just off the Memorial, and at the south end of Back Street.

Wharton was looking disappointed, even if profuse in his thanks. But the disappointment went as soon as we were outside.

"Back Street," he said. "We ought to have thought of that. When he left the café he probably had a look to see if his father had taken the car. While we're at it, we might as well do some timing."

We went to the café, and from there to Back Street at an unhurried pace. The time it took us was exactly three minutes. I ventured to point out that there'd been no guarantee of the correctness of the café clock on that Wednesday night. George said it didn't matter. Nelson Corbit was killed within twenty minutes of finishing his meal. Three of those minutes—say four for luck—had gone.

"There's something else," I said. "He might have gone along the High Street there instead of taking this fork. Then he could have cut through to Back Street by the passageway beyond Frosbeck's shop."

George said we'd better look at Back Street first and find where the surface had been patched, so on we slowly went. Timings didn't matter now and we watched the road. The first patch was found well short of Frosbeck's back premises and from there to the very end of the street we counted thirty-one patchings, some not much bigger than the palm of a hand and others a filling up of what must have been quite nasty pot-holes.

"Well, either he came this way or he didn't," George said. "Let's assume he did. Then what happened to him?"

"The car wasn't here," I said. "I think we can believe Stanley Corbit about that. So if Nelson was hit on the head and strangled here, where exactly was it done? I know this street wouldn't be used at all at night because it isn't any sort of a short cut, but it'd have been a damn risky business. There aren't many street lamps, I know, but there're some. There's one right against his father's back premises."

"What about *inside* the back premises?" George said. "Nelson had a key to them. Someone could have been waiting for him inside."

"Then it couldn't have been Turbey," I said. "Even if Turbey's got only his wife to prove he was at home, he still couldn't have disposed of the body. How could he have humped it all the way to the gravel pit, even the following night, without being seen?"

"What about Drew?"

"We're still back at the body. If Drew followed him and killed him, how'd the body get to the gravel pit?"

"Wait a minute," George said. "How far is it to the cinema where his daughter was? Not a hundred yards. Why shouldn't Drew have slipped along and fetched his own car?" I said we could ask the car-park attendant, but even so I didn't see old Drew humping that body over a gate and carrying it up that rough slope to the gravel pit edge. Admittedly Nelson Corbit wasn't a much bigger man than Drew, but a dead weight of over nine stone takes a bit of humping.

George said we'd test the idea in any case, and off we went to the car-park of the cinema. The attendant wasn't there and we had to go to a bungalow along the Stepford Road. He turned out to be an old-age pensioner who wasn't paid for the job, but made his money on tips.

"I never see Mr. Drew that night," he said. "I'd have told the police when they was askin' about him."

"You remember his daughter taking the car?"

He remembered her, he said. She'd left just after seven o'clock and the woman who was with her handed him sixpence as he gave the car the road.

But one thing was perfectly clear. The car-park had been fairly full that night and some cars—those of farmers presumably—had been there most of the day. Towards the end of the first house the attendant admitted that he'd been in his little hut having a bite to eat and tea from his thermos and a car could have been moved without his knowledge. After all, as he said, cars were parked free and entirely at their owners' risk.

We went along High Street and through the passage-way to Back Street again.

"I don't suppose by any chance Frosbeck happened to see Nelson Corbit go by on the Wednesday night," Wharton said.

"It's a million to one that he didn't," I said. "It was pitch dark even if his curtains weren't drawn. But there he is. No harm in asking."

Frosbeck had backed his car out of his garage and had drawn it up at the kerb as we came along. He gave us his usual quiet enquiring look. Wharton apologised for asking the question.

"You're quite right," Frosbeck told him. "It was dark when I got back from that short walk I told Mr. Travers about. I went straight upstairs and I didn't stir out again, not till eleven o'clock or so."

That was that. I asked him if he was going anywhere special in the car.

"There's a sale at Lamport tomorrow and Friday," he told us. "I'm going along now to have a preliminary view. You'd like to come?"

I said unfortunately I couldn't. But I liked sales, and if there was nothing doing I might accept his offer for one of the days of the sale itself. He said I'd only to let him know in good time. It was a first-class sale and quite a lot of big dealers would be there.

We moved on and neither of us was saying a thing. When we got to the junction with the High Street, Wharton said he'd get those clothes and shoes sent to the Yard. I said I'd see George at the hotel for lunch. It was half-past twelve in any case.

* * * * *

I'd nothing particular on my mind, but when I turned back I found myself going along Back Street again. Frosbeck's car was still at the kerb, but he wasn't in sight—not that I wanted to see him. It was Stanley Corbit I was thinking about, and something I ought to have done.

I don't know under what heading you would put it—inverted snobbery or a taking of one's self too seriously—but I'd had something on my mind. There are times, as I've said, when I can lie with fluency and freedom, and there are times when I'd hate to be thought a liar. Jekyll and Hyde, if you like, but I don't like mixing the Travers of ordinary life and the Travers who sometimes has to lie in the name of justice.

I looked in at the back and there was Stanley Corbit having a sandwich lunch in his office. I apologised, but he insisted that I should come in. I said we had no news for him and I'd come on an entirely personal matter.

"That Saturday morning when I came into your shop," I said. "I'd like you to know, in case it might have been worrying you, that I came as a genuine, private individual. I'd not the faintest idea all this business was going to occur."

He hardly knew how to take that explanation, even if he did seem dimly gratified. Then his business instinct got the upper hand. Did I still want to be notified if he ran across any good quality Whieldon? I said I certainly did.

"I understand there's a big sale on at Lamport tomorrow and Friday," I said. "Are you going to the preliminary view?"

He said he'd thought of going early in the morning to have a quick look before the sale began. His wife was very much better, but he didn't like to leave her till he was sure the neighbour could come in.

"It's awkward now Nelson's gone," he told me quietly. "Turbey's not a lot of use in the shop."

Nelson's funeral was on the Friday in any case, and so he'd have to leave commissions on anything in the Friday's sale. That was what he was telling me, and it seemed to be easing his mind to be talking about his son. He said it didn't seem little more than a week since Nelson had been at a sale.

"Not the one on the Monday, near Ipswich?" I said.

"That was the one," he said.

I told him how Mr. Ampling and I had gone with Frosbeck to Ipswich, and how Frosbeck had bought a mirror for me.

"Wait a minute," he said, and rummaged among some papers in a drawer. "I think I've got the catalogue."

He found it and flashed it for me to see. It was Nelson's marked catalogue, and there was my mirror.

"It was good quality?" he said.

I said it was a beauty, and I'd got it cheaply.

"I don't know," he said. "Forty-two guineas is a lot for a mirror unless it was something special. And then he had to have his profit."

"Forty-two guineas?" I said. "Who says it cost forty-two guineas?"

He shrugged his shoulders and showed me the catalogue. In the margin was a pencilled note—*F. 42gs.*

"Maybe you're right after all," I said, and then his hand went out to my arm.

"You will not mention this—please." His voice was urgent. "It is no business of mine what Mr. Frosbeck charged you for the mirror. Fifty pounds, perhaps—a hundred, it is no business of mine. But I do not want trouble with Mr. Frosbeck."

"You needn't worry," I said. "I'd never dream of mentioning your name to Mr. Frosbeck. As far as I'm concerned the deal's over. I bought the mirror and I'm satisfied. I've no need even to mention it to Mr. Frosbeck again."

But I was sure Corbit was wrong, and that was why I went straight to the hotel and rang the Ipswich auctioneers who had conducted that sale. None of the principals was there, but I talked to a very helpful clerk. I was a Colonel Smith of Stepford, I said, and I'd like to know who bought that mirror because I'd like to buy it from him. I gave him the lot number and the description so that there should be no mistake, and in a very few seconds he was telling me that the mirror had been bought by a Mr. Frosbeck, antique dealer, Helmsbury.

"Be a good fellow," I said, "and tell me what he gave for it. Otherwise I shan't know what to offer him, or whether he's robbing me."

He told me that straightaway. The price paid had been forty-two guineas.

I paid at the desk for the call and went up to my room for a wash before the meal, and slowly it began to dawn on me that somewhere something was radically wrong. When I came down again George had begun his meal, and while I was waiting for my soup he was telling me that Umberson had drawn a blank. In Stepford every woman who had a boy of any age had been questioned, and never a one knew anything about a wallet. Since Umberson had given it out that enquiries were being made in order that the sender of the wallet could receive a substantial reward, there seemed no question of anyone holding back.

"What's the matter with you?" he was suddenly asking me. "Got something on your mind?"

I admitted that I had, and I told him the whole story of that mirror.

"The very first morning I went into Frosbeck's shop," I said, "I saw a mirror I'd have liked to buy. It was marked forty guineas and it wasn't nearly such a good one as the one I did buy, though that doesn't at the moment matter. The point is that I said I wasn't prepared to go beyond twenty-five guineas or so for a mirror. Well, now, he gives forty-two guineas for the mirror I do buy and he lets me have it for my original limit of twenty-five guineas. A sheer loss to him of seventeen guineas, plus his profit. What's the reason?"

"Don't know," George said, "unless it was ground bait."

"But I told him I wasn't in the market for anything except a mirror. And listen to this, George. There was a question of some miniatures that were sold to Bernard Ampling."

I told him that story, and how I had thought at the time that that deal also might have been ground bait.

"Now I'm thinking differently," I said. "I think that Frosbeck wanted to make a friend of Bernard Ampling and he laid himself out to do so. But you can't say that in my case. I don't live here. It's even likely that Frosbeck won't ever see me again."

"What's his idea then? Trying to make use of you in some way?"

"That's what it looks like," I said. "As if he wanted me on his side for some reason or other. And, of course, all this mirror business happened well before Drew was killed."

"Frosbeck knew who and what you were?"

"He certainly did," I said. "We played bridge on the Sunday and I got my leg pulled by Bernard, now I remember, because I couldn't make a single finesse. Whenever I tried to place a card, I guessed wrong. Bernard said that if my detective powers weren't any better on behalf of Scotland Yard then it was about time they got some new blood. Everybody took the remark for granted."

Wharton grunted.

"Very well then, let's get down to brass tacks. Let's go so far as to say that Frosbeck knew that if he committed a murder, then you might be in on the enquiry. But Frosbeck didn't commit a murder. By no conceivable chance could he have committed a murder—Drew's murder, that is. I admit he might have killed Nelson Corbit, but there the question is why."

"Don't pin me down to hard facts, George," I said. "I know Frosbeck didn't kill Drew, but all the same he might have had some fore-knowledge he wanted to keep to himself."

"What fore-knowledge?"

"I don't know. It might have been something to do with Truebent. It strikes me there was something remarkably fishy about Truebent's late appearance at bridge on that Wednesday night."

"But why should Frosbeck shield Truebent?"

"Don't ask me," I said. "I haven't a single fact to go on, except the queer business of that mirror. But let me ask you a question for a change. Didn't you yourself think there was something lying somewhere at the back of Frosbeck? That he was just a bit too quiet and reserved?"

"That was when you were telling me about him losing his wife and his only son. All I said was you could see he was a man who'd had a nasty knock or two in his time."

"You said something else, George. You said he struck you as a man with something on his mind. The sort of man who's always thinking about himself or quite other matters than those he happens to be talking about."

"Well, if that's how it struck me, then that's how it did strike me," George said. "After all, he's had a fairly lonely life in Helmsbury. Practically nothing but his business and himself to think about."

"The more I think," I said, "the stronger the hunch is. Now take the very little we've learned from Frosbeck. It was Bernard Ampling who got him to tell us about that picture. Frosbeck himself has never volunteered a single statement to us. I think he must have known that Drew's movements on the Wednesday night were being enquired into, but it was only by luck that I learned from him that he was one of those who'd actually seen Drew. And take something else. But for the extraordinary chance of a piece of paper falling out of one of Frosbeck's old books I'd never have known that he'd changed his name. And what's more important, that he'd known Drew before he came to Helmsbury. But why didn't Frosbeck tell us that. You'd have thought it a natural thing for him to have mentioned it. Why has he been so consistently secretive?"

"Perhaps it's a kind of exaggerated keeping of himself to himself." He shrugged his shoulders. "Still, if you think there's something fishy behind it all, what do you propose?"

"This," I said. "I think I'd like to concentrate on Frosbeck for a bit. I'd like to know a whole lot more about him. He's ticking in a most peculiar way, George, and I'd like to know what's wrong with the works."

"Why not?" he said. "And how're you going to make a start?"

"At the very beginning," I said. "I'd like to have a talk with someone who knew Frosbeck when his name was Farmer."

"Why not?" George told me again.

CHAPTER XVI
MOTIVE FOR MURDER

I LEFT for London that same afternoon, and it was just a bit unlucky, if only from the taxpayers' point of view, that Matthews had already left in the car. But I travelled light and I'd fixed up a room at an hotel, and when I'd had a cup of tea the evening was before me. Not that I was minded to do much more than prepare the ground.

First I rang the Hampden police to warn them that I was coming. When I got to Hampden myself the local Inspector was waiting for me and I told him just as much as it was good for him to know. Then he and I took a walk to Main Parade.

The premises of Homeland Furnishings Limited were prominent enough, with the name in big letters across the front of the whole three shops. I had a good look at number twenty-nine—not that it told me anything, for the three premises had been made into one big establishment and there was merely a window to indicate the shop where Walter Farmer had once lived. If I had hoped for some evocation or sudden inspiration I was disappointed. That window and the upper stories now used as showrooms were telling me nothing about the William Frosbeck of a little country town.

"What I'll do, sir, is this," the Inspector told me. "There's a sergeant of mine who's lived here all his life and some of my men are local. 1938 isn't so far back as all that, so somebody ought to remember your man."

I said that what I wanted was someone who'd known Farmer intimately. He said that mightn't be too difficult either, and he'd see what he could do. We left it that he'd give me a ring in the morning, and as the tube station was near I made my way back to the hotel. The only other thing I did that night was to look at the telephone directory. Homeland Furnishings Limited seemed quite a big concern. If they had branches in the provinces I didn't know, and I hadn't a Stock Exchange Directory to consult, but they had a shop in Lower Oxford Street and twelve others in the suburbs. If nothing emerged from Hampden in the morning I thought I might see the secretary of the company and go into the acquisition of the Drew and Corbit properties. What that interview might tell me I had little idea, but chance, as I knew, had a queer habit of taking a hand.

But I needn't have planned so far ahead. The Hampden Inspector rang me at nine o'clock the next morning and said he had something for me, and he thought it was just what I wanted. Half an hour later I was meeting him at the tube station.

It was the proprietor of a bookshop, he said, and only three doors away from number twenty-nine. He was an elderly man of the name of Applehurst, and he'd known Farmer well. I said he might as well come with me and we'd see this Applehurst together. In three minutes we were there and I had a look at the shop before we went in. It was something that might have been transported from Charing Cross Road. There were the trays in front and the one window stacked high with books, and here and there a coloured print. When one cast an eye around at multiple stores and modern chromium it looked a queer survival. And a survival was just the thing I wanted.

It was a man of well over seventy who came forward as soon as we stepped inside, but he looked hale enough and he had almost a perky way with him.

"Here you are then, Inspector," he said. "And is this the gentlemen you were bringing along?"

We made our way past tall bookshelves and stacks of yet more books and into an inner room that had a stuffy cosiness. I showed my credentials, and he looked somewhat startled.

"But I thought you gentlemen wanted to know about Walter Farmer."

"We do," I said.

"But Farmer's dead," he said. "At least, I understood he was dead."

I said it didn't matter if he *was* dead. Our business was to do with the disposal of a certain estate.

"You mean he'd have come into some money?"

"That's what it amounts to," I said, and he was letting out a breath.

"Pity it didn't come a few years ago, then. It might have made all the difference."

And so to what he had to tell us, and again I edit a story so that events may appear in due sequence. And I was realising from the very outset that I was being uncommonly lucky. Applehurst and Farmer had been friends. Farmer had had a taste in books and both men played chess. Applehurst had known the Farmers intimately. He could tell me that there had been also a daughter who had died at a very early age, though that was to colour my final views and in no way to change them.

Applehurst had known Farmer's father, who also had been a bookish sort of man. He'd never been cut out for a business man, Applehurst said, and when he died the business had gone down pretty badly. Walter took some time to get it on its feet again, and then he became handicapped by two things—the impact of the depression and the continued illness of his wife. It was when he got as far as that that I felt a certain depression myself. All he had so far told me agreed with what I had heard from Frosbeck.

But he was going on. Mrs. Farmer was a woman to worry, he said. Farmer had spent most of his capital or savings on the business and there was the additional problem of Robert, the only boy. He was doing well at school and Farmer wanted him to go to Cambridge and be a doctor as his grandfather had been. But there was the nagging question of money. Mrs. Farmer had a serious operation and recovered from it, but business picked up somewhat and Farmer began to think his troubles and anxieties were over. That was when the blow fell.

Numbers twenty-five and twenty-seven had been a kind of drapery and fancy-goods store kept by a couple of women. A big draper store nearby was putting them out of business, and when their lease fell in they made no attempt to renew, and the premises were acquired by the furnishing firm of Drew and Corbit.

"A dirty, ruthless firm," Applehurst told us venomously. "I only saw one of them—Corbit—but that was enough. It was a filthy combine, it was. Well, you can guess what happened, too.

Inside six months Walter Farmer might as well have closed his shop."

"Did Farmer see these Drew and Corbit people?" I said. "Couldn't he have made some sort of protest before they actually opened?"

"I don't know that he actually saw them," he told me, "but I know he had some correspondence and they more or less spat in his face. They made him an offer for his business—a ridiculous offer—and that's what brought on his illness."

It was confused, and yet it wasn't, for one could discern a pattern as he spoke, despite his deeply bitter feelings about combines. Mrs. Farmer—a dear little body, Applehurst called her—worried herself into a fatal illness and Farmer broke down, too, and was taken to hospital. It was the boy, Robert, who tried to straighten things out through his father's solicitors. Farmer recovered somewhat and finally the business was advertised. It was ultimately sold with the stock at a ridiculous price and to a nominee of Drew and Corbit. Applehurst knew all that because Farmer's solicitors were also his own.

"What happened to them all then I don't really know," he told us. "Robert came to see me. Just before Christmas of 1939 it was. He was in the army and home on leave. I think he said his father had had a relapse and was in the country somewhere, in a home."

"You think he'd become a mental case?"

"I wouldn't like to say," he told us. "He'd had enough worry to make him mental and the boy didn't seem inclined to talk about it. Then later on I heard poor Robert was killed. I don't know who it was told me, but someone saw it in the papers. A real tragedy, if ever there was one. A real nice young fellow he was. I know I felt it at the time as much as if he'd been one of my own."

"And what about Farmer? Did you ever hear of him again?"

"Not a word," he said. "Someone or other must have told me, or else I had the impression he was dead." He shook his head. "One of the best men you'd ever meet. It makes me miserable to go back and think of it all. And that's your combines for you!

That's what they can get away with. And you can bet your life they made a good profit when they sold out to this other combine. Every time I look at their place it makes my blood boil to think of it. That's why I don't often look."

"But you're safe enough yourself?"

"That may be," he told me. "I'll last out my lease all right, but that's not the point. It's the principle of the thing. The way I see it is that Walter Farmer might have been living there today. Nothing short of three murders; that's what it is, and you two gentlemen can think what you like."

There was little more that he could tell us, though he did remember the name of the hospital where Farmer had been. He had wanted to see him once, he said, and had rung up beforehand, but he had been too ill to receive visitors. But that gave me another idea.

"What about his wife's relatives?" I asked him. "Were there any living?"

Her father was alive at the time of her death, that much he knew for certain. He'd been in the ironmongery business in Liverpool but had had a stroke and had had to retire. He'd recovered from the stroke but hadn't been allowed to come to the funeral.

"Do you remember his name?"

"I ought to," he said. "I've heard Farmer mention it enough times. What was it now? Cossley . . . Crossley . . ."

His lips began a shaping of various consonants.

"Not Frosbeck, by any chance?" I said.

"That's it," he said. "Frosbeck. The boy's name was Robert Frosbeck Farmer."

"He must have had money," I said. "An ironmonger's shop is reckoned to be a pretty paying concern."

"Oh, he had money," Applehurst told us. "But Farmer wasn't asking him for it. He had his pride, the same as I should have had."

That seemed to be all we could learn. When we thanked Applehurst for his help he asked to be put in touch with Farmer if he should happen to be still alive. As I shook hands with him I asked him if he'd seen the names Drew and Corbit in the papers recently, and I didn't tell him why.

"I've given up reading the papers," he told us. "And I don't listen to the wireless news either. Everything you hear gives you the miserables."

That brought him to the Palestine outrages and we hurriedly said goodbye. When we got to the police station I thought things out. To try to trace Farmer from the hospital might take some time, but maybe his solicitors might have some news. Applehurst had known their name, since they were his solicitors as well.

I had a longish wait till I could be put in touch with someone who had known of Farmer's affairs. Then I got all I wanted. Farmer had been in St. Hilda's Nursing Home at Porling in Sussex. He had been discharged from there in October 1940 and had then called on the solicitors and they had paid him a sum of approximately three hundred pounds, the balance held by them from the deal with Drew and Corbit. That was the last they heard of him. But they had an idea he had gone to Liverpool.

That had seemed logical from the first. Farmer had had to go somewhere and from someone he had obtained the money to buy that business at Helmsbury, so the best thing to do seemed to be to get in touch with Liverpool. At the Yard I saw the Assistant Commissioner, and urgency questions were rushed through. By that time it was two in the afternoon and it looked as if I'd never a hope of getting back to Helmsbury till the very last train, so I rang the police station and left a message accordingly.

I spent an hour at my club, I had tea, I got in touch over the telephone with Applehurst again and I paid periodic visits to the Yard, and it was not till seven o'clock that Liverpool had what we wanted. Percy Frosbeck died in March 1941, and his property had been left to his son-in-law, a Walter Farmer, who had been living with him. A condition of the will was that Farmer should assume the name of Frosbeck. This had been done, and William Frosbeck—he changed the Christian name, too—had left Liverpool in the following September.

Liverpool suggested that his movements thereafter could be traced through the bank. I agreed, but said it was not a matter of urgency, though we'd be grateful for the information at their convenience. And by then there was just time for a car to rush me to Liverpool Street where I caught the last reasonable train. It was well after ten o'clock when I arrived at Helmsbury and the Roebuck. Wharton was waiting for me.

"So there you are, George," I said. "No one could ever have a stronger motive than Frosbeck. That old bookseller Applehurst said as much."

"Let's assume it then," George said, and the tone of his voice meant that if anything went wrong the onus would be on me. "Let's say he was partly cracked—"

"That's going too far," I said. "Say he had an *idée fixe* if you like. His idea was that Drew and Corbit had killed his wife and son. By comparison, the ruin of his business was only an incidental and contributory factor."

"But if he did the murders, he must have been mad."

"That's just legal jargon," I said. "I admit that Frosbeck might have been slightly mental when he first had the idea. But he got well, and he still had the idea. It became a part of him. Everything he did was perfectly sane. He got in touch with Homeland Furnishings Limited and obtained the whereabouts of Drew and Corbit. He acquired a business here and he was prepared to wait. I'll wager, too, that neither Drew nor Corbit ever recognised him, even if they'd seen him before. Applehurst told me that he knew Farmer as a big, raw-boned, thinnish man, and clean-shaved. Down here he had the beard and he'd put on a lot of weight, and he must have aged considerably."

"But he could have killed both of them fifty times," George protested. "He'd been here for years."

"He wouldn't want that kind of killing," I said. "What's the good of merely killing a man you hate? Frosbeck would have to kill his man and tell him just why he was being killed. That's where revenge and satisfaction would come in. And he would have to protect himself. He'd have to be entirely unsuspected, so that later on he could do the other killing."

"Forget it," George said, and waved a testy hand. "Leave motive out of it. What you can't get away from is that Frosbeck has a cast-iron alibi for that Wednesday night—for Drew, that is. Drew wasn't killed till somewhere round about half-past eight, and he was killed at Truebent's woodyard. You had Frosbeck under your eye from before half-past seven till eleven o'clock."

"Except at from twenty-past nine to half-past when he was making coffee."

"Comes to the same thing," he told me. "Drew was dead then in any case, even if Frosbeck had wings." He shook his head. "You get that alibi broken down, then we might be getting somewhere."

"Well, we've broken down as tough alibis before," I told him. "I did a lot of thinking in the train and I don't know that I haven't a few ideas."

"Oh?" said George. "Such as what?"

"Leave it till the morning," I told him. "So far they're ideas and no more. But if you want a specimen ask yourself who besides Drew had enough information to suggest to Stanley Corbit over the telephone that an Inspector Brewer was interested in his son."

It was after midnight, as I said, and I was uncommonly sleepy. George was suddenly sympathetic. He even got the night porter to bring us in a couple more whiskies. I was wondering if he'd suddenly acquired some ideas himself.

But in the morning he was rousing me soon after seven o'clock, and when I asked him if he'd thought about that alibi, he said he had and he hadn't. I said quite untruthfully that I'd made little progress either, but I'd like him to go with me on a short walk. There was something we might look at which could have a bearing on the case.

Where we actually went to was as far as the Memorial and then along Back Street. Just short of Frosbeck's back premises we stopped.

"See that old-fashioned street lamp high on the wall?" I said. "Wouldn't that give a dim sort of light in the back rooms of the shop?"

"Looks to me as if it would," he said. "But what's the idea?"

"Tell you in a minute," I said. "Something else to look for first."

I moved close in to the shop side of the street. As we went by I gave a quick look through the window. I then had to stop and squint through sideways. Then I was motioning him to silence and we moved quietly on.

"What's all the mumbo-jumbo?" he was asking me as soon as we were out of earshot of the house.

"Something's still there," I said. "Something I remembered from when I was there before."

"What's still there?"

Then I told him. I told him a whole lot more. When the waiter brought our coffee I thought of something else: a something that made that alibi far less impregnable than it had seemed the night before.

Soon after ten o'clock that morning we were in the tea-shop with Frosbeck's shop in full view across the street. We had ordered coffee and we lingered it out. In fact we were having our second cups when Sergeant Matthews came past the shop. He stopped and looked our way and waved a hand.

"Right," George told me. "Here's where you do your stuff. For God's sake mind you don't slip up."

I kept to my side of the street and crossed at the fork. Matthews joined me there.

"You know what you've got to do," I said. "As soon as you see me in the doorway, you'll know it's all clear. You're sure Frosbeck has gone?"

He'd left ten minutes ago, he said, in his car and he'd called to his man that he'd be back before five o'clock.

He moved into Back Street and I went along High Street to the shop. Tom Polter was there.

"Morning, Tom. Mr. Frosbeck about?"

"He's just gone to that sale at Lamport," Tom told me. "Anything you wanted in particular, sir?"

"Of course," I said. "I remember now. Did he buy anything at the sale yesterday?"

Tom said he'd bought some Sheraton and glass and china and he was hoping to get a set of Heppelwhite chairs and some needlework pictures.

"Monday's the day you ought to come in, sir," he told me. "That's when they'll be in the shop. But the prices! You never heard anything like it."

"I very much doubt if I'll be here on Monday," I said. "That's really why I came in now. It suddenly struck me that I'd never had what you might call a good look round."

"Go where you like, sir, and do what you like," he told me. "Anything you want to know, just give me a holler, that's all. I shall be in here most of my time."

"I think I will then," I said, and I made a slow way through to the two back rooms. Then with an ear for the main shop I was tiptoeing quickly to the door that opened on Back Street. It was unlocked. Matthews nipped through. On top of a large carved chest was standing a smaller chest and a couple of copper cauldrons. We moved them quietly down and very gently I lifted the lid of the chest. Matthews's long legs went inside and as he drew his body down, I closed the chest again. Then I went back to the main shop.

"You don't happen to know, Tom, what Sheraton it was exactly that Mr. Frosbeck bought yesterday?"

That was a prelude to a quarter of an hour's gossip. A woman came in with a pair of candlesticks to sell, and I nipped back to Matthews. The chest was empty so I got the small chest in place again and the two cauldrons. There was dust on the lid of the larger chest and I knew I ought to wipe it off, for it showed where the smaller chest and the cauldrons had been moved. But just as I took out my handkerchief, I heard Tom Polter's cough, and I moved on. I was contemplating a large oilscape when he came through.

"There's nothing particular in here, sir," he told me. "Not the sort of stuff that'd interest you. But did you see that little lacquer cabinet in the other room?"

I had to go through with him and after that it seemed too risky to go back for that dusting. And when I finally left the shop I was feeling somehow pleased that I hadn't removed that dust after all. For if Matthews had found what we wanted, then things might work out in quite a different way. Tom Polter would be sure to mention to Frosbeck that I'd spent quite a long time in that back room, and Frosbeck would know that someone had opened that chest. And then, what? Did I want Frosbeck to escape the law? Frankly I didn't know. I lack the ruthlessness of Wharton. My job is to help find an answer to a problem, not to pull the lever for the drop. And in spite of what I knew, in spite of logic and sheer hard sense, I still had a furtive liking for Frosbeck himself. But that was something which I wasn't prepared to admit to Wharton.

He was at the police station and Matthews was with him.

"Was it there?" I said.

"It was there all right," Wharton told me grimly.

He shook the envelope and showed me the sliver of wood.

From four o'clock onwards we had men on watch, and every few minutes a runner would come with news. At a quarter to five Frosbeck came home. Some things—the needlework pictures, I imagined—were taken by Polter from the back of the car, and then Frosbeck garaged it. At twenty-past five the shop was closed. At just after six o'clock the housekeeper left, and presumably Frosbeck had finished his high tea and the washing-up had been done.

"About time we made a move," Wharton told me. "Get your men in position, Umberson. No rough stuff, mind you. Just collar him if he tries to get away, and then bring him here."

Umberson left and George seemed loth to move.

"This is going to be a tricky business," he told me. "It may be a short cut, I still don't like it. And suppose he won't talk."

I said we'd gone into all that. We had enough to hold him on suspicion, so what had we got to lose? But George still didn't like it, and he was shaking his head as we moved off. I was thinking cynically that the hesitation was all for my benefit. I was the one who'd been chosen to do the talking, and once more the onus might have to be on me.

It was quite dark when we reached the side door of the shop. One of Umberson's men drew up to us.

"Everything all right?" Wharton asked him.

"Nothing stirring at all, sir."

Wharton's hand went out to the door handle. He flashed his torch on the stairs, and we made our way up. The door from the landing opened and a light was switched on above our heads. Frosbeck looked out. He drew back into the room and we went through. You'd have expected a smile from him, but there wasn't one. On his face was merely that quiet enquiring look.

"We're here officially," I told him. "Superintendent Wharton would like your answers to several questions."

He moistened his lips and looked away.

"Yes," he said, and as if to himself. "I thought perhaps you'd be coming tonight."

"Something to do with the dust on top of a chest?"

It was as if I hadn't spoken. All he was doing was to wave a hand at the chairs by the table. Wharton shifted his chair near the door by which we had entered. Mine covered the door to the kitchen. Suddenly my heart was racing madly and it was a moment or two before I could begin to speak.

Chapter XVII

HOW IT WAS DONE

Frosbeck sat on the chesterfield and there was something almost frightening about the quietness of his manner. It put me off my stride, and though I'd thought I knew by heart each word I'd intended to say I began in the wrong place.

"Yesterday I saw Applehurst," I said. "Your old bookseller friend. He had an idea you were dead. I didn't disillusion him."

The slightest movement of the head was the only indication that he had heard.

"He told me the truth," I said. "If you'd been as frank maybe we wouldn't be here now. What you told me was forced out of you when I found that paper in that book. You had to extemporise. You knew we'd make enquiries. We couldn't let a coincidence like that pass without enquiry, and you tried to forestall it. And you managed to have a framework of truth, even if everything inside it was lies. You *didn't* make a good bargain with Drew and Corbit. You were squeezed ruthlessly out. Your wife did die as a result, but you didn't tell me that your son should have been a doctor. If he'd been at his medical studies in 1940 he wouldn't have been in the army. In other words, Drew and Corbit killed your son just as they killed your wife. That's how it showed itself to you. And you'd absolutely idolized both of them."

"What about it, Frosbeck?" Wharton was asking. "Is that much true?"

Frosbeck's hands lifted and fell. I waited a moment and then went on.

"We now have every step you made since you left the nursing home. We know you came down here with the deliberate intention of killing both Drew and Stanley Corbit. You could afford to wait. Neither of them recognised you, and I think you were rather pleased than otherwise to have to wait. I think you liked hugging that idea of revenge to yourself. It gave you a sense of power that they shouldn't know who you were. I know, too, that you must have been pleased when the two fell out, and when there was that trouble over Nelson Corbit. I think you used Drew to foment even more hostility between him and Corbit. But perhaps you'll tell us just one thing. Was it Turbey who sold that picture to Drew?"

"Yes," he said, and then his lips clamped tight again.

"Then it was you who put two and two together and found out about the rugs," I told him. "Everything was working your way at last. Instead of having to commit two murders—killings, if you like—you saw a way to kill Drew and incriminate Corbit. If Corbit was hanged for Drew's murder that'd be quite a nice revenge. That's why you took that pestle when you were in Corbit's shop. It would have his prints on it, and you kept it in your safe till the time came.

"Everything was to centre round that bridge party, for that was to give you your alibi. It was all bunkum about having to have five players. Truebent had to be late, it is true, but if he hadn't been able to come at all you'd still have found a fifth from somewhere. And so to what did happen and the mixture of genius and bungling that it was. For one thing, you had to make everything too complicated. You changed your mind about placing Drew's body, and just because of that local scandal about Truebent and Drew. You mixed up the original idea with a wholly new one. You couldn't see that if your scheme was to succeed it had to have a stark simplicity. Instead of dumping Drew where Corbit could have killed him, you made an additional suspect out of Truebent. But if Truebent killed Drew, there wasn't any need to place the pestle. You see what I mean?

"But to get back to that Wednesday night. You rang Drew and told him you'd something definite on Nelson Corbit. You'd learned that Drew was alone in the house and you said that if he came here at seven o'clock you could show him irrefutable proof that Nelson Corbit was responsible for those church robberies. He was to keep everything strictly to himself and come in by Back Street, and you'd be on the look-out for him. You *were* on the look-out for him, but I think something went wrong. You'd intended to take him to the garage and stun him there, but either he came just a bit too soon or you'd gone inside for a moment, but in any case he found the door to Back Street open and he came in. You were too late to stop him, but you probably said something perfectly natural; and when he was either coming further in or else going out with you, you struck him with the pestle in your gloved hand.

"It doesn't matter that he'd been stunned in the shop instead of the garage because you could nip across with the body. What you intended to do was truss him up and gag him and leave him till a later convenient moment, and then you'd nip down to the garage and tell him just who you were and why you were killing him, and then you'd strangle him and put his body in the boot of your car. He'd have died at about nine o'clock, in other words, and you'd have had an irreproachable alibi. But something else went radically wrong. *Nelson Corbit was wrong.*

"He'd just had a meal at a local café and was coming along Back Street to see if his father had taken the car home, and he saw Drew in front of him. He wondered what Drew could be doing there at that time of night, and he followed him. He saw him enter your shop by the back way, and he came closer. Two things might have happened then. There was sufficient light from the street lamp for him to have seen you strike Drew. Or he might have come forward from where he was standing in the deep shadow just as you were nipping across to the open garage with Drew in your arms. I think the latter. I think he said, 'Hallo, what's up?' You stepped back in the shop and said Drew had had an accident. He stooped to have a look and then you struck him, too. You strangled him. You had to. There wasn't any other way out. Then you put his body in that big chest under the window. What you couldn't know was that he'd just stepped on some road-repair tar. Some of that tar had adhered to his boot. Some of it came off the sole of his boot against the end of the inside of the chest. We found it there this morning."

"Anything to say?" Wharton asked him.

Frosbeck shook his head. He wasn't even looking at us. His eyes were across the room as if his thoughts were miles away.

"So much for that," I said. "But there was another disaster. You'd struck Drew too hard, and he was dead. Your alibi wasn't worth a penny. You'd read up about everything in that copy of Glaister's *Toxicology and Medical Jurisprudence* you've got there in the bookcase, and you knew you were absolutely without an alibi. But you put Drew's body in the boot of the car all the same. There was nothing else you could do, but no wonder you were hot and bothered, as Bernard Ampling told you, when we got here at just short of half-past seven. You'd not long finished telephoning to Stanley Corbit, luring him out to Truebent's woodyard, and you'd had to examine your clothes for blood spots and wash your hands, and so on. You'd probably had only a second or two to spare when we arrived.

"Then came the bridge and why you had five players, not four. It was when you were sitting out that you'd thought originally of slipping down and finishing off Drew, but that wasn't necessary now. You'd also arranged to have another precautionary look while you were supposedly making the coffee. *But you didn't have to make the coffee.* That coffee was already made and it and the milk were kept hot in the Aga oven. All you had to do was to pour it out of the saucepan, put it on the tray and bring it in. That would have given you ten minutes downstairs by the back way while we were on another rubber.

"Still, that doesn't matter so much now. You took Mr. Ampling and myself back to Stepford, as carefully arranged. It was a pitch-black night, and on the way back you stopped your car just short of or past the woodyard and you took Drew's body a little down Endover Lane and dumped it on the sawdust. You'd muddied his boots and then pressed them into the sawdust to give the impression that he'd been walking about in the neighbourhood, and I rather think you covered the body with a layer of sawdust. Originally it was vital that the body should be discovered the very next morning. The time of death could then have been established at nine o'clock or so, when you had a perfect alibi. Now it didn't matter. If the body weren't discovered for a day or two, all the better. Then the time of death couldn't be accurately established to within an hour or two. And for that you still had something of an alibi. And, of course, you had no motive whatever for killing Drew. Or Nelson Corbit.

"I think you dumped Nelson's body the following night, and I think you didn't have Truebent or anyone else in mind when you put it where you did. It was just that you'd seen that water—on the Monday when we went to Ipswich, perhaps—and you'd had a subsequent look on the Thursday at the lie of the land. But you must have been sweating all the same about your Drew alibi. Until you had that stroke of luck that put everything right back where you wanted it. When I told you that two people had seen Drew out for a walk on that Wednesday evening and how the time of his meal meant all the difference to the stomach content and the time of his death. Glaister had told you all about that.

That had been your worry. All you had to do was tell me you also had seen Drew out walking—just as he was almost home, in fact. And he'd told you he was just going to have his tea. But he wasn't. You didn't see him at all. We know now—after wasting days of time—that he must have had his tea at five o'clock or before, not at six as you'd said. So there you were in the clear again, and there you'd have been now if you hadn't made that slip about the mirror."

His eyes met mine and they didn't move. It was embarrassing and almost hypnotic, and I had to look away at Wharton.

"Frosbeck never expected me to find out about the mirror," I told him. "Even Tom Polter didn't know what Frosbeck paid for it, for Frosbeck's own catalogue which was in the shop was marked as what Frosbeck told me he gave for it."

I looked back at Frosbeck, and his eyes were still on mine.

"There was the irony of it," I said. "It was Nelson's catalogue of that sale that told us the real price you paid. His father happened to show it to me in his shop. You'd felt something of a twinge of conscience about Stanley Corbit, or else you felt for his wife. Or it might have been that you didn't want any further revenge on him since he'd also lost his only son. That's why you sent him the money you'd taken from Nelson's pocket. Stanley Corbit," I said. "The man you tried to frame for Drew's murder, and but for him we shouldn't be here now."

There was a sudden silence in the room. Wharton's hand moved. It was going to his pocket where he had the warrant. Another moment and he would be giving the words of caution.

"Isn't there anything you'd like to say?"

Frosbeck's tongue went slowly along his lips.

"Yes," he said slowly. "Only perhaps that nothing matters very much—now. But there's something I'd like you to see."

He had got slowly to his feet. Wharton suddenly stiffened and I knew he was watching his hands. But Frosbeck turned quickly and was through the door at his back. It was his bedroom door and it all at once came to me that he was going to fetch those photographs of his wife and son. He was going to make some defence. Some justification.

There was a click as the key turned in the lock of that bedroom door. Wharton was across the room like a flash. His fifteen stone drew back and his shoulder crashed into that door. It drew back again and I heard the door splinter by the lock. But I heard something else too—the deafening sound of a shot.

"Well, a hell of a mess we made of that," Wharton was telling me when we at last got back to the Roebuck that night. "If ever a man ought to have been strung up it was him."

I put that deftly aside.

"What did you think he was going to that room for?"

"I thought he'd written some confession or other," he told me. "We'd given him time enough. Now we'll never know if all those theories of ours were true."

"They were true enough, George," I said. "I won't say every detail was right, but the main outline was. If not, why did he shoot himself? Mind you, I know there're odds and ends we'll never know. Whose prints were on the letter about finding the wallet, for instance. Perhaps they were the housekeeper's, or a customer might have handled the paper."

I went to the bar and fetched a couple of whiskies.

"Ah well," said George resignedly as he took a swig. "It's over and done with. That's one thing. A bit lucky, though, that we had that idea about that mirror."

I didn't remind him that it was hardly a question of *we*. What I did say was that that other business of the church robberies was over, too.

"That chap, Turbey," he suddenly said, and scowled. "He's one I'd like to get my hands on."

"The evidence has all gone," I said. "We know he took that picture himself. Slipped it under his coat, as you said, but how can we prove it?"

"I'll make it my business to see him again all the same," George said, and his look was that other Colosseum one, of the same lion when he's missed his first snap at the plump Christian.

"Nothing much for you to do here now," he went on. "As soon as you've written your report, there's nothing to keep you here. I'll stay on and clear everything up."

"What's the idea?" I said. "I buy you a drink and all you do is try to rush me off the pay-roll."

"It wasn't that," he told me mildly. "All I thought was that you might like to get back to The Pleasance and go on with your holiday."

"I couldn't do it, George," I said. "I can't tell you why, but I suddenly hate the sight of Helmsbury. I couldn't start that holiday all over again."

That was why I sat up till all hours making out my own report. After breakfast in the morning George went over it and owned himself satisfied. I was planning to go back to town by the midday train, and when I said I ought to go to Stepford and say goodbye to Bernard Ampling, he said Matthews could take me there and back in the car.

Bernard seemed surprised and disappointed that I was going back to town. He hadn't heard of Frosbeck's death, so I told a white lie, that the case was now in Wharton's hands and I had some oddments to clear up in town. I'd dreaded the idea of knowing about Frosbeck, for I knew that somewhere deep down he'd had an affection for the man. All I had myself was something of a pity, and it was a pity that I didn't want evoked.

Then I mentioned a something else.

"By the way, Bernard, what was the mystery of those rugs of yours?"

"You mean to say you never worked it out?" he said, and his eyes had a mischievous twinkle.

"To tell the truth I'd forgotten about it," I said. "You be a good fellow now and tell me all about it."

"There's very little to tell," he said. "Langdon is pretty hard up and there's precious little for luxuries. Ethelberta knew he ought to have a holiday and he wouldn't take one. Said—quite rightly—that he couldn't afford it. She thought of those two rugs. They used to be in their drawing-room, but she said they'd be nicer in her bedroom, and she put something in their place.

Having got them to her bedroom she next passed them on to me. I got Frosbeck to have them valued and I gave her a hundred and sixty guineas for them. You ought to have seen her face when I gave her the cheque."

"I get you now," I said. "And that's why you didn't want the vicar to go into the dining-room."

"Exactly it," he said. "At least till we thought he'd forgotten all about those two rugs."

We were moving along the path towards the car when he was telling me that, and then he was asking me why I was looking rueful.

"I'm beginning to think like you," I said, "that I'm not too good a hand as a sleuth."

He took it as a good joke. And his last words to me as the car moved off were that if I should happen to see Frosbeck would I tell him that he was trying to fix some bridge.

The car moved off. We passed the chapel and Endover Lane, and I was thinking that it hadn't been so much of a joke after all. Maybe I'd never be the perfect story-book sleuth, at least in the full-blooded Whartonian way. I was like the philosopher, only it was sentiment with me that persisted in breaking in. The sentiment, for instance, that asked Matthews to take a turning off the Endover Road that would bring us to the police station without having once more to pass Frosbeck's shop.

THE END

www.ingramcontent.com/pod-product-compliance
Lightning Source LLC
Chambersburg PA
CBHW031015190726
48286CB00003BA/852